ROUND ONE

BY

MARIS BLACK

KAGE

Maris Black
Maris@marisblack.com

Edited by Jonathan Penn (Romantic Penn Publication Services)

Cover model: Mike Chabot

This novel is dedicated
To all of the MMA fighters
Who risk their lives and health in the Octagon
& to all of the fans
Who love them.

1

IRONICALLY, the thing that changed my life was the sound of the radio playing in the background while I was plowing my girlfriend on a Friday afternoon. By all rights, I shouldn't have even noticed the voice on the radio— because I was balls deep, her head was thrown back, and the headboard was tapping out a cadence of love on the dorm room wall. But I did hear it, and a series of events was set in motion that, like dominoes lined up just so on a gymnasium floor, would not be stopped.

I had swung by Layla's room after my last class, partly because I wanted to see how she had done on the essay I helped her with, and partly because it had been almost a week since we'd had sex. Okay, I didn't actually give a damn about the essay. With our busy schedules— Layla's cheer practice and club meetings, and my heavy class load— it wasn't easy to carve out time to take care of business. To put it in the simplest of guy terms, I was backed up. So when I knocked on her door that day, I had exactly one thing on my mind: getting laid.

Layla answered the door in a filmy bathrobe, which surprised me because it was the middle of the day. I could see her nipples pushing against the sheer floral fabric, and the shadowy strip of pubic hair at the junction of her thighs— cheerleader thighs that had been perfectly sculpted by years of squats and lunges.

"What if it hadn't been me at the door?" I asked sternly, giving her revealing attire a suspicious once-over. She just smiled and stepped aside to let me come in, and I pushed past her, catching a whiff of her signature mix of hair products, shower gel and perfume.

Layla was easily one of the most beautiful girls I'd ever seen— a blond-haired, blue-eyed China doll with delicately arched brows, a plush little mouth, and a body that looked diminutive next to just about anybody. I was nearly her polar opposite in looks. Five-eleven, muscular, dark-haired. I wasn't extremely tall, especially for a basketball player, but standing next to her I felt enormous. She tweaked my protective instincts like no one ever had.

That is, until she opened her mouth.

You see, Layla's mother had married a Mexican man when Layla was very young, and she'd grown up on the Latin side of town. Her tough barrio accent opposed her delicate Aryan appearance to a comical extent. She looked like she needed protecting, but she sounded like she might cut you if you rubbed her the wrong way.

We had met at the beginning of the semester when she took the seat in front of me in Western Civ II. About halfway into the first day of class, she turned around, fastened her crystal eyes on me and said in that incongruous barrio accent, "You wanna quit kicking the back of my seat, chulo? I can't pay attention to the fucking lecture."

I think my mouth hung open for the rest of class. I just couldn't believe that hard-boiled voice had come out of the pale waif in front of me. Before I could forget, I had typed the word *chulo* into my cell phone browser and looked it up, thoroughly expecting it to be the Spanish equivalent to *fag* or *asshole*. Instead, I had been pleasantly surprised to discover that what she'd actually called me was… *cute.*

Our relationship began as a tentative friendship consisting of sharing Western Civ notes and talking after class on our way out of the building. I liked the fact that she was a cheerleader, and she seemed fascinated with my ability to be both good-looking and smart. Within a couple of weeks I'd asked her out on an official date. Our budding romance garnered a lot of dirty looks from the other guys in class, and I ate it up.

Now, after four months, she and I had fallen into a comfortable rhythm. Conversation was easy, sex was easy… just like today. After she let me into her room, we barely spoke to each other. I loosened the tie on her robe and let it fall to the floor, pushed her down onto the bed, and she opened her legs to me.

I always tried to make sure she got hers first, because there was no telling how long I might be in the mood to go. I went down on her until she was a trembling wreck, then climbed on top and pounded her tiny body with long, hard strokes, dragging out the pleasure as much as I could.

Several minutes later, we were interrupted by fate.

"Too hard, Jamie! Owww. " Layla's cries punctuated the ends of my thrusts, the breathy little sounds popping out of her throat more like hiccups than actual words. "Slow down, you're hurting me."

But my mind was already somewhere else.

"Shhh," I hissed, stopping suddenly and leaning over to turn the radio up. A male announcer was yelling in that overly-excited style reserved for car dealership commercials, gun sales, and sporting events of questionable merit.

"...the Phillips Arena tonight at eight!" the announcer crowed. *"Brutality Sports MMA Extravaganza! Tickets on sale at the box office!"*

The voice continued, but that's all I heard. My mind was spinning with possibilities. I looked at the clock.

Four-fifty in the afternoon. Shit!

"I'm really sorry, babe, but I've gotta go," I said, snatching unceremoniously out of Layla's sweet body and discarding the empty condom into the wastebasket. I grabbed my shorts off the floor, pulled them on, and stepped into my sneakers.

"You're leaving right in the middle of sex?" Layla leaned up onto her elbows and stared at me, bending her knees and laying them over to one side in a demure pose pulled straight from a lingerie catalog. Her perfect tits were partially obscured by the blond hair spilling over them in waves. "What could possibly be more important than sex, papi?"

"My future," I told her, pulling my t-shirt on and slinging my messenger bag over my shoulder. "I just figured out what I'm doing for my final project, but I've got to get over to the Journalism Building before Dr. Washburn leaves. I don't know what time his last class is. He's probably on his way out to his car by now. I'll make it up to you, okay?"

And to myself.

"What is your project?" she asked, but I was already out the door, wondering why in the world she thought I had time to chit-chat if I didn't even have time to get a nut.

I ran all the way from Layla's dorm to the Journalism Building, ignoring the occasional cries of protest as I pushed roughly past the people standing in the halls. Dr. Washburn was just locking his office door as I rushed up behind him, trying to catch my breath.

"Caught you!" I said too loudly, and he jumped.

"Dammit, Jamie. You nearly gave me a heart attack." Dr. Washburn pushed his wire-framed glasses up higher on his nose and narrowed his watery blue eyes at me. "What can I do for you? My last class is about to begin."

"I have an idea for my final project. I want to cover tonight's MMA event down at Phillips Arena, but I need you to call and get me a press pass. Can you do that?"

Dr. Washburn squeezed his eyes shut and rubbed his short, reddish beard, his agitation clear. "That is a great idea, Jamie, but why did you wait till the last minute? I'm about to be late for class."

"I didn't know about it until today. My stupid roommate… He's always driving us crazy with that MMA stuff, so I don't even know how he hasn't said something about this. Please, I'm begging you. I know it's short notice, but I don't have any other options. You don't want me to fail, do you, Doc?" I dropped melodramatically to my knees, poking my bottom lip out and giving him my best puppy dog eyes. "You know you're my favorite professor, right?"

It was almost cheating, really, dropping to my knees in front of poor Dr. Washburn. The way I cut my eyes up at him from beneath my bangs as I begged could probably be classified as flirting, and I had always suspected he found me attractive. The uncomfortable heat in his eyes as he looked down at me told me I had guessed right.

Being the object of that kind of attention, even from men, was nothing new to me, and I wasn't above using it to my advantage on occasion. Flirting came naturally for me. I knew I was good-looking. Everyone had always told me so.

I had brown hair that I kept cut short in back, but with long bangs that swept over one eye. Warm brown puppy dog eyes framed by long lashes gave me an innocent look, as did my plump, pouty lips. My mother had the stereotypical red hair and lightly freckled skin she got from her full-blooded Irish mother, but somehow I'd gotten a good dose of my grandfather's half Spanish looks. Add to that the fact that I'd pretty much mastered the art of boy-next-door charm, and I could be pretty persuasive when I wanted to be.

Like now.

Dr. Washburn cleared his throat nervously and extended a hand down to me. "You're laying it on a bit thick, aren't you Mr. Atwood? Stand up." He helped me to my feet with a grunt and nudged his glasses up again. "I'll do my best to get you a pass, but I can't promise anything. It's up to the event promoters, really."

I grinned. "Thanks, Doc. You won't regret it. I'm gonna rock this project."

"You'd better," he warned. "I want to see you graduate with honors next year, Jamie. You're too good, too smart, to just skate by. And you've certainly got the charm to make things happen." He gave me a pointed look that let me know my efforts to flirt my way into a press pass had not gone unnoticed, and that perhaps I wasn't as smooth as I thought I was.

I smiled and bowed to him, which earned a hearty laugh. Then, without asking, I grabbed the Sharpie out of the top of his notebook and scribbled my name and number on the cover. "Call or text me and let me know something, okay? You gotta come through on this."

"I'll try, but like I said, I can't promise anything." He frowned as a tone sounded over the hallway speaker, signifying the beginning of class. "God, look what you've done. You know how much I despise tardiness. You've made me guilty of the thing I rail about the most." He hurried away down the hall without another word, and I wandered out of the building.

I considered going back to Layla's dorm room and finishing what we'd started, but instead headed out to the parking lot to my car— a thirteen-year-old white BMW with a sluggish engine and a fraying convertible top. A piece of waterproof tape held the back window in. My roommate Braden had informed me that a new top would cost more than the car was worth, and I'd told him he was full of shit. No way a new top could cost that much. But I researched it online, and as much as it pained me to admit it, Braden was right.

So I was stuck with a car that would probably be held together by bubble gum and fishing line by the time graduation rolled around. Meanwhile, Braden— who was much more of an asshole than I was, and therefore less deserving, right?— tooled around in a sleek black Audi that probably rang up to about forty grand. Hell, that was close to my mom's yearly salary as a nurse.

At least I had it over Braden in the looks department. He may have been rich, but his appearance was as plain as it got. His mix of brown hair, brown eyes, and medium skin tone was perfect for blending in, like human camouflage. He also had an aversion to working out.

As I drove the mile and a half from campus to our condo, my brain was swirling with excitement about my upcoming evening. It didn't get much cooler than having a press pass to a big sporting event, even if it was a pseudo-sport like MMA.

My roommates were certainly impressed. Braden, our resident MMA expert, had already bought tickets for him and his girlfriend, Miranda. I still didn't understand why he hadn't mentioned it. I mean this guy was so crazy for the sport, he'd probably been having wet dreams about the upcoming fight for weeks.

"I thought you hated MMA." Braden glared suspiciously at me, like he thought I must be hatching some diabolical scheme. "What ever happened to it not being a legit sport? You said it was barely a step above pro wrestling. You said—"

"I know what I said," I interrupted. "Look, I'm still not a big fan of MMA, okay? But it's a pretty big sports event, and it's here in town, and it's just a few weeks until my project is due. It's like fate, you know? Like the *deus ex machina* swooping in to save my ass at the last minute."

"Deus ex— whatever that means. Can't you speak English? We're not all in the Mensa club, dude."

"I'm not in Mensa, either. That's even less legit than MMA. And I pretty much defined the term in the sentence for you. Ever heard of context clues? You don't have to be a genius to listen, Braden."

"Boys, boys," Miranda interrupted. "Are you going to fight all night? Because I don't want to hear it. I'd rather stay home."

"Well, anyway," Braden said irritably, fluttering his hand in the air like a bird having a seizure. "I think you're secretly a fan of the sport, but you think it's beneath you. That's what I think. I think you have this idea that fighting is a bunch of brainless cavemen, and you want people to think you're too smart to enjoy it."

"Oh, is that right?" I laughed and looked to my other roommate, Trey, for backup. He ignored me and kept playing his video game, looking like a little turtle, with his cap of curly brown hair, freckled nose, and roundish glasses.

"You wanna ride with us?" Miranda interrupted in her no-nonsense way, running her fingers through the blunt ends of her straight, dark hair. "We've got plenty of room. Is Layla going with you? She and I can get ready together."

"Nah, if I even get to go, it's just going to be me. This is business, not pleasure."

I didn't say it, but I doubted that sitting through a bloody massacre with Layla could be classified as pleasure. She could barely stand being in the same room when I was watching sports, which was baffling, because she was a college cheerleader. She was present at every football and basketball game the school played, yet she had only a rudimentary understanding of the rules of those sports. I had a sneaking suspicion she wouldn't even have known when to get excited during the games if it wasn't for the cues from the cheer captain.

But that wasn't why I dated Layla. Sports was the last thing on my mind when it came to her. She was gorgeous, popular, and willing to suck my dick. Plus, she was incredibly lovable once you got past her jarring first impression, and my family had gone nuts over her the one time I'd taken her home for the weekend.

"I'm glad you finally decided to bring someone home," my mom had said. "She's such a sweet girl."

"And not bad to look at either," my dad had added with a laugh. "Can she cook?"

His unapologetically sexist comments earned him a sharp elbow to the side by my mom. But he'd winked at me, and mom had smiled and crinkled her freckled nose, and I knew I had their blessings to take things to the next level.

Only that next level had never materialized. Layla did her thing, I did mine, and we met up once or twice a week for sex. Most nights, we talked on the phone for a few minutes before bed, but we had never actually spent the night together in the same bed.

She had invited me over a few times, but I'd always declined, and she hadn't pushed the issue. She seemed to respect my need to keep some space between us, even if she didn't understand it. Truthfully, I didn't understand it, either. While I considered her my girlfriend, loved her as a friend, and enjoyed having sex with her, anything that suggested true intimacy or the commingling our separate lives still made me uneasy.

I knew she wouldn't expect to be invited to the MMA event. We both knew that wasn't us.

As I trotted down the hall to my room to grab a towel for a quick shower before the fight, I heard Braden trying to explain my relationship to Miranda. "Jamie and Layla aren't like us, babe," he said. "She actually gives him a little breathing room, unlike some people I know."

"Is that supposed to be a hint?" Miranda laughed out loud. "Okay, big boy. You want breathing room? I'll just go out drinking with Kaylee and Lisa tomorrow night instead of hanging here with you like I always do. They've been begging me all week."

"Um, I don't think so," Braden said irritably.

"Then quit complaining."

I heard what sounded like loud kissing coming from the living room, and I shook my head, pulling the bathroom door closed behind me. Those two puzzled the hell out of me. Individually they seemed like the most independent, take-no-shit people, but put them together, and you had a couple who couldn't seem to get enough of each other. It almost made me wish I could figure out how to have that with Layla.

But as the warm water spilled down over my head, I felt an undeniable pang of guilt. The truth was, I didn't actually want that kind of closeness with Layla, or anyone else for that matter. Did that make me selfish?

Was I destined to be one of those serial womanizers who bounced from girlfriend to girlfriend and woke up one day to discover my forties had come and gone and I still didn't have a family? Was I going to be like Uncle Martin, my dad's lawyer brother who showed up with a new woman at every family reunion? On the surface, Uncle Martin seemed to be living the life he wanted, but I had studied him a few times when he thought no one was paying attention. Something about the wistful look in his eyes as he watched the established couples and their children interact gave me the distinct impression that all was not wine and roses in Martin's world.

I didn't want that kind of life, but sometimes it felt like that's exactly where I was headed.

2

WHILE I was getting dressed, Dr. Washburn texted to say that a press pass would be waiting for me at the Will Call ticket window, and I celebrated so loudly the neighbors probably heard me. I pulled on my skinny khakis, a midnight blue stretch button-up over a black t-shirt, and my black leather shoes. Then I pieced my bangs out with a bit of hair gel and slicked the rest back into a ducktail.

Lastly, I picked up my favorite necklace, a crude silver Claddagh strung with double strands of black rawhide that tied in the back, leaving the strands hanging free down the back of my neck. The small beads knotted on the end of each strand clacked gently when I moved just right.

The symbol itself, two hands holding a crowned heart, was a nod to my Irish heritage that my mother, and I by way of osmosis, found to be such a source of pride. Mom had given my older sister a

Claddagh ring for her sixteenth birthday, and I'd been so jealous. When I turned sixteen, Mom had the more masculine-styled necklace custom made for me. Since that day, I'd rarely gone without it.

I tucked the strands into my collar in back and checked myself out one final time in the mirror. By the time I met my friends in the living room, I looked and smelled like a million bucks. Okay, maybe only a couple hundred bucks since I shopped at Target, but it was good enough to make Miranda raise her eyebrows.

Phillips Arena was hopping an hour before the show was set to begin. Braden drove the Audi carefully through the parking garage, sandwiched in line between two late-model beaters. The ticking sound from one of the engines bounced around deafeningly in the enclosed garage, prompting a familiar tirade from Braden.

"Dammit, why do people drive such hunks of shit? Don't they have any pride at all? When a car sounds like that, it's time for the junkyard."

"Not everyone can afford to buy a new car, sweetie," Miranda said quietly from the passenger seat.

I sat in the backseat and kept my mouth shut. More power to Miranda for wanting to teach her man a little humility, but I'd lived with him long enough to know he'd always be a spoiled rich brat, bitching from the womb to the tomb about problems he would never have the misfortune of understanding.

His dad gave him everything he wanted, including the three-bedroom condo he and I shared with Trey. Braden had the master suite with his own bathroom, while Trey and I fought over the one in the hall. Not a bad deal, considering Braden's dad owned the condo and only charged Trey and me a hundred dollars each, plus our share of the utilities, food and expenses.

My parents would shoot me if I lost my killer living arrangement, and I didn't have sex to barter with like Miranda, so I knew better than to mouth off at Braden too much. Friendship was the only thing I had, and that was a slippery slope at best with a guy like Braden. We'd already lost one roommate when he got a little too pushy, accusing Braden of not doing his part to keep the place clean. That guy had lasted all of one month before he'd been replaced with Trey.

Now the three of us were about to be wrapping up our third school year of living together, all of us juniors, sweating finals that were coming up in three weeks. I'd been worried I wouldn't be able to come up with a suitable final project for Dr. Washburn's class, and it counted for fifty percent of my grade. That was why I was so excited about the MMA fight. With this opportunity, my journalism degree suddenly seemed within reach.

"You're not sitting with us?" Miranda asked when we were standing in line at Will Call. She sounded disappointed, which in turn seemed to annoy Braden.

"No, babe," he grated. "He's here for work, like he told you. Let the guy do his job."

My job. That sounded good. Grown up.

"What kind of job are you going for?" she asked. "I don't think you've ever told me."

"I'm hoping to be a sports writer, or a publicist for a sports team. Something like that. Maybe even a sportscaster."

"So you might be on TV?" She bounced excitedly on her toes, her brown eyes twinkling. "I could definitely see your face on TV. You'd be a celebrity." She turned to her boyfriend. "We'd know a celebrity, Braden. How cool would that be?"

"Name a sportscaster," Braden challenged her.

"What?" She gave him a blank stare, the smile falling from her face. "I don't know any."

"Not such a big celebrity after all, huh?"

I bit my tongue to keep from retorting against the obvious insult. It helped that I understood where his animosity came from; Braden was afraid his girlfriend was attracted to me. For a guy who had so much going for him, he was awfully insecure about his girl.

"I don't want to be a celebrity," I said. "I just like the idea of a profession that combines my two greatest loves: writing and sports."

"Oh." Miranda nodded politely, the stars fading from her eyes.

"My name is Jamie Atwood," I said to the girl at the Will Call desk, bending to speak into the hole at the bottom of the window. She checked something on her computer and produced a laminated press pass for me. My heart climbed into my throat as I took the official-looking badge and turned it over in my hand. It may seem cheesy, but to me it was the first sign that I'd almost arrived— was almost a professional.

Almost a man.

Miranda and Braden turned off at their section, Miranda waving over her shoulder as I continued on toward the backstage area. My heart was hammering in my chest now, and I felt a little light-headed. What the hell was I supposed to do now? I hadn't really thought past getting the press badge, and now that I was actually expected to do something, I was at a loss.

Think, Jamie. What do reporters do?

I wracked my brain, trying to come up with any knowledge I'd gained from my journalism classes, realizing belatedly that working in a classroom setting just doesn't prepare you for the reality of being in the field. Maybe in trying to wow my professor, I'd bitten off more than I could chew.

I suspected the rest of the students were doing reports that didn't require hands-on work, and here I had signed myself up for a crash course in the realities of making an ass of myself. Because I was pretty sure that was what was about to happen.

A giant with tattoos covering his arms and a mass of scraggly facial hair guarded the door to the backstage area, and I was willing to bet his face had never stretched into a smile. He eyed my press pass and waved me on through without incident, and I breathed a sigh of relief.

Backstage was crawling with people. Organizers rushed from one place to another, radiating nervous energy as they worked to ensure everything was going as planned. There were security guards, men in suits, and guys who looked like fighters but weren't here to fight.

I'd watched enough MMA shows with Braden to know that the fighters on tonight's card would be prepping in private rooms with their trainers and coaches. I wouldn't be able to interview any of them until afterward, if at all. As for fighters who would not be fighting, there were a few of them milling around backstage talking to reporters already.

I'd never been so intimidated in my life. Besides the fact that I was here in a professional capacity but knew next to nothing about how I was supposed to conduct myself, I was surrounded by guys who were in crazy physical shape. My muscles seemed almost like facsimiles of the real things in comparison to the sinewy muscles that stretched along the bones of the fighters. These guys had honed their bodies into killing machines in martial arts training facilities around the world, while I had languished on the cushioned seats of stationary weight machines at the YMCA, half-assing it when I got a little winded.

To say I felt physically inferior was an understatement. Watching fights on TV had not prepared me for how these guys would look in person, or for the overwhelming hum of testosterone-infused excitement in the air. I could feel my entire being vibrating beneath my skin.

I froze when I caught sight of a young fighter standing in the center of a group of people. Two men in suits hovered close to him, flanking him like guardians, effectively and wordlessly establishing themselves as part of his entourage. A couple of women with press passes and cameras slung around their necks gazed at the fighter with a kind of rapture as he talked, and I couldn't blame them.

The fighter had longish hair, a dark chocolate color infused with subtle caramel highlights. It was pulled back from his face and twisted into a tight little topknot. Don't ask me how I knew he was a fighter, because he was dressed like he was ready to hit the runway.

His face was vaguely suggestive of a Latin heritage, with a strong jaw, large, black-rimmed eyes, and a straight nose that looked like it had miraculously never been broken. Beneath the designer clothes, his skin had a healthy-looking tan, as if he'd just come back from a week at the beach. But something in the way he carried himself left no mistake as to what he was.

This guy was a professional ass kicker.

Before I knew it, my feet had carried me right over to the small group, and I found myself standing beside the reporters. I knew I was staring, but I couldn't help myself. I'd never seen a person with such presence. He wasn't bulky, though. On the contrary, he looked lean and lethal like a panther, with golden-green eyes to match.

If the guy's fighting was anywhere near the level of his looks, he was destined to be a star— just the kind of person an aspiring publicist might like to align himself with. Then it occurred to me that if he was much of a fighter, he'd probably have battle scars. Maybe he was just a pretty face after all.

"I wish we could see you fight tonight," one of the reporters said. "I'll bet that would be something."

The guy shrugged. "I'm just kicking back tonight, supporting my training partner, Jason Kinney. Plus, my next match is against Davi Matos, one of the fighters here tonight." For a moment he looked uncomfortable, as if he had said something he shouldn't. "Uh, I may be fighting him. I'm not sure yet. Anyway, it's good to get in close to the action, see what a guy is made of. You can't really tell on TV, you know."

I pulled out my cell phone, switched to video mode, and started filming his response.

"Is it that much different in person?" The other reporter leaned in closer, waiting for an answer that took a moment to come. "It seems like with the camera close-ups on TV, it would be the other way around."

"It's hard to explain." The fighter paused, looking directly at me for the first time since I'd arrived. "There's a feeling you get when you're close to something. Seeing it right in front of your face takes it to a whole different level. You can feel the fear and the excitement, the rush of adrenaline, smell the sweat, hear the force of the blows and the snap of bone. You can tell if someone's confident or if they're scared shitless."

Out of the corner of my eye, I saw the ladies wrinkle their noses at his raw choice of words, but I stepped in closer, mesmerized. This was exactly the kind of thing I wanted to hear. I repositioned my phone slightly to get a better angle on the fighter.

"What's your name?" he asked me, and he may as well have focused a spotlight on me.

I laughed nervously and called on my keen wit to rescue me. "I thought I was supposed to be asking the questions."

Yeah. Nothing keen or witty about that.

As his face hardened slightly and the others glared at me, I rushed to make amends. "Jamie Atwood," I said. "That's my name."

I figured I might as well just turn around and leave right then, because I'd clearly botched the whole interview thing, but he graciously stuck out his right hand. He didn't smile, but at least he wasn't walking away or knocking me out. "I'm Michael Kage," he said. "You can just call me Kage. Who do you work for?"

"Work for?" I asked stupidly, snorting out a laugh that would have sounded more appropriate at a Star Trek convention than a fight. My skin felt clammy against his warm, dry palm as we shook hands.

"I mean who are you reporting for?" he reached out and tugged gently on the press pass hanging around my neck.

It may sound strange, but when he reached out for me like that, I felt the heat of a flush creep across my face. It reminded me of high school, when the hot senior guys would talk to the freshman girls, making them giggle and blush from nothing more than a simple touch. In other words, this Kage guy must have been made of 100% testosterone, because he had succeeded in making me blush like a schoolgirl.

"Oh, who am I reporting for. Right. I'm here on behalf of Georgia State University." I started babbling like a jackass, telling shit I had no business telling, digging myself in deeper with every word that came out of my mouth. "Actually, I'm not a real reporter yet. In fact, I probably won't be a reporter at all. I'm actually not here in an official capacity, I guess." Insert awkward laugh. "I mean, I am, but it's just for a school project. I'm a journalism major, but what I really hope to be is a publicist."

"Yeah? What all does a publicist do, besides sending out press kits and shit like that?"

It was impossible to tell if Kage was being condescending, or if he was truly interested in the job description of a publicist. He might have been wearing a killer suit, but the rough edges of the guy were still clearly visible. He smirked at me, daring me to impress him.

And I wanted to.

"Well, Mr. Kage, I suppose we do whatever needs doing to make sure that a client is well-known and well-liked. Good publicists are story-spinners and star-makers, but bad ones… Let's just say a publicist can make or break a career, no matter what the client has done."

I don't know where those pretentious words came from. It was as if I were suddenly playing a role, and my character knew a heck of a lot more about being a publicist than I did. It must have sounded good, though, because Kage took the bait.

He raised his eyebrows. "And you know how to do all of that?"

"Of course." I gave him a cocky grin, his apparent interest giving me way more confidence than I had any right to have. "It's my specialty."

And there it was. The lie that had the potential to get me in trouble. My mother always called me her little flimflam artist. Said I could sell ice to an Eskimo, which is a ridiculously overused cliché, but she made her point.

"No shit." Kage turned fully toward me, his eyes wide. "What if I did something really, really fucked up? Could you get me out of it?"

"Why, are you planning on killing someone?" I laughed, but he didn't, so I cleared my throat. "Uh, yeah. I'd do my best to keep you smelling like a rose. I'd even help you hide the body if you paid me enough."

I was at the mercy of my ego, talking shit I probably couldn't back up if my life depended on it. But who really cared, anyway? He could tell me he was a brain surgeon, and I could tell him I was a fighter pilot. Neither one of us would ever know the difference.

The lady reporters stared at me, and one of them put her hands on her hips, clearly irritated. "Fascinating, I'm sure," she said flatly. "But I'd like to know more about this upcoming fight of yours, Kage.

What promotion will it be with? Do you foresee a future with the UFC?"

Without missing a beat, Kage turned to the reporters and smiled. It was the first time I'd seen him purposely attempt to be charming, and I had to admit, he was damn good at it. Dimples for days. "Actually, ladies, I need to take off. Gotta get to my seat so that I don't miss any of the fights. It was nice talking to you, though. Maybe we can catch up some other time."

He sent a subtle wink in my direction, and my heart sped up. I felt like I'd just been invited to sit at the popular table. Like he and I had something between us, some secret that the ladies weren't privy to.

But then Kage just turned and walked away, followed by the two silent men who had been hovering behind him. He didn't speak, didn't say goodbye or nice to meet you, or even kiss my ass you little wannabe.

Damn. So much for the popular table.

The reporters spared one last prickly glare at me before clicking away on their sensible heels, leaving me by myself and reeling from shame. I had come here planning to keep my head down, learn enough to ace my school project, and get a little job experience. But it appeared that I had only succeeded in running everyone off.

THE tournament was everything Kage had painted it to be and more. I'd never attended a live fight of any kind, and it was so much different than watching it on television. I wondered if any of my other MMA-obsessed friends had ever seen a live fight, or if Braden and I were the only ones.

I was able to push my way out from backstage into a press-only seating area, but all of the seats were taken, so I stood off to one side. I was squished uncomfortably between two overweight reporters, one of whom smelled like corn chips and stale cigarettes. But it didn't take long to forget they were there altogether. Being so close to the action was surreal.

I recalled Kage's words about smelling the fear, and I thought I knew exactly what he meant. On TV, the action was sterile, just another sporting event with rules to follow and some exciting action to watch. But when you were here watching from mere feet away, it became real. It was a transplanted street brawl, with real people and real injuries. It was one guy trying to beat the shit out of another guy, and someone was going to lose. Someone was going to have to limp home with a broken ego, possibly even some broken bones or scars.

It was terrifying and exhilarating all at once, and as I watched through eyes stretched wide, my teeth dug painfully into my bottom lip, I thought maybe I was already addicted.

I decided to try to get some action shots of the fights, but it became clear soon enough that my photos were not going to be anywhere near Sports Illustrated quality. Cell phones were great for taking selfies and posting them on social media sites, but if I was even going to try to pretend to be a sports reporter, I'd have to have a good digital camera. That would be a perfect gift to ask my parents to get me for my twenty-first birthday coming up in a few weeks. Until then, I'd just have to make do with blurry fight shots.

I was particularly interested in chronicling the fight between two Brazilians— Kage's future opponent, Davi Matos, and some guy whose name I didn't bother committing to memory. Honestly, I didn't care about Matos beyond getting his name right for my assignment. Somehow I'd gotten locked in on the first guy I'd come in contact with in the world of mixed martial arts, and now everything was about Michael Kage. Already my brain was trying to figure out how to spin this whole project to focus on him, and he wasn't even fighting.

After Matos finished wiping the floor with the other Brazilian, I got an uneasy feeling. The guy was impressive. It made me nervous for Kage, who had the demeanor of a fighter, but whose face looked entirely too pretty. If this match was any indication of things to come, Kage would probably be the one limping home when it came to fighting Matos. Maybe this fight would scare him enough to back down.

I scanned the crowd for him, but there were too many faces to sift through. I couldn't find him— couldn't see if he was scared.

After watching two more fights, I'd come to the realization that I knew virtually nothing about mixed martial arts fighting. Sometimes Braden ordered a keg on pay-per-view nights, and we watched the fight and got smashed. I'd always been an armchair spectator, more concerned with keeping a full beer in one hand and my girlfriend's ass in the other than what was going on inside the octagon.

I could recognize a few submission moves, knew the basic kicks and punches like anyone would, but the rest of it had flown right over my head. Fighting just wasn't my thing. I was more of a ball man, myself. Give me a basketball, football, baseball, soccer ball—

hell, even a tennis ball— and I knew what I was doing. But fighting was foreign territory for me. I felt bad for the thoughts I'd had earlier about Layla, about how she knew nothing about the sports she cheered for, because tonight I was no better.

As the last fight was ending in a knockout, I began to make my way out of my seating area and into a stream of people madly dashing for the door. I knew the parking garage would be mayhem within minutes, and I wondered where Braden and Miranda were. Then I realized I didn't have to wonder, because I had one of those newfangled communications devices in my pocket. I pulled my cell phone out and texted Braden.

"Where are you?"

Nothing. He probably couldn't hear the alert on his phone in the noisy arena.

I noticed reporters from the press seating area were all moving in the same direction down a hallway off the main lobby, so I followed. They led me to a large conference room with a hand-written sign on the door that read *Press*.

Yep, this is my stop.

I hovered for a few minutes outside the press room so that I could at least listen to the questions other reporters— real reporters— were asking the fighters, but I was afraid to go in. I was also afraid Braden was going to leave without me.

"Don't ditch me," I texted, belatedly wishing I'd driven myself.

I opened the browser on my phone and Googled *Michael Kage* on a whim. There were a couple of social media profiles, a headshot of some unknown actor, and several unrelated results that made me scratch my head that they'd even shown up in the first place.

Apparently, Michael Kage was not a household name in the world of mixed martial arts, and learning that left me inexplicably disappointed. Guess I thought I'd met a celebrity.

I leaned against a wall and studied a couple of fighters who were in my line of sight, looking the worse for wear after having recently beaten someone senseless, or having been beaten senseless themselves. Davi Matos came near, and I just stared.

Like Kage, he had an undeniable presence. He passed so close to me, I felt the air stir, but his eyes never lighted on me. Thank goodness. That guy made me nervous. Up close, his face looked like it had been through a meat grinder. Apparently his opponent had gotten off a few damaging shots before he got submitted.

The two lady reporters who had snubbed me at the beginning of the night stood in the group inside the room. One of them kept yelling questions out of turn, like she thought she was in the movies or something. I rolled my eyes.

I turned my attention back to my cell phone, getting ready to call Braden.

"Learning anything?" said a voice from behind me, and I spun around to come face to face with Michael Kage.

I startled, looking guiltily up at him and shoving my cell phone behind my back before he could see that I'd been researching him. "What are you doing?" I said, for lack of anything better. My heart had sped up again. Something about this guy really had my ticker going wild, like his very presence caused an adrenaline dump in my system.

"Getting ready to go eat. I'm starving. Any nice places around here without a long wait?"

"Lou's is only a few blocks away. They've got a killer cheeseburger, and they're quick."

"Cheeseburger." Kage laughed, showing those rampant dimples. "You're funny, college boy. I meant something a real man would eat."

He took a step closer. One step closer than propriety dictated.

"What's the matter, you don't like cheeseburgers? That's downright unpatriotic."

Instinctively, I took one step back, reclaiming my personal space. But Kage stepped forward again and gave me what could only be described as a look of challenge. This time, I stood my ground.

"You don't get a body like this by eating fast food." He said, patting his belly. There was so little give, he might as well have been hitting a suit of armor. "How's your project coming? You got everything you need?"

I shrugged. "I wish I could have gotten better photos. The action shots are blurry. I need a new camera if I'm gonna be doing this kind of stuff."

"Wanna take one of me?" He grinned and crossed his arms over his chest, plumping up his biceps. I fumbled for my phone, quickly switched to camera mode, and took a picture. Then he struck another pose, this time with his usual face that looked like he was ready to whip some ass. It was shocking to see him change like that, as if he'd slipped into another personality and back again.

"I appreciate you helping me out," I told him. "If you want to know the truth, I'm a little starstruck right now. I've never met a real fighter before." I bit my lip nervously. "Would you mind taking a selfie with me? It would make my roommates so jealous."

"Yeah?" He raised a brow. "Well, I'm all for making people jealous."

We leaned in close to each other, and I held the phone out as far as I could to capture the image. The two well-dressed thugs who had been flanking Kage all night chose that moment to step out of the shadows. "We need to go, Kage," one of them said. "Plane's leaving in less than two hours, and we still have to stop for food."

"Fuck." Kage rubbed a hand irritatedly over his eyes. "All right, let's go. Catch you on the flip side, college boy." He turned to go, his friends leading the way. But just at the last second, he glanced back over his shoulder at me with a cocky smile and graced me with another of his little winks.

Jesus, that guy was something else.

"It's Jamie," I called after him, watching his back disappear into the crowd. "Hey, where can I see you fight?"

I don't know if he heard me or not. The three of them disappeared into the crowd as if they'd never existed, leaving me wondering what the hell I was going to write for my project, since I'd spent all night trying to bond with a fighter even Google had never heard of.

3

SOMEHOW, I pulled an A out of my project. Between the bits Kage had told me, the stuff I could learn from the internet, and getting to watch the fights in person, I was able to craft an interesting and informative report about how fighters prepare for upcoming matches.

My roommate Trey, an art major who wanted nothing more than to get into a good film school, recorded a video of me doing a mock newscast. I flipped through the photos and video footage I'd shot of Kage that night, but I didn't use any of them. They seemed too personal. Instead, we used a few of my grainy action photos along with some actual tournament footage found online. I created a makeshift news desk out of the kitchen table, and Trey hung his green screen behind me, then superimposed a newsroom background on it during editing. The end result was enough to put every one of my classmates to shame.

"You looked very professional in your video, Mr. Atwood" Dr. Washburn told me after class. "I wouldn't have thought you owned a traditional suit."

"Only because I was a pallbearer in my aunt's funeral last year." I admitted. "Not much opportunity for formal attire when you're a college student."

"No, I suppose not. Especially when you're an underachieving college student."

I rolled my eyes. "Not the underachiever speech again. I would have thought you'd be tired of that by now."

"I never get tired of encouraging students. Not if I truly believe in them." He rested a hip on his desk and crossed his arms. "Jamie, I see you languishing away, settling for mediocre, and it makes me want to give you a swift kick in the pants. Because when you put your mind to it and really call up that passion that's inside you, you're capable of so much more. I want to see you get fired up about something. This project was the first thing I felt like you've really put your heart into, and it was a refreshing change."

"Doc, no offense, but I've been hearing that same speech since I was in the first grade."

"Well, maybe it's time to listen to it."

I turned his statement over in my head. On the surface, it sounded like a platitude, but he did make a good point. If I kept hearing the same thing coming out of different people's mouths, maybe there was some truth to it.

"Look, Jamie," he continued. "I'd be glad to stand behind you in any kind of recommendation, review, reference, referral… whatever you need—"

"Does it have to begin with an *R*?" I interrupted with a grin.

Dr. Washburn rolled his eyes in annoyance but didn't miss a beat. "However… in return I want to see you putting out some real effort. Take an active part in shaping your life. Partying and video games may be good enough for your friends, but you deserve more than that, and all you have to do is reach out and take it."

I nodded, at a loss for what to say. The man seemed so earnest, I was actually beginning to believe what he was saying. But my mind was also full of doubts.

"You know, I was lost at that MMA event," I admitted, stuffing my hands into my jeans pockets and giving a sheepish grin. "I didn't know what the hell I was doing. Half the stuff in my report just came from research after the fact. At the event, I looked like some idiot who had found a press pass on the floor, stuttering and scared to speak to anyone. It got me thinking that I'm in the wrong major. What if I'm just no good at it?"

Dr. Washburn laughed. "Welcome to the world of real journalism, Jamie. The stuff you see on TV may be tied up with a pretty red bow, but you have no idea what hell someone may have gone through to get it that way. That's where the talent comes in. You work with what you have, do your best, and learn as you go."

"You really think so? I was feeling like such a fraud, like a cheater or something."

Dr. Washburn leaned forward and put a hand on my shoulder, peering up at me through his glasses. "You did fine. You taught everyone in this class some things today, and you entertained us in the process. That's what journalism is all about. Educating and entertaining your audience, using whatever you can get your hands on, however you can get it. Within reason, of course."

A light suddenly came on inside my head. It wasn't about being perfect; it was about getting the job done. With his simple words, it felt like Dr. Washburn had just opened up my entire future for me, and I couldn't help smiling all the way home after our talk.

I FLOATED through the end of school with a kind of euphoric confidence, earning straight A's on all of my final exams. Several times, I thanked Dr. Washburn for what he'd told me. I don't know if he'd understood how profound his words were when he said them, but they had really made an impact on my attitude. I was starting to realize that my outcomes were dependent on and directly related to the amount of effort I put in.

"What's got you so fired up about school?" Layla asked me over lunch the day before our last exams. "You seem different. I've never seen you so concerned about your grades before. You're not going all nerdy on me, are you?"

She was teasing, I knew, but it rubbed me the wrong way. Suddenly I was that little guy in elementary school again— the one with glasses and a book in his hand. The one who joined the football team to seem more like the other boys.

"Everything is not about sports and partying, you know. *Some* of us have aspirations." I picked at my spaghetti with my fork, dragging the overcooked noodles around on the plate.

"I have aspirations, Jamie. I'm not just some air-headed cheerleader. I'm going to be a school teacher. That's an important job."

There was hurt in her eyes, and I immediately felt guilty. I reached over and slid an arm around her narrow shoulders, pulling her into a one-armed embrace. “I’m sorry, Layla. I didn’t mean that you don’t have aspirations. It’s just… I guess I just don’t like being called a nerd. I heard it enough when I was a kid. Do you really think I’m a nerd? I play basketball.”

“Of course not. I was only joking.” She rested her head on my shoulder. “You’re like what Dr. Bayne would call a renna… renna...”

“Renaissance Man?” I supplied the term begrudgingly, because knowing it just further solidified my nerd status.

“Yeah, that’s it. That’s what you are.”

But the whole conversation over lunch left me feeling unsettled. Not because I thought I was a nerd, though I guess if I was honest with myself, I had to admit it was something I’d always been worried about. What really bothered me about the exchange with Layla was that it had felt so strained, and it wasn’t the first time. More and more over the past few weeks, I was getting the impression that the two of us were drifting apart, with only a gossamer cord of desire still keeping us tethered to each other.

“Do you love me, Jamie?” She asked suddenly, lifting her head from my shoulder and searching my eyes with her own. I knew what she was searching for. I was also sure it wasn’t there. The knowledge made my stomach roll.

“You’re my girlfriend,” I said lamely. “We’re together, aren’t we?”

She just kept looking at me like she was waiting for something better to come out of my mouth. Something with emotion. It wasn’t going to come, though, and we both knew it. And if by some miracle

I'd been able to get the right words to cross my lips, she wouldn't have wanted them anyway. Not if they were coerced and only half true.

Instead of giving her what she thought she wanted to hear, I squeezed my lips together and looked away. I took the coward's way out. But then she surprised me— no, a better word would be shocked. She shocked the shit out of me with what she said next.

"I've been talking to someone else," she said quietly. "For a while."

My head snapped back around, and I was suddenly able to look at her. "What?" I could feel how wide my eyes were, and how indignant my expression was, even though I had no right to be indignant. "Another guy? You've been cheating on me?"

My brain struggled to process the words. My pride told me I must have misheard.

Layla pulled away, surprisingly calm as she folded her hands into her lap and regarded me with a sober expression. "I haven't cheated on you, Jamie. I wouldn't do that. But… I've thought about it. Well, not about actually cheating on you, but about going out with this other person. You and I are just—"

After a few drawn out seconds, I whispered, "Over?" I looked into her eyes. "Are we going to be able to stay friends?"

"I think so." She smiled wistfully. "You don't seem too upset."

My heart was beating fast. I felt like I should say something profound, something to make it all okay, but it wasn't okay. We were breaking up, and it was awful because I didn't seem to want to fight to change that.

Dammit, why can't I just be a good boyfriend? I need to do something.

"Maybe we could—" I began slowly, but Layla cut me off with a resolute shake of her head.

"It's okay, Jamie. I understand you don't want the same things as me, you know? That's why I just needed to move on. I may seem tough, but deep down I'm just a girl. I can't help it. I want the fairy tale."

"And this other guy… He gives you the fairy tale?"

"I don't know. Maybe." Layla shrugged and scanned the room, and I couldn't help feeling like she was looking for a way out, like she'd rather be anywhere but sitting here talking to me about relationships. Because the truth was, ours was over. Maybe the other guy was waiting for her somewhere in the cafeteria, watching all of this go down.

If he was watching, he didn't get much of a show. We could have at least argued, shared a few tears, but instead it felt like nothing, and the nothingness was ultimately more painful than any drama we might have had. I just sat there awkwardly, feeling the nothingness like a boulder in my gut, not wanting to stay, but not knowing quite how to say goodbye and get up and walk away.

And that was how I became single again. Emasculated in the cafeteria by a tiny blond cheerleader with a Mexican twang.

MIRANDA didn't seem surprised when I got home and announced to everyone in my living room that Layla and I had broken up. In fact, except for Trey's halfhearted *Really?* and Braden's overly-shocked

No!, there was no reaction to my earth-shattering news. Trey and Braden continued playing their video game.

"It's about time," Miranda said, earning a suspicious glare from Braden. "I mean, you two were just not compatible. Did you know there was a rumor that she was seeing Matt Foster?"

Fuck. One of my teammates?

"She didn't tell me it was him. Just said she hadn't cheated on me, but that they had been talking." I plopped down on the sofa next to Miranda. "We're still friends, though."

I feel numb. I must still be in shock.

Miranda snorted. "Okay."

"What? We *are* friends."

"I said okay."

She clearly didn't believe me, and I didn't bother trying to convince her. Either Layla and I were friends, or we weren't. She'd be busy soon with her new boyfriend and probably wouldn't have time for friends, anyway, so what was the point?

"I got all A's so far," I said, changing the subject.

"Nerd," Braden accused, still without taking his eyes off of the game.

"I'm not a nerd," I protested for the second time within hours.

Braden snickered. "Yeah, right. You make straight A's without studying, you wear those Clark Kent glasses when you read, and you've started dressing like one of those male models in the magazines. What are they called? *GQ*, or *Cosmo*. Some shit."

"*Cosmo* is a women's magazine, hon," Miranda corrected.

"Whatever," Braden said. "He knows what I mean. Jamie, you need to stick to the basketball shorts and snapbacks. That's what the chicks dig. I'll bet that's why Layla broke it off with you. Matt Foster doesn't try to be GQ. He dresses like a jock."

"I dress like a jock a lot of the time," I pointed out indignantly. "And my body is way hotter than Matt Foster's."

That claim actually got Braden to look up from the game long enough to give me an amused look. "The shirts you wear are too tight. Guys need breathing room. And those skinny little pants you wear when we go out are ridiculous." He elbowed Trey like he'd just made the joke of the century.

"You're just jealous, Braden. I look damn good in tight t-shirts and Clark Kent glasses." Out of the corner of my eye, I noticed Miranda nodding in agreement. "Besides, we've got to start growing up at some point, man. You think you're going to wear snapbacks and basketball shorts to your first job? I guess that would be okay if you're a pro ball player, but that won't fly in the real world." I looked to Miranda and then Trey for backup, but they were no help. "Trey, I'm not a nerd, am I?"

Trey laughed. "What's so bad about that? I'm a nerd, and proud of it."

"You got that right." Braden piped up. "College is for partying, man. You're gonna be forty years old looking back on this time wishing you'd sowed your wild oats like me."

"Yeah, you think so?" Trey asked him. "I'm okay with that, because when I'm looking back, I'll be sitting in a nice house counting my money. Meanwhile, you'll be crying in your beer in some one-room hovel wishing you'd done your homework and taken life seriously."

Braden waved him away, obviously not buying into Trey's vision of the future. "My daddy's got money, man."

The room was thick with Miranda's sudden disdain for the turn the conversation had taken. "Sowing your wild oats, huh?" she asked her boyfriend pointedly.

"Figure of speech, babe," Braden said. Then he let loose with a barrage of virtual gunfire on the video game, jumping to a standing position and pounding frantically on the buttons on his controller. "Motherfucker shot me! Did you see that? We've got to get better internet, because this shit is lagging. No way he could have gotten me. Did you guys see that?"

Trey threw up his hands. "Thanks, man. Nice going. You just got me killed."

Miranda rolled her eyes at me. "I guess this is what they mean by sowing oats? Wearing a hole in the sofa playing video games?"

"Hey, it's better than going out and banging other chicks," I pointed out. Miranda didn't seem too thrilled that I had put that particular thought into words, and I didn't relish exploring the idea further with her. "Give me that controller," I told Braden. "Let the master take over. I'll prove to you there's no lag."

"It's your funeral." He handed me the controller and headed off to the kitchen. "Anybody want a sandwich?"

Trey raised his hand like he was in class. "I'll take a PB&J."

"Let me rephrase that," Braden said. "Anybody named Miranda want a sandwich?"

Miranda got up and followed him into the kitchen, leaving me and Trey to battle bad guys on the game. I needed some brainless man-fun. Anything to get my mind off the fact that I'd just been dumped.

THAT night, I went to the gym later than usual.

The place smelled of chlorine and sweat. It was a smell I'd come to associate with being healthy, and the second it hit my nostrils, I got a surge of adrenaline. I strode across the crowded space to secure a locker for my cell phone and wallet, taking in the familiar sights and sounds of the gym— muscles pumping, men grunting, the clang of heavy weights hitting the floor. Treadmills whirred, ponytails bounced, and sneakers tapped out a choppy rhythm on the treadmill belts. In the background, sneakers squeaked on the basketball court, and children squealed beneath the gushing fountain in the indoor pool, which should have been closing any minute.

My brain shifted into workout mode, and I turned everything else off.

Whether I was straining to eke out that eighth rep on a weight machine, pushing myself to failure, or zoning out on the treadmill for an hour, it was always cathartic. Focusing on pushing my body gave my mind a much-needed vacation. I didn't have to think about school, or relationships, or whether I could afford to go out with my friends on Friday night. It was just me and the machines, and we had only one goal in mind: physical exhaustion.

When I was almost finished with my Thursday night arm routine, a guy sat down on the machine directly in front of me. It was one of those awkward situations where both of us were forced to stare directly at each other as we worked. I was doing lat pull-downs, and he was on the ab crunch machine. I'd never seen the guy in school. He was slightly shorter than my six-foot height, with light hair and a broader build. I was of the opinion that people who took part in sports had a slightly different musculature than people who only worked out in a gym environment, and this guy had a gym jockey look about him. Not that it wasn't a good look on him, because it definitely was.

Normally, I would have tried to engage him in a little chat to dispel the awkwardness of staring right at each other while we worked out. Except for my horrible attempt at impersonating a reporter during the MMA event, I'd never had a hard time talking to people. But after Layla knocked the wind out of my sails, I hadn't felt much like socializing.

As I watched, the guy slipped his t-shirt off and slung it over the arm of the machine. Then he began to crunch his very tight, very prominent abdominals, keeping his eyes trained on his six-pack as if to visually confirm that the muscles were engaging. When I realized I was studying his muscles just as intently as he was, I looked away and reminded myself to resume my own exercises.

I could tell a difference in my own appearance during the off season. I kept myself in shape, which was easy considering my natural tendency toward a long, lean muscularity. Baseball, basketball, and football had all been important to me in high school. I'd juggled all three sports until my junior year when it got too much for me. Carrying a full load of Advanced Placement classes and trying to play every sport they offered began to feel like a slow suicide, so I reluctantly dropped baseball. By college, football had fallen by the wayside as well, mainly because I had little chance of doing anything at a big university other than riding the bench.

The decision had also been affected by my desire to focus on preparing myself for a successful career, and also by my secret fear that I couldn't hang with college-level athletes in such a physically demanding sport. My parents seemed relieved when I announced my plans to drop football. I think we all breathed a little easier knowing I wasn't going to have to compete with guys who would probably stomp me in the dirt. I did still play basketball, though I often considered retiring that jersey, as well.

Quitting ball wouldn't be so bad. I could always stay in shape by frequenting the gym, just like the guy I was currently watching work his abs. I mean, he was no Michael Kage, but he looked good.

Dammit, now I was thinking of that stupid fighter again. It felt like he'd appeared in my life for the sole purpose of making me feel like shit in comparison. I had looked at his pictures on my cell phone until I was sick to death of seeing him. Especially the ones where I was in the frame with him.

I wondered what his abs looked like under the dress shirt he'd been wearing at the event. No doubt amazing. Some guys had all the luck. Sure, Kage worked his ass off for that body, but the face… he was born with that. Ever since I'd met him I'd been preoccupied with the idea of getting in better shape, but I knew no matter how hard I tried, I'd never be able to attain his level of attractiveness. I wondered if he'd found me attractive, or if maybe he looked at mere mortals like me and felt pity.

And now my girl just dumped me. Can I get any more pathetic?

I hopped up from the weight machine in the middle of a rep, quickly sprayed and wiped the seat and handles, and hurried down the long corridor to the back of the gym. I grabbed one of the white towels off the cart just outside the door to the shower room and went inside.

Leaning over the bench that ran beneath the wall of tall gym lockers, I propped a foot up on it and unlaced one of my sneakers. That's when the guy from the ab machine rounded the corner, a towel slung over his shoulder along with his shirt. When he saw me, he stuttered to a halt at a locker near the door and began to remove his own expensive shoes, not bothering to untie the laces. I was careful not to look in his direction, but at one point, as I pulled my t-shirt over my head and slung it into the locker, my eyes accidentally found him anyway. To my surprise, he was looking right at me.

He smiled tentatively, and I glanced away like I'd just been caught peeping through the keyhole of a brothel bedroom. *Shit.* I was usually very careful to not look at other guys in locker rooms, but I wasn't exactly my usual self that night. I swallowed hard and worked my sweaty shorts and boxer briefs down my legs and wrapped the rough towel around my hips. Then I headed for the showers at the back of the room.

Even though we were alone in the locker room, the guy entered the shower stall right next to mine. I could see his head and shoulders out of the corner of my eye the whole time I was bathing, and I knew he could see me, too. It was awkward as hell, and I found myself wondering why I was in this predicament anyway. Had he purposely followed me into the locker room? Why was I here, anyway? Normally I just drove straight home and showered.

"You need some shower gel?" the guy asked from the other side of the low wall.

"Huh?" I was startled enough to almost lose my footing.

"Shower gel," he repeated. "I noticed you didn't have any. Would you like to use some of mine?" He held up a black bottle of shower gel, sans top. "You can use it for your hair, too."

"Uh, sure… I guess," I stammered, reaching for the bottle. As I poured a dollop into my cupped palm, I read the label aloud. "*Tom Ford*. I thought he only made clothes."

The guy shrugged, took the bottle back from me. "What's your name?" he asked.

I felt my eyes widen, and I looked at him like he'd just asked for my social security number. "Um…"

"Never mind," he blurted. "You don't have to tell me if you don't want to."

"No, I do. I want to." I lathered my body quickly as I spoke, without regard for accuracy of coverage. "It's Jamie. My name's Jamie Atwood. Can I get another squirt of that soap?" I smiled, trying to warm up and relax.

He spilled some out into my palm, and I rubbed it into my hair. After I'd finished rinsing my hair under the showerhead and wiping soap from my eyes, I said, "You know my name. What's yours?"

"Cameron Walsh," he answered.

He wasn't creepy, wasn't trying to look over the wall or anything, but his eyes never left mine. It felt strange and oddly exhilarating as we held gazes for what seemed like minutes, both searching for something else to say and coming up blank. When it got a little too intense, I was the one to break the stare, glancing down and watching the last tiny bubbles of Cameron's shower gel gathering at the edge of the drain before being sucked down.

"Well, I guess I'm gonna get out of here." Cameron finally found his voice, and I was relieved. Relieved that I hadn't had to speak first, and relieved that he was leaving. Better not to find out just how strange a gym shower conversation could get.

I felt like I'd just been hit on. Hell, I knew I had. It wasn't the first time a guy had ever shown interest in me, and I'd never gotten up in arms about it. I just considered it a fact of life. But this one had seemed different— bolder.

Not tonight, buddy. Not ever.

I pretended to shower until Cameron had left the locker room. Then I got dressed and headed out to my car. Instead of going straight home like I normally did, I took a detour and drove straight to the local pick-up bar, The Collegiate. It was where all of the single guys on the basketball team hung out, and I figured since I was now a single basketball player, that was where I belonged. Besides, a guy was almost guaranteed to find something he could take home in there.

Since fate seemed to be kicking me in the ass that day, I was only slightly surprised to discover Layla and her new boy toy cozied up together at a back table in The Collegiate. It made me angry for more reasons than one, but mainly because Layla deserved to be taken somewhere better than this shit hole for a first date. But she also deserved better than me, so who was I to talk? I hadn't even been able to muster enough interest to ask her not to break up with me.

At that point, my appetite was gone. And I don't mean my appetite for food. I sat down at the bar and ordered one of the fifty-cent well drinks the club used to get the girls compliant, which in turn brought the guys through the front door every night.

One girl after another sat next to me to order their drinks, but I never even cast a full glance at any of them. They never stayed more than a couple of minutes, either— probably because of the arctic chill emanating off of me. Just after I got my second Screwdriver, Matt slipped onto the stool beside me.

"Hey, man," he said. "You okay?"

"Not really," I grated.

He rested his forearms on the bar. "Look, we never went out while you two were together. I just want you to know that, okay? I didn't steal her from you. She said you two just grew apart."

I finally turned to look at him. "It's not even that. So we grew apart. Fine, I accept that, and she and I are still friends. But dude… what are you thinking bringing her to a place like this on your first date? She's not some piece of meat. She's a great girl, and she deserves better than this. Why don't you pretend you've got some fucking class and take her out to a nice restaurant?"

My response was not the one he was expecting. He floundered, obviously wanting to say something though his mouth wasn't producing words.

"That's what I thought." I swallowed the last half of my drink in two large gulps and set my glass back on the bar. "You don't even know this is wrong, do you?" I slid off my stool and left the bar, sparing a glance at Layla on my way out. She looked appropriately uncomfortable, and I just felt really, really bad for her. Jesus, I hoped she would find someone better than that asshole. And someone better than me.

4

MY CELL phone rang just after noon the next day. I rolled over and squinted against the light filtering through the blinds, opening and closing my mouth in a futile attempt to smack away the horrific case of cotton mouth I had. I found my phone on the floor beside the bed, nearly dead, and flipped it over to see who was disturbing my coma.

Dr. Washburn?

I answered hesitantly, wondering what he could possibly want. It was almost like getting a midnight call from the hospital or the police station.

"Jamie, hope I haven't caught you at a bad time," he said.

"No, Doc," I groaned. "What's up?"

"Something quite interesting happened this morning. I got a phone call from Las Vegas concerning you. Do you have anything you'd like to tell me?"

I wracked my brain, trying to come up with any possible reason Vegas would be calling. I'd stopped off at a convenience store on my way home the night before and picked up a case of beer, then gotten exceedingly wasted. In fact, my head felt like a subway accident, and my mouth tasted like I'd sheared a sheep with my teeth. But I was fairly certain I hadn't gone to Vegas.

Still, I could play along.

"Who called? Was it the mob looking for the money I won counting cards, or the transvestite hooker I married in the Elvis chapel? Because I swear I thought she was eighteen."

"I'm sure you did." Dr. Washburn chuckled. "But in all seriousness, some big shot from Vegas called and requested you for an internship."

That woke me up. "What? Why me? Do juniors usually do internships?"

"Well, technically you're a senior now," he pointed out. "But no, normally people take internships after graduation. However, this would only be a summer position. Summer break is sixteen weeks, so you would be in Vegas for roughly fourteen weeks. A hell of an opportunity to get some experience without interfering with school. That is, if you're willing to give up your summer vacation."

I laughed, wincing at the pain in my head. "Sounds like you're pretty excited about it."

"Of course I am. I'm always thrilled when my students show initiative. I just wish you'd told me you were applying so I wouldn't have been blindsided. I'm afraid I was a bit clueless when the man called, but I think I recovered nicely."

I was shaking my head as if Dr. Washburn could see me through the phone. "I didn't apply to anything, Doc. This is just as much of a surprise to me as it is to you. More in fact, because you got the call first. I'm finding out from you. How the heck did they get my name?"

"I was told you had been recruited at the MMA event you attended several weeks ago. You must have talked to someone or done something, Jamie. They requested you specifically."

My head was spinning. Immediately, my memory was assaulted by the image of Michael Kage winking at me as he took off behind his goons to catch a plane.

Catch you on the flip side.

And I'd bet money that plane was headed to Las Vegas.

"Wow." I said. No other words would come to me.

"Does something ring a bell now? You weren't drinking at that event, were you? It's strictly forbidden."

"No, of course not. But I never officially put in for a job. I think I would have remembered that."

"Well, you must have some idea how this came about."

"Hmmm, let me take a stab in the dark, and you tell me if I'm warm. I'm going to be interning as a publicist for an MMA fighter named Michael Kage. Am I right?" My heart rate picked up at the mere thought of it. Could there possibly be a sweeter gig on earth? Forget all that moping and moaning I'd done in my mind about him being sent to make me feel like shit. The truth was, I would have killed to intern for him.

"Well…" Dr. Washburn cleared his throat. "I'm afraid I'm not allowed to tell you the specifics of the position until you sign a non-disclosure agreement."

"What the fuck, Doc?"

"Language…" he chided.

"What the heck, Doc? I have to sign a paper?"

He sighed none too patiently, and I swear I heard him drop into lecture mode. "The people who need the services of a publicist often require a certain amount of security to protect their privacy. As a publicist, there's a good chance you will be exposed to information of a sensitive nature, Jamie. Personal information. If you're going to make a career of working with celebrities, you'll need to understand that they can't let just anyone into their inner circle."

"Michael Kage's inner circle? In Vegas?" I think I actually giggled. "Yeah, there's no way I'm passing that up."

"No thinking about it?" Dr. Washburn asked. "You don't have any questions for me?"

"Yeah. I've got two questions. Where do I sign, and when do I start?"

GETTING ready to go to Vegas was a bit of a challenge. I had to make arrangements for everything without alerting my friends to the fact that there was anything out of the ordinary— a near impossible feat when you considered that my head was about to blow off from the excitement. So many times I almost caved. Almost gave it away. But then I've never been good at keeping secrets.

The non-disclosure agreement I signed, with Dr. Washburn and a notary as witnesses, had not forbidden me from mentioning that I had an internship in Las Vegas. It only forbade me from sharing anything that could be considered identifying information or information of a personal nature, just like Dr. Washburn had said.

From what I could understand with the limited information provided beforehand, I would be staying in a hotel owned by Michael Kage's uncle, Peter Santori. The Alcazar, as it was called, was a posh five-story hotel just off the Vegas strip, boasting a small casino, a Mediterranean restaurant, and a spa. The website didn't have much detail besides a few photos of well-appointed guest rooms and a swimming pool lined with colorful tiles.

I couldn't help but wonder, with all of the flashy themed resorts within a mile on the main strip, why someone would choose to stay at a place like the Alcazar for a couple hundred dollars a night, when they could be right in the middle of all of the Vegas action on the strip for a measly thirty-nine bucks. I knew this because I had used a good portion of the five excruciating days before my flight to research Vegas on the internet. I'd pretty much memorized prices and show times, restaurants and attractions. Funny thing was, I didn't actually care about any of it. I was just champing at the bit to get out there, and at the moment, internet research was as close as I could come.

Many times, I tried to dig up any information on my new client— damn, I loved the sound of that!— but his electronic footprint was nearly non-existent. I discovered a couple of social profiles that I was pretty sure belonged to him, but I was too chickenshit to make a connection with him on any of them.

Besides, I'd be seeing him in person in just a matter of days. The thought of it tied my stomach up in knots and made it hard for me to sleep at night. I wondered what it would be like getting to spend more than a few stolen moments with him. Would he be scary, nice, snobby, or mean? Would I enjoy working for him, or would he send me home with my tail between my legs? These types of questions plagued me day and night until I thought I would lose my mind. And not being able to talk about it was the worst of all.

"What's got you so worked up?" Braden asked after Trey had left to go home for vacation. "You've been really quiet. Not your usual smart-ass self. Is it the breakup? To be honest, I didn't think it was gonna be that bad on you. You've always been so… free."

"Thanks," I said with a smirk. "I'm just feeling anxious about summer vacation. It's been a while since I've spent much time at home, and I'm afraid I won't know how to act. Maybe I'll want to come back here, you know?"

"Same here," he admitted. "Every time I go to my parents' house, I feel like I'm sleeping in someone else's bed. Does that mean we're growing up? This condo feels more like home now."

I nodded my agreement, realizing that, in essence, I was lying to my friend. There was just no way around it. My allegiance had to be to my future and to my client rather than my buddies. Even my family had little knowledge of how I was spending my summer. I'd told my mom I had an internship with an athlete, and that I'd be in Las Vegas. Beyond that, the woman who'd birthed me nearly twenty-one years before was completely in the dark.

I couldn't tell Braden shit. If I gave him a sentence, he'd demand a thesis. Best to just let him think this summer was like every other one so far. Home for sixteen weeks and back again, with an occasional visit to the condo when the whole family thing got to be too much. Only this time, I wouldn't be coming back at all over the break.

By the time my plane took off, I thought I might need a Valium to calm my nerves. But I was relieved that I wouldn't have to lie to people's faces anymore or war with my inner self to keep from spilling my guts to someone… anyone… *everyone.*

How do you keep such exciting news a secret without losing your mind?

At the other end of my flight, there were two burly men in dark suits waiting for me. They were the same guys who had been with Michael Kage the night we'd met, and one of them held a poster board with my name misspelled on it.

Jammey Atwood.

I let it slide, though. Men who looked like they'd just stepped off of the set of *Goodfellas* could spell my name however they damn well pleased. As long as they didn't shoot me and dump me in the Colorado River, I figured I could be gracious enough to overlook the fact that they were phonetically challenged.

WHEN the car pulled up to the front of a hotel on the Vegas Strip, I just about shit my pants. I suppose I'd expected my new job to be in the sweat-scented office of some dingy little back alley gym. This was something else altogether. The building had a glass front that showcased a glittering lobby in a sophisticated color palette of blues, greens and grays. As one of the goons opened the glass door, I was assaulted by the sights and sounds of the darkened casino that lay beyond the lobby.

"Nice," I said lamely. It was the first word I'd uttered since climbing into the car. And by car, I mean sleek white Range Rover SUV limo. Apparently, this was what rich dudes were being driven around in these days.

The goons ignored my comment, which was not surprising. They'd spent the entire ride pretending I didn't exist. Now one walked ahead, and I followed, feeling goon number two close on my heels as we crossed the diamond-patterned carpet to the front desk. A porter stepped up beside us, pushing a cart that held my two suitcases and duffel bag. They looked underwhelming, a little too trailer trash for this establishment. The only thing that could have been more embarrassing than my ragged luggage was a set of plastic grocery sacks.

"This is Kage's new intern," the first goon told the young man behind the counter. "Mr. Santori said put him in a suite."

"Sure thing, Aldo." The tiny blond desk clerk, whose name was Steve according to his silver name tag, tapped on his computer keyboard. "Best available?"

"Whatever." Aldo grated.

Steve frowned at my testy chaperone. "*Jesus*. Who pissed in your cornflakes, Aldo?"

Aldo literally growled. "Aaron and me got babysitting duty today, as you can see." He hooked a meaty thumb over his shoulder in my direction.

Steve smiled at me, and his gaze roamed freely over my body. I was wearing a t-shirt— a tight red one that Braden would have shaken his head at— and a pair of low-slung jeans, but I got the impression that Steve's imagination was ripping them right off of me. "Cute baby. What's his name?"

Aldo shrugged. "Trouble."

"This baby does have ears," I pointed out. "And my name is not Trouble, it's Jamie Atwood. Nice to meet you." I held out my hand, and Steve shook it. Delicately and deliberately, and a little longer than necessary.

"Nice to meet you, too. Oh, it says here that the Sky Room has already been reserved for a Mr. James Atwood. I've heard that one is absolutely gorgeous, but I've never gotten to see inside it."

"I could let you take a look sometime," I said. "No problem."

"That is so sweet of you." Steve's smile sparkled. "Isn't he just adorable, Aldo? Look at those kissy lips."

"Oh for Pete's sake," Aldo groaned. "Are we finished here? I've got somewhere to be."

"Go," Steve told him with a shooing motion. "I've got this under control. Just get out of here before you get your negativity all over me."

Aldo and his silent partner Aaron disappeared in a whoosh of air, and I was left with Steve and the porter, who may as well have been one of those cardboard cutouts that populate movie theater lobbies.

Steve stared at me after the goons were gone. "What the hell did you do to Aldo?"

"Nothing!" I was indignant. "Why would you think I did something? I don't even know those guys. They just picked me up from the airport and drove me here." I thought of the MMA event where I'd first met Kage, remembering the way they flanked him the entire time. "Actually, I've seen them before, but I swear I've never done anything to either of those guys."

Steve looked skeptical, but he just smirked and handed me a key card for my room. "Okay, go hop on one of those." He indicated a bank of silver elevators directly behind me. "Third floor, turn right, all the way at the end of the hall. You can't miss it. It's the only one with double doors." He winked, like there was some private joke I had yet to be let in on.

"Thanks, man." I headed to the elevators with the porter dragging his luggage cart behind me.

When we stepped off the elevator and turned right, I sucked in a breath. At the very end of the hall was a set of fancy double doors, intricately carved and painted a creamy robin's egg blue. "That's my room?" I directed the question at no one, because I still wasn't sure if my cardboard porter could even speak, but he surprised me when a mouthful of words came tumbling out.

"That's more than a room," he told me. "It's like a small apartment, really. There are two on each floor, except for the top floor. No guest rooms up there— only Mr. Santori and Mr. Kage live up there."

"Oh." We stepped up to the double doors, and I stood there like I was afraid to go in.

"This isn't the biggest or the fanciest hotel around, but Mr. Santori keeps it nice," the porter said.

"It looks pretty nice to me," I admitted, the reverent tone in my voice giving away my lack of sophistication.

The porter laughed. "Son, this is Vegas. The idea here is bigger, better, brighter, flashier, louder… That's why I like the Alcazar. Mr.

Santori knows about taste and restraint. Stick around Vegas long enough, you'll get sick of flashy."

He plucked the key card out of my hand and opened the doors for me, stepping aside so that I could enter my new temporary home. To say I was stunned would be an understatement. The robin's egg blue from the door was part of the color scheme within, but it was combined with a subdued palette of white and cream that was more *Architectural Digest* than Vegas strip. No gold lamé or heart-shaped hot tub here. A large window revealed the breathtaking Vegas skyline in a way I never thought I'd see it— from my own place.

Yeah, this was only going to be my place for a few months, but I figured it counted anyway.

With the porter standing just behind me, I took in the view, noting that my mouth was hanging askew but not bothering to fix it. This room deserved a slack jaw.

"What's your name?" I asked, feeling like I needed to either speak to the guy or send him on his way.

"Charles, sir." He sounded like one of those 1940's movie butlers. His face was gaunt and sallow, more suited to a wino than a butler, but his posture was ramrod straight. I got the distinct impression that Charles was less about putting on airs and more about doing his job properly. After all, who wanted a sloppy porter? I liked him instantly.

"I'm supposed to tip you, right?" I asked.

"If you like," he said easily.

"Uh..." I reached into the pocket of my jeans and fished out a wadded up receipt from the airport coffee shop and a small pill of dryer lint.

Charles chuckled and held up a hand to stop me. "I have plenty of receipts and lint in my own pocket. Maybe next time? Vegas is one of those places where it's a good idea to carry a little cash in the pocket at all times." He winked at me, putting me instantly at ease. I told myself I'd give him double next time, though double of what, I wasn't sure.

After Charles was gone, I made sure the door was locked and secured, then I ran across the living area and jumped onto the white leather sofa. I stared up at the high ceiling, and at the large picture window, and wondered what I had done to rate this kind of summer. Hell, even if the job sucked, the hotel suite alone was worth the trip.

I pulled my cell phone out of my back pocket and started taking pictures, flitting from one place to another like an excited kid. I snapped pictures of the living room, the view, and the king sized bed. The bedroom wasn't actually a separate room, but the bed was situated on a large platform that distinguished it from the living area. The bathroom looked like a spa, with tumbled stone tiles, a glass sink and shower, and a stack of custom soaps that resembled river rocks. I took a picture of those and immediately texted a slide show of my new digs to my mother.

"Wow," she texted back. *"When did my little boy get so fancy?"*

"Today," I replied.

"How is the job?" she asked.

"Don't know yet. Just got here, Ma."

"Oh, yeah. Well, keep me posted. Love you. P.S. Are those rocks on your counter?"

I laughed out loud and decided not to reply. Let her wonder. It made things more exciting.

The first night passed quietly. I opted not to go out. No reason to go anywhere when I had a great place, room service, and a seventy-inch wall-mounted LCD. I could even see the TV from the bed, which was a plus when porn time rolled around. I rented *Huge Pom-Poms 2*, and after I fast-forwarded over the credits and the intro scene, the next twelve minutes were absolutely fascinating. Then I went to sleep with a smile on my face.

Chapter 5

THE NEXT morning, I felt fresher than I had in a long time. Possibly ever. There were no birds singing outside my Vegas window, but a lot can be said for waking up in what is essentially a palace. All I needed were some harem girls, a hookah, and a couple of servants to complete the fantasy.

After a hot shower, during which I giggled to myself about bathing with rocks, I dressed for success. My heather-gray skinny dress pants cuffed at the ankle, showing a strip of argyle socks above black dress shoes. I opted for a black button-up shirt with a white t-shirt underneath. I smoothed the wrinkles out with the hotel iron and admired myself in the full-length mirror near the bed, unhitching a couple of buttons at the top— just enough to show the collar of my undershirt. I bent to temptation and tied my Claddagh necklace around my throat. It may not have been the most professional piece of jewelry, but how could I leave it off? Over the years, it had become almost a part of my body. I felt naked without it.

My hair was uncooperative, sticking out in a couple of spots in such a way that I resembled a horny little devil, and I attempted to tame it with a dollop of hair gel. After ten minutes of fighting, I had the flyaways tamed, the ducktail in place, and my bangs curtaining one eye just the way I liked it.

"Hello, stud," I said to my reflection. Then I flipped my phone out and took a selfie to send to my mom. I captioned it *First Day on the Job*, then hit send.

"*Good luck, baby!*" My mom texted back. "*You look beautiful as always.*"

I wondered why I was being so overly concerned about how I was dressed, anyway. It wasn't like this was a real job. It was an internship— a test run. People expected interns to be slightly unkempt and a bit surly, right? At least that's how it always was in the movies. The intern comes in, with a progressive attitude and a healthy disdain for authority cultivated through years of college classes and keggers, and breathes new life into the stodgy work atmosphere. After a couple of weeks, everyone is loosening their ties and taking longer lunch breaks. The girls are bringing their babies to work, everyone is openly embracing diversity, and the men are bonding over beers and darts at some cutting-edge club in the hipster district. Creativity has a renaissance.

Yeah, nice fantasy, dude.

The reality was that this was Vegas, and everyone in the office of the Alcazar was at least as progressive as me— even the granny answering the telephones. She wore tortoise-shell Catwoman glasses with a black chain, a pink cashmere sweater, and a matching pink streak in her platinum hair.

"Can I help you?" she asked in a smooth, professional tone. Her work voice. I was willing to bet her regular speaking voice was several steps lower and a lot less refined.

"I'm Jamie Atwood," I said. "The new intern."

"Intern?" She cocked her head to the side, as if she didn't have the foggiest clue what I was talking about but was reluctant to admit it.

"We've got an intern?" A man poked his head around the half wall at Catwoman's back, but when he saw me, his face fell. "Oh, a male intern. It figures. I was about to be going all Bill Clinton up in here. So what are you going to be doing for us, male intern?"

"Uh… publicist?" I was becoming increasingly less sure of myself. In fact, I was beginning to question whether I'd even come to the right hotel. Everyone seemed surprised— and less than thrilled— to see me. "Did you guys not know I was starting today? The name's Jamie Atwood. Maybe there's a memo or something?"

The man rounded the receptionist's desk and shook my hand. "Mark Gladstone," he said, slipping his hands easily into the pockets of his expensive dress pants. His dark hair was perfectly tousled, his shirt starched to perfection. "I'm afraid you've caught us a little off guard. We weren't told we were getting an intern. Never had one before, so…" He hesitated, rubbing the back of his neck, looking toward the receptionist as if for ideas. "What do you think, Cathy? Should we put him back there next to Alicia? Bet she'd love that. She really goes for those pretty boy types."

Cathy scoffed. "Don't do that to the poor boy. He wouldn't get a lick of work done, and neither would she."

Mark gave me a conspiratorial look and dropped his voice a notch. "Alicia is very… outgoing. If you catch my meaning." He raised his eyebrows, and Cathy snorted.

"Outgoing, my ass. That girl is a slut, plain and simple." She shook a finger at me. "You stay away from her if you know what's good for you. There are plenty of nice girls in Vegas if you know where to look. Across town, though. Not around here."

I nodded. "Thanks for the advice. I'm here to work, though. Not looking for a girlfriend."

Mark huffed like he was personally affronted. "Who said anything about a girlfriend? You're way too young to settle down. Hell, I'm too young to settle down, and I've got at least five years on you. How old are you?"

"I'll be twenty-one in three weeks and a day. The twenty-ninth."

The door opened behind me, and a cool draft hit my back. Cathy looked up, surprised, then started shuffling papers like she was trying to look busy.

Mark clapped me on the back. "Hey, we'll have to take you out after work on your birthday and buy you some drinks. It's not every day a guy becomes legal in Sin City! Don't plan anything for the night of the twenty-ninth. I'll handle everything."

Mark, who looked the part of the quintessential office stud, sounded altogether too excited about introducing me to the debauchery of Vegas. Like he would take great personal pleasure in escorting me through the gates of Hell. My mind conjured up an image of me snorting mounds of cocaine off of a roulette table as Mark Gladstone cackled maniacally, surrounded by mobsters, carnies, and hookers… and one really awkward-looking donkey.

"Sounds nice," I told him, pushing the disturbing image out of my head.

"You'll have to get in line, Mark," said a voice from behind me— a voice smooth and deep like dark chocolate. It was surprising that I recognized the voice without turning around. Except for the noisy video on my phone, I hadn't heard Michael Kage speak since the night we met. But now he sounded familiar, as if we'd only paused for a moment in conversation.

I whirled around, feeling the smile take over my face. He was dressed in running shorts and sneakers. Sweat had seeped through almost every inch of his t-shirt, causing it to cling to the curves of his muscles. Muscles that were only hinted at in the suit he'd worn the night of the event but were now on audacious display here in this professional setting. Somehow the incongruity of his style of dress and the locale made it almost obscene— like a shirtless guy in a restaurant.

Kage ran a hand through his unruly dark hair, pushing sweaty tendrils away from his face. A few strands still clung to his temples. "I think it's only right that I should be the one to take Jamie out on his birthday, since he belongs to me." Both Cathy and Mark seemed to do subtle double-takes at his comment. "I hired him as my publicist, so he's working for me."

"Ahhh…" Cathy breathed. "That explains it. We were trying to figure out where the little whippersnapper belonged. Now we know." She glanced pointedly at Mark. "You got here just in the nick of time. I'm afraid Mr. Gladstone was about to change his sexual affiliation just so he could pull a Bill Clinton."

"Uh-huh." Kage narrowed his eyes at Mark. "Get your own intern. This one's mine."

Mark waved his hand in the air dismissively. "I want a girl intern, not a boy one. Could you put in a good word with your uncle for me?"

"Sure. Why don't we get you a private secretary who's fresh out of massage therapy school? Put you in an office upstairs, with a bed in it? Fully stocked with flavored condoms and a box of sex toys."

Mark positively beamed. "Now you're talking."

"Yeah," Kage said. "I'll get right on it."

He turned his attention to me. "So how is it going, Jamie? Did you get settled into your room okay?"

"Oh, yeah. That place is phenomenal. Love the rock soaps."

Cathy wrinkled her nose at Kage. "Looks like someone else could use some soap right now."

Kage smiled almost shyly and grabbed the tail of his t-shirt, pulling it up and using it to wipe his sweaty forehead. I caught a glimpse of his glistening washboard abs before he dropped it back into place.

"You wanna grab some lunch?" he asked.

"Me?" I snapped my gaping mouth shut and looked around to confirm he was talking to me. "Sure. Uh, now?"

"No, not now." His tone suggested I might be a little soft in the head. "It's only ten after eight. I meant at noon."

"Of course." I blushed so hard I was positive my hair turned red.

"Mr. Santori," Cathy interrupted, speaking to Kage. "Where should we put your intern?"

"My uncle didn't make arrangements for him to have an office?"

Cathy shook her head slowly.

"Well, give him an office then. A nice one."

"Really?" Mark gaped. "I've been here two years, and I'm still in a cubicle."

"Not my problem, brown-nose. You've been kissing up to the wrong Santori." Kage banded his strong fingers around my arm just above my elbow and pulled me down a wide walkway flanked by cubicles. All of the employees, which appeared to comprise two men and four women, had their noses stuck out of their cubicles, watching us.

One girl, about my age with dark blond hair, smiled as we passed. If she was supposed to be the office slut, she hid it well beneath her conservative clothing and wholesome face. "Hi, Kage," she said under her breath.

"Alicia," Kage said flatly, and I couldn't help wondering if there was a story there.

When we got to the back of the office, I asked the question that was currently driving me crazy. "Why do some people call you Kage, and you introduce yourself as Michael Kage, but Cathy just called you Mr. Santori?"

He shrugged. "Michael Kage Santori is my legal name. But I don't like Santori, so I dropped it."

"That makes sense."

"Does it?"

The brusqueness of his tone made it feel like he was putting me in my place for something, though for what I had no idea. Still, I wasn't stupid. I didn't bring up the name thing again.

When we got to the back of the office area, I noted three empty cubicles, one of which I assumed belonged to Mark Gladstone. There were several doors back there, too. "Any of these offices empty?" Kage asked loudly to no one in particular.

Alicia came up beside us. "They're all taken, Kage. Management, you know."

I had the sudden fear that Kage was going to start busting down doors and tossing managers out on their asses. Alienating an entire office full of people and establishing myself as the pet of the boss's spoiled nephew was not what I had in mind for my first day of work.

"It's fine, Kage." I leaned closer, so that only he could hear what I was saying. Well, he and possibly the blond girl Alicia, who was standing much too close for comfort. "I can work in a cubicle, I don't mind."

"Well, I do mind," he said. "You're working for me, and I don't want any of these fuckers knowing my business."

"Ahhh." I was beginning to see his dilemma now. He wasn't playing favorites; he was protecting his interests. I felt a little ashamed for misinterpreting his motives, and for thinking he was spoiled.

"Yeah, you sit out here in a cubicle, and whoever is nearby can hear every word you're saying." He speared Alicia with a hard glare, and she finally had enough sense to walk away. "I don't mean to be rude. I'm just a little pissed because my uncle was supposed to get you an office. I asked him to. Maybe you could just use a cubicle for a while until I can arrange something different. Do you have a laptop?"

"In my room," I said.

"You'll need to use it for business, I guess. But stay on the hotel Wi-Fi, okay? Not the office network. It's heavily monitored, so all of your embarrassing personal stuff on there…" He smiled mischievously. "Well, you get the idea."

"Heavily monitored?" I gulped, feeling like I'd taken a job at the CIA rather than a Vegas hotel. "What makes you think I've got embarrassing things on my laptop?"

"I'd be disappointed if you didn't."

His smile was contagious, and I couldn't help giving it right back to him. Of course, he was right. I did have embarrassing things on my laptop. Doesn't everyone?

"Yeah, that's what I thought," he teased. "Anyway, you have fun getting settled in here with the natives. We're just winging it, you and me, okay? I've never had an intern before, and you've never been an intern before, so let's play it by ear. You figure out what you need to do your job, and I'll make sure you get it even if I have to bust some heads. Fair enough?"

"Fair enough," I said, still smiling.

"I'll stop back by to get you for lunch, okay?" He looked down at his sweaty attire. "And I promise I'll be clean."

He left before I could reply, and I found myself standing in a strange office, in front of a strange cubicle, surrounded by a bunch of strange people. I sat down in my chair and pulled out my cell phone to call Dr. Washburn. Getting some emergency advice was my first order of business.

"Dr. Washburn, I'm in deep shit."

I heard the professor's nasally chuckle on the other end of the line. "Hello to you, too, Mr. Atwood. What can I do for you?"

"I'm sitting in a cubicle," I said, then dropped my voice, remembering Kage's warning about being overheard. "I don't know what to do, Dr. Washburn. I figured they'd tell me what to do, you know? Like an assignment or something. This is jacked up."

Dr. Washburn chuckled again. "Calm down, Jamie. Think. You must realize this job you've accepted is largely an artistic endeavor. It's not piecing together a car on an assembly line or making pre-prepped fast food burgers. You're creating something from scratch. No one can tell you what to do, because you are the one who will be planning everything. You're the expert. Do you understand?"

"I think so," I groaned. "Oh, God. I thought I'd be putting together press packets or something. Calling places to arrange things."

Again with the infuriating chuckle.

"Doc, could you please quit laughing at me? This is serious."

"I know, Jamie. Listen, all of those things you just mentioned are legitimate things you may be doing. But you will be the one to come up with the plan. Essentially, you will be giving yourself assignments rather than waiting for someone else to give them to you. Autonomy is something you have to get used to in the working world. It's not like high school or college. Who do you think comes up with the assignments to give to you in my classes?"

"You?" I asked hesitantly.

"Me. Not the dean or the school board. I have to come up with that stuff out of my own noggin. That's what you're going to have to do, as well."

I paused for a moment, my heart beating fast, realizing I may have been in over my head. "So where do I start?" I asked finally.

"Do some research on the internet. Try to find articles or books about publicists, especially sports publicists, and find out specifics about what they do. Recommendations, pitfalls, anecdotes... Whatever will spark some ideas about the types of things you should be doing. Then get to know your client, Jamie. That's the most important thing."

"That makes sense." I liked the idea of getting to know my client a lot more than doing research.

"Give it a couple of days, then call me and tell me what you've learned. Okay?"

"Okay, Doc. Thanks."

"You're welcome. And Jamie... stop stressing. That won't do anyone any good."

It was my turn to chuckle. "Says the man who freaks out if he's one second late to class."

I could hear the frown over the phone. "That's different."

BY LUNCH time, I was engrossed in an excerpt from a biography of a publicist who had represented a bunch of high-profile athletes. The trials he faced in making some of those guys look good had me shaking my head. Dog fighting, alleged murder, domestic abuse, cheating, and let's not forget the ever-popular use of performance enhancing drugs— or PED's as the media so loved to call them. You name it, these athletes had done it, and then turned around and hired someone to get them out of it.

Of course, it wasn't all a desperate game of clean-up for the publicists of the world. Advertising campaigns, wardrobe choices, speeches, and public appearances were some of the other less dramatic things they dealt with on a daily basis.

Overall, I felt pretty productive for a guy who didn't know what the hell he was doing. I was jotting down some ideas on a notepad that Catwoman Cathy had given me when Kage showed up for lunch. His approach was so stealthy I didn't realize he was there until his shadow fell across my paper. I jumped and spun around in my task chair.

"Hi," he said calmly, as if he had no idea he'd just scared the bejesus out of me.

"Hi." I worked to slow my banging heart.

"You look different." At my confused look, he reached up and tapped lightly on the frame of my glasses.

"Oh, yeah." I quickly snatched them off of my face and set them on the desk. Then I flipped my notepad face down on top of them and stood up. "Will my laptop be safe here?"

"Maybe." He shrugged. "I don't think anybody will steal it. You got anything on that pad of paper you mind someone seeing?"

"Paranoid much?" I regretted the question right after it cleared my lips, but Kage didn't appear to take offense.

"Lotta nosy people around here," he said. "They like knowing what I'm up to, and I like to keep a little mystery."

I laughed. "You're definitely a mystery."

"Yeah?" He grinned, obviously pleased to have me guessing.

"I'm not sure if that's a good thing, Kage. I'm your publicist, and the first order of business for me is getting to know my client."

"You'll know me soon enough. In fact, you may be regretting signing on for this job in a couple of weeks. You're gonna get sick of seeing me."

For some reason, that comment made me feel awkward, and I shoved my hands into my pockets and looked away. I couldn't come up with anything to say. All I could do was turn that thought over in my mind— spending time with Michael Kage. So much time I'd get sick of seeing him. I didn't think anyone could get sick of seeing someone who looked like he did, but I did consider that I might need to take up drinking to calm my nerves around him.

He was so incredibly larger than life. I'd never met anyone who made me feel so insignificant, so lacking. Either he sensed my unease and purposely came to the rescue, or he was oblivious to it, because he continued smoothly.

"Let's get out of here. I'm starving."

Again, everyone stared at us as we passed between the cubicles and exited through the office door. Kage led me on a winding path through the hotel lobby and the casino, down a hallway, and through a set of soundproof doors. I knew they were soundproof, because on one side of them the noise of the casino was deafening, and the other side was like putting my ear to a sea shell. Through the high-pitched ring of sudden silence in my ear came the tinkling of light music from the down the hall— something ethereal like New Age.

The music was coming from the restaurant, dimly lit and furnished in dark leather and wood. A gentle flicker of candlelight added a romantic flair. *The Grotto* was chiseled into a rustic stone sign above the arched doorway, which was hung with Spanish moss and twigs.

A young woman in a peasant-style dress met us at the door. Her hair was pulled severely back from her face, which was conspicuously clean-scrubbed. The unassuming style of her greeting furthered the impression of being served by a simple peasant girl.

"Do you prefer a particular table today?" she asked Kage.

"One of the private courtyard booths."

She grabbed a couple of menus and tucked them under her arm, cutting her eyes up at him several times. I was ashamed to realize that I could totally relate. He just had the kind of face that you had to keep checking, to confirm that it was indeed as unnaturally handsome as you remembered.

And yes. Every time, yes.

"No menus, thanks. Just tell Enzo we're here."

She replaced them in their discreet holder behind the hostess podium and led us through the quiet restaurant, through a set of French doors, and onto a covered patio populated by wrought iron bistro tables. Some of the diners glanced up at us as we passed, then resumed eating from crude earthenware dishes that somehow, against the backdrop of the Grotto, looked more sophisticated than the finest China.

Booths were built along the back wall of the building, and the other three sides were enclosed by tall shrubs. Flowering vines crept along and through the shrubs, creating the impression that we had entered an ancient garden somewhere in Europe. The shrubs blocked out the high noon sunlight to the extent that it appeared to be twilight within the confines of the patio, an illusion supported by strands of twinkling lights that dangled from the rafters.

After the hostess had seated us and walked away, I studied our booth. It was roomy but intimate, crafted from heavy polished wood and granite. A hurricane lamp affixed to the brick wall cast a flickering glow across Kage's face, and I regarded him with a mixture of surprise and awe. "Is this your restaurant?"

He leaned back in his seat, sprawling in a manner that was all man. "Nothing is mine, Jamie. This all belongs to my uncle."

I turned his comment over in my head and weighed it. An odd way to put it, I thought— a sad way, really. *Nothing is mine.*

"Well, you know what I meant," I said, for lack of a better response. "This is amazing. It feels authentic. I mean, I've never left the United States, and certainly not the twenty-first century, but if I could imagine a really upscale medieval restaurant…"

"Thanks." His terse dismissal of my compliment stung a bit. Had me wishing I hadn't said anything about ownership.

I squirmed in my seat. "Um, so you said no menus. Are we… not eating? I can pay for my own if that's a problem."

That coaxed a laugh out of him. "You don't have to pay for your food. I'm just ordering for you."

"Oh. Okay." I wasn't sure what to make of someone else ordering for me. It had never actually happened before, not since I was a little kid and my parents forced me to get stuff I didn't want off of the kid's menu. To be honest, except for my parents, I don't suppose anyone ever had a desire to order for me before. Maybe it was just that he was confident that he knew what was good at his own— his uncle's— restaurant. They probably had a specialty or something.

It didn't take long to find out. Within minutes, there was a stout, bearded gentleman standing beside our booth and beaming down at Kage. "So glad to see you brought a friend, Kage. Someone new I get to impress with my unequaled culinary skills." He set a couple of water glasses down in front of us.

"Enzo has an ego on him, Jamie. But trust me when I say he can back it up in the kitchen. The man can cook his Italian ass off."

Enzo beamed some more. "What can I get for you today, my darling? I'm thinking the salmon."

"You do like fish, right?" Kage asked me, and from the look on his face, I thought "no" would definitely be the wrong answer. Besides, I did like fish.

I nodded, and Enzo hurried off to prepare our salmon.

Kage relaxed even more and offered me an apologetic smile. "I eat clean, so there's not a whole lot of variety. But it's always good food. Especially here, I know it's the best ingredients, the freshest fish. All of the vegetables are organic and in season. I personally make sure of that. So if you order room service, you don't have to worry about what you're getting, okay?"

"I remember from the first time we met, you're very serious about your eating. No hamburgers, right?"

"Right. Fast food is the devil."

"Is eating like you one of my job requirements?" I asked, only half joking.

Kage didn't even crack a smile. "No, but you said you wanted to get to know me. What better way than to live like me? At least for a while. I figured I'd take you to watch me train some, you could maybe work out a little yourself."

"Ordering for me, making me work out… If I didn't know any better, I'd think you were trying to whip me into shape." Again, I was only half joking.

"You look like you're in pretty good shape already." Kage glanced away almost shyly, and for a split second I thought I saw a crack in his ever-present confidence. "I mean, you work out, right? Lift some weights a couple of times a week, maybe play a little sports. You keep your weight around one-fifty-five, and your caloric intake is decent at around twenty-five-hundred a day, but you're getting way too many carbs. And you don't drink enough water." For emphasis, he picked up his water glass, raised it toward me in *cheers*, then took a swallow.

Dumbfounded, I picked up my water glass, returned Kage's *cheers*, then killed half of it before setting it back down. "So how the hell do you know all of that?"

He shrugged. "I can look at you and tell."

"Can you tell what size underwear I have on? How about my birth sign? Because I have to admit I'm a little freaked out right now by your amazing powers of perception."

He narrowed his eyes at me. "Ummm… Taurus?"

"Nope. Gemini." I gave him a smug smile. "Just this morning you walked in on that wannabe intern-molester inviting me out to celebrate my birthday in three weeks. Remember?"

"Dammit, I forgot!" Kage slammed his fist on the table. "I don't know the Zodiac signs by heart, but I definitely could have Googled that on my cell phone. Shit." He leaned forward, resting his forearms on the table so that his hands were within a couple inches of mine. "As for the underwear…" His voice was low, and he glanced dramatically toward my lap and back up again. "I'm guessing about a thirty-two to thirty-four, medium."

I felt the color rush to my face, opened my mouth to speak, and snapped it shut again.

Kage stayed leaned across the table for a long moment, gloating. Apparently, when it came to physicality, the guy really knew his stuff. Not surprising when I thought about it. He manipulated his own body with exercise and diet to a degree far beyond what the average fit person did, so it stood to reason that he would be sensitive to that type of information.

I had to wonder how many times a day he looked at himself in the mirror. Hell, if I had a body like that, I'd probably live in front of the mirror.

After Kage straightened up and pulled himself back to his side of the booth, we fell to talking about my plane trip. I told him I didn't think Aldo and his silent twin were very friendly, and he laughed like I'd told a joke. He didn't offer any insight into the pair, though, so I was left to wonder still whether they treated everyone like scum or if it was just me.

A few moments later, the food arrived. Grilled salmon and a couple of large skewers of vegetables that included eggplant, tomatoes and zucchini. The waitress gave us each a bowl of yogurt sauce.

"Keep the water coming," Kage told her.

We didn't speak during the meal. The food was out of this world, but my nerves had my stomach tied in knots. Kage was fucking intense when he ate, as if he had one goal, and every other thing in the whole universe had slipped his mind. He ate quietly, almost reverently, moving through his food at a steady pace until it was all gone. Then he looked up to find me staring as I nibbled along.

"What?" he asked self-consciously. "You've never seen a guy eat before?"

"Of course I have, but not quite like that. You're very focused when you eat." At the hint of a crease between his brows, I quickly added, "Not in a bad way."

"Guess I just enjoy my food," he admitted. "Sometimes I—"

My phone interrupted him, playing a ringtone I recognized all too well. "Shit, I'm sorry," I told Kage with a grimace as I answered it. "Hey, babe. I'm in the middle of a… uh… meeting. What's up?" I offered Kage an apologetic smile as I listened to Layla on the other end of the line.

"Oh, I just wanted to talk to you, I guess," she said hesitantly. "But if you're busy, I can call another time. When is good for you?"

"Uh, let me call you back. I'm going to be pretty busy for the next few days with my new job, so I'm not sure when I'll have a minute."

"Okay, papi," she said sweetly, using her favorite term of endearment on me. That one definitely had me scratching my head, and I had to wonder where her fantastic new boyfriend was while his girl was calling me. Maybe he'd gone home for the holidays.

When I hung up the phone, I noticed Kage was looking out over the other diners on the patio. Trying to give me as much privacy as he could without leaving the table, I suppose.

"Sorry about that," I said. "My girlfriend."

He blinked. Didn't say anything.

I realized that I'd made a mistake, calling her my girlfriend out of habit. But the truth was, I didn't want to take it back now that it was out of my mouth. If Kage knew I'd been dumped, he'd look at me with pity in his eyes and think what a pathetic loser I was, and that was something I couldn't stand. So I went with the harmless lie and hoped I'd never have to prove it.

"She's back home," I continued. "Or actually back at college. She lives in the same town where I go to school. Where you and I met, as a matter of fact. She's a cheerleader. Blond hair, blue eyes, pretty. I'm fucking babbling, aren't I? I'm sorry."

God, I was a horrible liar.

Kage gave a one-shouldered shrug. "Why do you keep apologizing to me, Jamie? You think I'm gonna fire you if you take a phone call from your girlfriend?"

"I hope not." I laughed nervously. "I'll try to keep it professional from now on. She just— It's hard when I can't tell her what I'm doing or where I am."

He didn't say anything back. Just kept looking at me with that unshakable poker face.

We lingered over our lunch for a few more minutes as I ate the last of my vegetables. I'd never liked tomatoes, but I ate them because I didn't want to let Kage down. He was so serious about nutrition. Just as I ate the last bite, he tossed his napkin onto the table.

"Ready to go?" he asked, seeming to be in a hurry all of a sudden. The talkative, charming guy who had ordered my lunch and gleefully guessed my underwear size was gone.

"Sure." I had to practically run to keep up with him as he blazed a trail back through the restaurant and to the business office.

"See you soon." He left me off at the door with a quick nod, and I didn't have the nerve to say anything to him. I'd really blown it.

It had been terribly unprofessional of me to let a phone call interrupt my very first business lunch ever. Kage had been too polite to call me out on it, but the guy was radiating disappointment.

I'll redeem myself, I thought. *I'll be the best damn publicist a fighter ever had.*

On that thought I slipped back into the office, hoping to go unnoticed. I should have known that would be too much to ask for. Mark, the office sex offender, had a well-dressed hip leaned against Cathy's desk. When I turned around, both of my new coworkers had me pinned in their high beams.

I almost laughed.

Alicia poked her head around the corner, not bothering to try to camouflage herself or her intentions.

"So?" Mark asked bluntly. "How was lunch with *The Machine*?"

"Huh?" I stared blankly at him.

"Michael "The Machine" Kage." His sarcastic air quotes and goofy face made it clear that he was not a fan. "That's what they call your boss man. You didn't know that?"

"Dude, I just started. I can't be expected to know everything on the first day." My tone was flippant, but to be honest, it stung a little that I didn't know that piece of information. I was representing a fighter, and I didn't even know his nickname. That seemed like a pretty base level thing to know about a fighter.

It was pride, of course. I wanted to be immune to anything the people in this office threw at me. I wanted to be able to say, *Nice try, buddy. But me and Kage… we're thick as thieves.* At this point, that wasn't possible.

Right now, Kage was an enigma, I was the clueless new guy, and everyone around here seemed eager to watch me make an ass of myself.

I smiled and worked my way back to my cubicle, noting how everyone was still eyeballing me. Alicia's curious gaze burned a hole in me as I passed by, and the whole office seemed to be holding its breath.

Yeah, if day one was any indication, it was going to be a long, strange summer.

Chapter 6

MY SECOND day of work was a Friday, so while everyone else was dying for the day to end so that they could start their weekends, I was just getting warmed up. I had no Kage to guide me. *Or distract me.* He sent me a text to tell me we'd meet sometime during the next week to discuss the "plan" I was supposed to be devising. I was glad he'd texted, because the thought of looking him in the eye and trying to act like I knew what I was doing was terrifying. I had a lot of homework to do if I was going to become an expert publicist by Monday.

Yeah, right.

I gave it my best shot over the weekend, though. Following the tips I'd learned from the internet on Thursday and Friday, I crafted a loose plan and set up a website and multiple social media profiles for Kage. It was going to be a lot of grunt work getting those things established, but I promised myself I'd hunker down and get it done.

What else did I have to do? I was a lonely guy in a strange city trying to prove I was fit for employment.

When Sunday proved to be too boring to handle, I called my mom.

"I hope you're taking care of yourself," she said. "You sound tired."

"Not tired. Bored."

"Son, how can you possibly be bored in Vegas? Isn't that the most exciting travel destination in the entire country? There's supposed to be something for the whole family. Shows, dancing, partying till the sun comes up… Remember, what stays in Vegas stays— wait, I think I got that wrong."

I laughed. "You've been watching too many tourism commercials, Mom. Get off the Lifetime channel, okay? It gives you women a distorted view of the world. There's no rich Prince Charming waiting to sweep every plain Jane off her feet, everyone's mother does not die of cancer, and dll have you believe."

She was silent for a moment, as if I'd hurt her feelings with my insolent social commentary.

"Hey, don't take what I say personally," I told her. "I'm just in a crappy mood."

"It's okay, Jamie. I know you didn't mean it. It's just…" She let out an anguished whimper. "I just got a call from the doctor last week."

"Is everything okay?" My heart was racing.

"They just want to look at something again. On my mammogram. I'm just paranoid because of what happened to your aunt. These things run in families. It's probably nothing."

It didn't sound like she thought it was nothing.

I called Layla before I went to bed, because I hadn't returned her call, and because I had no one to talk to about my mom.

"So good to hear from you, Jamie. I thought you might not ever call me back. I can't blame you after what I did to you."

"It's okay, Layla. I'm not upset about that. If you're not feeling it, you're just not feeling it. I'd never want you to stay in a relationship that wasn't doing it for you a hundred percent."

"That's the thing," she said hesitantly. "I was happy in our relationship for the most part. I think I just got a little nervous. It felt like it was going nowhere, but that's stupid 'cause we're young. There's no need to have a ring on my finger or something to know you care about me. I've got years before I need to start thinking about settling down and having kids, you know?"

"That is true," I said.

"So what I'm trying to say is that maybe I jumped the gun on breaking up with you. I mean, you weren't horrible to me. You were good to me. You're just a little… distant, I guess. My parents are all up each other's ass all the time, you know? And my friends? They're like fucking Siamese twins with their boyfriends. But you're just not like that, maybe."

I bit my lip, wishing I hadn't called, trying to think of what to say. "But you want the Siamese twin thing."

"Yeah, but—"

"No buts, Layla. You were right to break up with me. You and I want different things. Hell, I don't even know yet what it is that I want. I'm just crossing my fingers that I'll know it when I see it. For now, though, I think it's best for me to be single."

"Then why did you call me?" Her voice quivered.

"I thought we were friends. I guess I shouldn't have. I'm gonna go now, okay? I'm sorry for everything."

I hung up, and the tears came. I cried for Layla, and a little bit for me, but mostly I cried for my mom. What hell she must be going through, and there was nothing I could do about it.

No good had come from the two phone calls I'd made. Both recipients had broken down in tears. In the end, I decided that in the future, I'd just suffer my boredom by myself.

MONDAY and Tuesday passed by in a blur. I didn't see Kage at all, and my mind was plagued by thoughts of my mother, waiting for a call telling me everything was fine.

By Wednesday afternoon, I had thrown myself totally into work and the idea of trying to be the best publicist money could buy. Dr. Washburn didn't mind my occasional phone calls to ask him questions. Or at least if he did, he didn't let on.

"You're totally cooler than I thought you were, Doc," I admitted after he'd given me yet another pep talk.

His scoff was audible over the phone line. "You didn't already think I was cool? Why am I even helping you?" But there was a teasing quality to his voice that let me know he wasn't serious.

"Because you love me," I said. "Because I'm your favorite student. Admit it."

"Okay, I will admit that I have developed a soft spot for you. But only academically. On a personal level, I find you barely tolerable."

"Oh, that was harsh!" I laughed quietly. "Hey, I know I've given you a hard time in the past, but I was hoping maybe you could find it in your heart to give my barely tolerable personality another chance. At least before it's time to issue final grades next year?"

"I don't know. Can you quit being a smart ass?"

"Can a puppy quit being cute?"

"Oh, so you think you're cute, do you?" He laughed a little too heartily as he hung up the phone, leaving me alone once again in my bare cubicle among strangers.

After a few minutes, Mark Gladstone poked his well-groomed head around the corner. "How goes it, intern?"

I spun around in my task chair and shrugged. "Pretty good, I guess. My job is still in its infant stages, I guess you could say. Not showing much of a return yet, but we'll get there."

"Haven't noticed your boss around much. He giving you input, or are you pretty much on your own?"

"To be honest, I haven't seen much of him. We had lunch that first day, but that's it."

Mark nodded and crossed his arms over his chest. "Yeah, nobody sees much of him from what I understand. Hell, I almost passed out when he stuck his head in here on your first day. He comes through here every once in a while, when he needs payroll to cut him a check for something."

"Doesn't seem like you two get along very well," I said, hoping I hadn't overstepped any boundaries.

"Yeah, well, I know it doesn't seem like it, but Vegas is a small town. Kage and I went to high school together, so there may be a bit of bad blood there." He stepped further into my cubicle. "The problem was that I was popular, and Kage was— well, people thought he was kind of weird. So there was sort of this jealousy thing going on."

"I see." I didn't want to call him a liar, but I definitely couldn't imagine Kage being jealous of a guy like him. If anything, it would have been the other way around.

"I got a lot of pussy," Mark continued. "Kage didn't. I guess you could say he was an outsider. As far as I know, he only had two friends."

Mark's description didn't make me think any less of Kage, but it did make my heart squeeze for him. All that money and talent, and he was considered an outcast by most of his peers. I wondered if he got picked on— if that's what made him learn to fight. Bullying had sent many a kid running for the martial arts gyms and the security of knowing that, if it came down to it, they could take care of themselves. As for myself, I had turned to sports and learned the art of blending in.

Mark kept running his mouth, but I had stopped listening. He didn't say anything more about Kage, so I wasn't interested. Finally, he wandered off and found another victim for his vocal attack. At four-thirty, my cell phone rang, and I was surprised and pleased to discover it was Kage.

"Hi, my little intern. How are you doing?" He sounded laid back, with a confident familiarity that bordered on seductive.

"Um, I'm doing fine. How are you?"

"Great. I was calling to see if you wanted to watch me train in the morning. Or do you prefer to sit in a cubicle?"

"No," I said quickly. "I don't prefer to sit in a cubicle. I'd be honored to watch you."

Honored? Way to geek it up, Jamie.

"Okay. I'll pick you up at your door at nine in the morning, then. Wear something comfortable. You won't be going in to the office at all tomorrow."

I hung up the phone and sat staring straight ahead at the back wall of my cubicle for a good ten minutes. I hadn't realized how excited I would be to talk to Kage again. It was almost unbearable to think that I'd have to wait all afternoon and all night to see him. And to get to watch him train. That was the most exciting thing of all.

IT SEEMED like nine o'clock in the morning took weeks to roll around. I'd been ready for over an hour when I heard a heavy knock at the door.

Kage was dressed in sweats and a t-shirt, and his shoulder-length hair was freshly washed, still wet and slicked back from his face. He looked enviably handsome as always.

"You ready?" he asked, making no secret of once-overing my attire.

"Ready and willing," I quipped, then winced inwardly at the suggestiveness of the comment.

"Yeah?" He grinned. "I hope you're willing to be bored to death, because I'm afraid that's what's about to happen."

"I doubt it. Have you ever worked in a cubicle? I mean, I'm not complaining. I appreciate my job, really I do. But it will be a welcome change to watch you train. That's all I meant." I pulled the door closed behind me, and we walked toward the elevator. "I don't want you to think I don't appreciate my job. You don't think that, do you? Sometimes when I'm nervous things come out all wrong." I pressed the elevator button for the lobby and glanced over at Kage. He was smiling at me. "I'm babbling again, aren't I?"

"A little," he admitted. "But it's okay. I kinda like it. Lets me know I'm getting to you."

"Well, I'll keep doing it then. You're the first person who's actually given me license to act socially awkward. I have to admit, it's very freeing."

After an ironically silent elevator ride, Kage led me through the lobby, down the hall by the Grotto, and through a large door with a keycard lock on it. Then we were in a large gym with all sorts of workout equipment, mirrored walls, and a padded floor.

"Wow, is this all yours, or do the guests get to work out here, too?"

"Just me," he said. "You can use it when you want, but don't tell anyone else. It's private."

"Of course not. I'd never tell anything you told me not to tell. I signed a paper, remember?"

"A paper?" he asked, his brows coming together in confusion.

"Yeah, the NDA. The non-disclosure agreement my professor and I had to sign so that I could do the internship."

"Hmmm… I had no idea about that. My uncle does stuff like that. What did it say, if you don't mind me asking?"

It was my turn to give him a confused look. "Of course I don't mind. It's your business. It just said we couldn't tell anyone I work for you. Like we have to keep your name confidential, and the hotel name, your uncle's name, and any personal information I might learn… Basically, I can tell people I'm interning for someone in Vegas, but that's about as far as it goes."

"So your family doesn't know you're working for me?"

"Nope."

"That's crazy. I was wondering why you said you couldn't tell your girlfriend what you were doing. I was like, what the fuck? Why would someone not be able to tell his girlfriend he got a new job? You care about someone, you don't keep secrets. At least that's how I feel about it."

"Yeah," I said awkwardly, wishing like hell he wouldn't bring up the girlfriend I'd lied about.

He cocked his head to the side and bit his lip. "What if I tell people you're working for me? Is that permitted?"

I thought about it for a second. "I don't see why not. You didn't sign anything, did you? I mean, the whole NDA is a safety measure to protect you, so that I don't tell private things you don't want me to. If you tell your own business, it's not private anymore, right?"

"You want me to tell your girlfriend you're working for me? We could call her right now, and I'll tell her myself."

Would he stop already with the girlfriend?

"Um… that's not necessary. But thanks." I tried to smile.

"How about your family? They should know where you are. Your mom is probably worried sick."

"Actually, it would be nice if you could tell my mom. She's really excited and positive, but I can tell she's dying to know the details."

"Yeah, okay," he said. "You want to call her now?"

I laughed. "No. We can do it later."

Kage nodded and removed his shoes and socks. I followed suit, and then we made our way to the center of the gym.

"This is Marco, my primary trainer." He indicated a shorter, balding man who was readying some equipment. "Marco, this is my intern."

Marco turned around and gave me a sharp looking-over. "Pleased to meet you, Jamie," he said in a heavy Brazilian accent, clearly already familiar with who I was. "Kage and I are very excited about what you're going to be doing for him. He says you're the man when it comes to these things."

"Uh…" I faltered, but Kage thoughtfully swooped in to save me from humiliation.

"Marco's main area of expertise is in Muay Thai, but he's very well-rounded, so he works with me on pretty much everything." Kage's voice was full of pride for his coach. "Sometimes I work on boxing down at Ed's Boxing Club. Then my Jiu Jitsu coach comes in on some afternoons. Just depends on his schedule. Other than that, it's pretty much just me and Marco."

"Don't forget the sparring partners I've been bringing in for you," Marco said. "You make it sound like I keep you locked away in a dark cellar. Whether your uncle likes it or not, I do get you exposure. It's good for you to work with people rather than alone all the time."

"Well, I've added another person, as you can see," Kage told him. "Jamie is going to be observing us some."

"Oh." Suddenly Marco didn't seem quite as pleased to meet me.

I figured it must be because he didn't like to be scrutinized. I probably wouldn't like it if Kage's uncle started sending in some high school student to observe my intern work, so why should I expect this high level MMA coach to be thrilled for some college guy to be watching over his shoulder.

Still, the first day of watching Kage train was a revelation. First of all, I'd never imagined how long and grueling it would be. I was thinking back to the few karate lessons I'd taken in middle school. An hour a week, and that was it. So I thought maybe Kage trained an hour a day.

Boy, was I wrong.

Marco was on full-time salary. Most days Kage trained for three hours in the morning and two hours in the evening, in addition to his early morning three-mile run. That was just a regular laid-back day for these guys. Apparently, they trained even harder in the week leading up to a fight.

During training sessions, they wore safety gear— shin guards, sparring gloves, headgear, mouthpiece. Sometimes Kage shucked his shin guards and headgear and just wailed on Marco. I couldn't imagine being a human punching bag for a living, but Marco took it like a champ, alternately barking out orders and taunting his eager student. *"Good, good, great head movement,"* he'd say. Or *"You hit like a girl. Are you wearing pink panties under those shorts?"*

Sometimes Marco talked such shit to Kage it was a wonder he didn't just walk out. I kept expecting things to get serious, for the practice blows to become real blows, but the two of them just worked diligently at besting each other without either one ending up in the hospital.

Morning workouts included a one-hour warm-up and general strength and flexibility workout. Then they would focus on stand-up work, which included punching and kicking. Footwork and head movement were also honed to a fine art during these sessions, ensuring that Kage could confuse his opponent while dodging whatever strikes came his way. Sometimes they'd work punch or kick combos over and over and over, calling the numbers again and again, until I found myself chanting along with them. In the afternoon session, they'd take it to the ground for grappling practice. The end of each session was reserved for anything-goes sparring matches.

I was shocked at the amount of physical labor Kage did every day. No wonder he looked so damn good. What he did was a far cry from going to the gym for an hour three nights a week. Hell, I got worn out just sitting on the sidelines and watching him pushing and pulling the prowler sled the length of the gym, and that was only a fraction of one of his rigorous routines. I'd participated in countless basketball, football and baseball training sessions over the years, and this was more intense.

"I wish I had a good camera," I said offhandedly to Kage as we made our way to the elevators after the first morning's practice. "I kept thinking I'd love to take some action shots of you to use for promotion. You look amazing out there."

"I look what?" he asked with an impish grin. "I didn't quite hear you."

"You look amazing," I said, over-enunciating loudly.

"How so?" That grin of his was so infectious, I found myself smiling shyly.

"Well, Mr. Ego, you're impressive. I mean, you're beyond impressive. I can't even begin to tell you how blown away I am after watching you work out. I've never been much of a fan of the fighting sports, but I have to say… You've got me. I can't wait to see you fight."

He punched me lightly— well, lightly for him— in the arm. "Hey, you passed the test."

"What test?"

"The yes-man test. You see, I only surround myself with yes-men. If you had said I looked like shit, I'd have to let you go."

"I don't believe that. Not for a minute."

Kage chuckled quietly as the doors slid open. "This is your stop, Jamie. See you tomorrow."

Chapter 7

AT EIGHT-THIRTY on the following morning, a guy from some professional camera shop showed up at my suite to deliver a top-of-the-line digital video and still camera. When I say top of the line, I mean the camera guy was jealous as hell.

After I sputtered for five minutes about how surprised I was to be receiving it and how I would never have been able to afford such an awesome piece of equipment, the guy said, "We don't normally do deliveries. So what, do you have a sugar mama or something?"

"No, of course not." I smiled from ear to ear, marveling at Kage's generosity. "It's from this really amazing guy."

"Oh," he glanced around my expensive suite. "He get you this place?"

"Yeah, I could never afford something like this myself. I'm just a college student from a middle class family."

"Now you've got a killer place and a great camera. I mean, look at that view. Imagine the shots you can get right from this window."

"That's a great idea. I'll be honest with you. He's spoiling the hell out of me, and I don't know how I'm going to leave all of this to go back to school in Atlanta next semester. It's gonna be tough."

"Sugar daddy won't spring for a penthouse down in Atlanta?"

I looked at him like a deer caught in the headlights. "Oh, it's not like that!"

"It's cool, man. I used to be a stripper before I got this gig last year, so I know how all that shit works." He winked. "I'm down with it."

I sighed and closed my eyes, wondering how to explain a situation I was legally prohibited from discussing any further.

The guy cleared his throat and held up the camera. "So… If you'd like to have a seat on the sofa, I'll show you how this bad boy works. Your really amazing guy also bought you a half hour lesson."

I contained my excitement enough to join him on the sofa without making a fool of myself, and over the next half hour he proceeded to explain the intricacies of using my brand new, ridiculously complicated digital camera.

He was still explaining features when Kage knocked on my door. I jumped up off the sofa, flung the door open, and threw my arms around his neck. Well, maybe it wasn't so much throwing my arms around his neck as it was wrapping them gingerly around his shoulders in the world's most awkward man hug.

Kage didn't hug me back. Instead, he clasped his hands behind his back, making me feel even more awkward. It wasn't my usual M.O. to hug guys, but then I'd never received a gift that cost thousands of dollars. Even my car hadn't cost that much.

"Sorry. Maybe I should have tried a handshake instead." I patted him on the back a couple of times, then backed away and smiled. "The guy's here with the camera. I don't know what to say, Kage. I'm… Well, I'm speechless."

"No babbling?" he teased.

"Nope. Not this time. I must be in shock."

I turned to face the camera guy, ready to introduce Kage, but then I remembered the NDA. I wasn't sure if this was covered under that or not. I also realized that maybe the hug hadn't sent the right message about our relationship. While I was pondering these things, Kage stepped around me and shook the guy's hand.

"I'm Michael Kage," he said. "Did I interrupt the lesson?"

"Only by a little bit. I just have a few more things to show him, and then he's all yours." He wagged his eyebrows.

Kage stepped over to the chair and sat down. "Just pretend I'm not here then."

It was impossible to pretend he wasn't in the room. Not only was he always the most powerful presence in any room, but now his eyes were glittering like diamonds. I thought maybe he was as excited as I was. He just sat there in that manly sprawl of his and watched us with those sparkling eyes. When the lesson was over, the camera guy stood up and handed me the camera, and I turned it over in my hands, admiring it for the hundredth time. Then I looked up to find Kage watching me closely.

I smiled. "This is so un-fucking-believable. I can't wait to take a million pictures of you. If this thing does what he says it does, we'll be able to see every drop of sweat on your body."

"Wow." The camera guy took an exaggerated breath. "I've just got to tell you, this is a really nice piece of equipment. You *are* a really amazing guy, and you obviously care a lot about him. Everyone should be so lucky."

"Yeah? You think?" Kage gave me an amused look, then got up out of the chair and joined me on the sofa. He took the camera from me and examined it for a few seconds. "Pretty nice," he said.

The camera guy smiled like we were two puppies playing in a cardboard box rather than a couple of jocks on a couch. "Call me if you guys need anything, okay?" Then he left.

As soon as he was out the door, Kage set the camera down on the coffee table and leaned back onto the opposite arm of the sofa, clasping his hands behind his head. "So… why does that guy think we're fucking?" He didn't look angry, only extremely amused.

I felt my cheeks flush bright red. "How should I know?"

"Oh, you know all right." He bit his lip on a cocky smile, which clued me in to the fact that he was enjoying yanking my chain. "What did you say to him? I mean besides that you'd like to take a million pictures of my hot, sweaty body?"

"Hey, you know what I meant!"

He laughed. "I do. But he obviously didn't."

I took a deep breath. "I may have also mentioned that you were an amazing guy."

Kage nodded, waiting for me to continue.

"And that you were spoiling me silly. And…" I covered my face and groaned. "And that I dreaded going back to my old life at school."

"Well, I guess that sounds vaguely suggestive."

"That was after he asked if I had a sugar mama." I started laughing then. "I didn't think about how it sounded. Just started going on about this amazing guy. God, what an idiot I am. I was just excited about the camera."

Kage had one leg bent up on the sofa, and he nudged my thigh with the toe of his sneaker. "I'm glad you like it."

"I know it's not a gift, that it's just something for me to use while I'm working for you, but it's still great. Most people wouldn't even get to borrow something this nice. I promise I'll take good care of it."

"Well, I had actually meant it as sort of a work-related gift. You've got a birthday coming up, and what better gift than one I can write off as a business expense?"

I shook my head in disbelief. "Are you serious? I get to keep it?"

"Before you give me too much credit, remember my uncle is loaded. I have nothing. So really the only credit I can take is for knowing how to use the company expense account."

"Thanks for being enterprising, then."

I got the camera packed up in its case with its three fancy lenses and stood the tripod behind the sofa. Then we went down to meet Marco for the morning session.

I sat on the sidelines and watched as usual, snapping all manner of still picture and video with my new camera. But my mind kept going back to that hug. How strange that I did it in the first place, and how awkward that he hadn't returned it. It was a possibility that he was just grossed out that I was touching him, but it didn't seem that way. It seemed like he welcomed the attention in a shy way, but he didn't know how to show it. It reminded me of Mark Gladstone's thoughtless comments about Kage being an outsider.

There was an unexpected tenderness growing inside me for the mysterious fighter, getting stronger with every day and every surprising thing that he did. I found myself wanting to make friends, but as much time as we were spending together, I got the distinct impression that we weren't actually getting any closer at all. That Kage merely allowed me to be near him, hovering like a tiny satellite around his brilliance. In this case, it was I who was the outsider.

KAGE said he had plans to meet a friend that night, so we all skipped the afternoon session. I went back to the office and did some work on my laptop.

I couldn't pretend it wasn't driving me crazy to know the identity of the mysterious friend. It must have been someone important for Kage to ditch practice. Marco had been surprised, so it obviously wasn't a normal occurrence.

At quitting time, I followed the meandering herd of Alcazar employees toward the front door. My suite was beckoning with its endless stream of TV and free Wi-Fi, and its luxurious bathroom, and its river-rock soaps that had eroded down to smooth pebbles. Another mind-numbingly uneventful evening in Vegas lay sprawling before me.

That is, until Mark Gladstone blocked my way. He leered down at me with his white teeth and perfect hair, still completely put together after eight hours of work. He slipped his blazer off his shoulders and draped it over his arm, looking like he'd just stepped out of the pages of a menswear catalog. Then he very deliberately unhooked the next button of his dress shirt, giving me a glimpse of black chest hair.

"Jamie, my boy," he said, his voice deep and dramatic like a movie trailer voice-over. I could almost hear an ominous soundtrack backing his words. "It's time to go. Time to introduce you to the city of sin."

"But… but I'm underage still. My birthday's not for two more weeks." I'd been drinking since the tender age of fourteen, but it sounded like a good excuse.

"Not a problem," he said. "I'll just order you Shirley Temples all night."

All night? That sounded like a long time.

I glanced in the general direction of my room, then back at Mark. "I'm not sure. I have my laptop with me." I held it up like it was the missing puzzle piece. My saving grace. The irrefutable reason I could not go.

Mark shrugged. "We'll take it upstairs."

Damn. This guy's got an answer for everything.

Unwilling to be easily dissuaded, Mark followed me to my suite and walked right in behind me without being invited. Not that I particularly minded, but it looked like a gym locker had exploded in the bedroom, and snack wrappers littered the coffee table, proof of my late-night snack machine raid from the night before. Funny how your own mess never looked that bad while you were alone, but once someone else laid eyes on it, it was downright disgusting.

Maybe I should put that maid service sign on the doorknob.

I didn't even get a chance to apologize, which I was totally going to do, because Mark beat me to it. "Don't worry about the mess," he said. "You're a college guy. You're allowed to be a slob."

It's a good thing my back was to him, because my eyes got wide, and I mouthed a few choice insults. I hadn't really wanted to go out with him in the first place, and now I wanted to even less. But I was also beginning to feel like the lamest person to ever hit the strip in Vegas, and I figured it would do me some good to get out. Going with Mark would save me from having to explore a strange place alone, so against my better judgment, I went.

Besides, Kage had blown off our afternoon session to go out and have fun. Maybe I ought to do the same. No sense holing up in my room for yet another night of work.

We walked a few doors down from the hotel to a trendy bar full of Mark Gladstone clones and women who looked like they'd just clocked out at the office. Of course, they had freshened their lips and hair. I got the distinct impression that this was an after work pickup spot, nothing more, nothing less. Sort of like the Vegas office drone version of the Collegiate back home.

A couple of women eyed me hungrily, cluing me in quickly to the fact that I was fresh meat around here— chum to the circling sharks. I didn't like it one bit.

Mark ordered a Shirley Temple for me. Which apparently is Vegas speak for straight cherry vodka. I nearly spewed it all over the bar.

"Whoa, we've got a lightweight here," Mark said jovially, patting me on the back like he was burping a baby.

Jesus. Could this guy get any more condescending?

"Not a lightweight," I gasped between hacking coughs. "I was just expecting ginger ale and grenadine. This is more like rubbing alcohol and cough syrup."

"Well, this is the grown-up version of the Shirley Temple. Time we were putting some hair on that chest of yours." His eyes dropped to my chest, and I swear even though he couldn't see through my shirt, I felt almost violated. For a moment, I thought I could relate to women on that subject.

"Okay, that wasn't creepy at all," I mumbled under my breath.

"Pardon?" Mark asked.

"Nothing." I slumped my shoulders and finished my Robitussin cocktail while Mark wagged his eyebrows salaciously at a pair of bottle blondes down the bar from us. I groaned inwardly when one of them settled her hopeful gaze on me. "I gotta go to the bathroom," I told Mark.

"Well, why don't you do it at the next bar? We need to get out of here."

I glanced at the girls and back at him. "I thought you were working something there."

Mark gave me a pitying look and shook his head slowly. "Don't ever take the first offer, Jamie. I'm just warming up. There's plenty of night left to explore."

The next place we stopped was more of a dance club with a slightly younger crowd. Mark ordered two Jack and Cokes and led me to a table near the dance floor. He nearly spilled our drinks, because his eyes were trained on the gyrating dancers and he wasn't paying attention to where he was going.

"Whoops," he said with a laugh and put my drink in front of me. I sipped mine through the tiny cocktail straw and sulked.

"Is this your usual after-work tour?" I asked, trying to make conversation.

"Yeah, I hit several bars. Then I pick my poison and get busy. That's what I love about Vegas. I never have to go home alone." His obvious bragging was more sickening than the first drink he'd bought me. "You see anyone you like, Jamie? Wanna go dance with someone?"

I shook my head, wishing I'd never agreed to go out with him.

"Aw, go on," he urged, gesturing toward the dance floor with his drink. "Go have some fun. Pick a couple of young ladies to bring back to the table."

And there it was. The reason I was here. Mark wanted me to pick up young girls for him.

Fuck. This is not good.

Three more drinks, and I was almost drunk enough to be Mark's ho-bagger. I was watching the dance floor with some interest when I noticed a couple cutting it up near the center of the dancers.

The guy was built, really good-looking, and his female dance partner was riding his back like he was a bucking bronco, her short sun dress barely covering her ass. She wore flesh-colored strappy sandals, and her ankles were hooked around his waist. I had to give them an A for originality.

The fact that the bucking bronco was none other than Michael Kage was just the icing on the cake of my night. I shook my head to make sure I wasn't hallucinating.

But as I watched, it became ever clearer that it was indeed my client— or was he my boss?— giving that girl a rodeo ride.

"Oh, Jesus," Mark groaned when he spotted them. "I heard he was dating her again. Who the fuck do I have to blow to get a girl like that?"

I turned my head drunkenly toward Mark and squinted. "Maybe that's your problem. Blowing someone usually gets you a boyfriend, not a girlfriend."

Mark ignored my derisive comment. "Do you see this? She's a goddamn Victoria's Secret model now."

"Really?" I gave Kage and his partner another look. "That's impressive. Way to go, Kage."

"You haven't met her already?" Mark's tone was oddly accusing, and I drew back.

"No. What's her name?"

"Vanessa Hale," he breathed reverently. "You've never seen her in the catalogs?"

"Uh, I'm afraid I don't subscribe. Though come to think of it my girlfriend has them lying around her dorm room all the time."

Damn, I've gotta quit calling her my girlfriend.

"Well, if you have a pulse I don't see how you could have missed Vanessa Hale. She's the hottest thing on the planet."

I looked again. Kage was smiling so broadly, I was betting there was laughter coming out of that perfect mouth of his. Vanessa's long brown hair swung across his face as she held onto his thick shoulders.

"She *is* very pretty," I admitted. "Beautiful hair."

Kage's hair was down, and it mingled with hers as they played on the dance floor. I felt a pang of jealousy as I watched them having so much fun, and here I was sitting with Mark the molester.

Just as the song ended, Kage started galloping toward the edge of the dance floor right in our direction. I wanted to sink into the floor, but instead I sat there like a deer in the headlights as he spotted me.

His step faltered, and the smile fell from his face, leaving a distinct frown in its place. He looked from me to Mark and back again, then bent his knees and allowed Vanessa to slide to the floor. The pair approached our table, her still smiling, him regarding us in a suspicious way that had me wondering if I'd still have a job by morning.

Maybe this wasn't such a good idea after all.

"Mark," he grated, stopping in front of our table. "I see you've decided to show my little Gemini the ropes even before his birthday."

"You remembered my sign," I said stupidly, noticing that he had a dark half-moon in the soft flesh beneath his left eye.

A black eye on a fighter should not have been shocking, but it was the first time I'd seen anything marring the perfection of Kage's face. I had the ridiculous urge to reach out and touch it. To ask him if it hurt.

God, I was drunk.

He didn't even glance at me as he growled at Mark. "I thought I made myself clear when we talked about this in the office. Maybe I need to use plainer language."

His right fist flexed at his side. It didn't look like a threat so much as a reflex, which made it all the more intimidating.

"You snooze, you lose," Mark said with a cocky smirk.

In that moment, I realized Mark truly was an idiot. He was the kind of guy who would climb into a lion's cage just to prove he was a man, and Kage was the lion who would eat him just because he could.

Vanessa Hale leaned in toward me, swaying a little on her feet, sticking her heart-shaped face right in front of mine. "Oh, Mikey, this is Jamie? He's adorable. If my lashes were that long, I'd never have to wear falsies on a photo shoot again." She studied me with big eyes that looked green under the low lights. Tendrils of dark hair curled at her temples and twisted around her narrow shoulders. "Can he hang with us? Pretty please? I'd love to get to know the guy who's going to help you get famous."

"I don't think so," Mark interrupted. "Jamie and I were just about to find a couple of hotties to spend the rest of the evening with. We've got a few on the line already, and we were just narrowing our selection."

Oh, Jesus. How lame does that make me sound?

"Jamie has a girlfriend," Kage said matter-of-factly, as if he'd never considered for a moment that I might cheat. I liked that.

I didn't correct him about the girlfriend thing, though, because I would've had to admit I'd lied. That was the problem with lies; they had a tendency to compound and to get out of control. I figured in this case, silence was the best plan of action.

Kage waved a hand dismissively at Vanessa. "Whatever you want, Nessy. If he wants to come with us, it's fine with me. I'm just ready to go home and watch a movie or something." He seemed awfully sullen compared to the guy who had just been galloping around the dance floor with a famous model on his back.

Vanessa grinned, assuming already that she'd gotten her way. With a face and body nice enough to rate a Victoria's Secret gig, I was pretty sure she was used to getting her way in all things. Personally, I didn't particularly want to let her get her way, but the prospect of having a legitimate escape from Mark was too tempting to pass up.

I leaned over and whispered in his ear.

"Sorry, dude. Between you and a Victoria's Secret model, I've gotta go with the model. I'm sure you understand."

Mark gave me a sour look, but he knew he'd been outbid for my company. "Go," he said. "Have fun, and fill me in on Monday. See if you can get some pictures."

I stifled a laugh. Mark really was a shameless sleaze bag.

Chapter 8

KAGE'S apartment was similar to mine in style, but about five times bigger. I had no idea how many bedrooms it had, but the center was an enormous great room with a living area, a dining area, and a stainless-steel kitchen. The view from the wall-sized window was astonishing.

Vanessa danced into the apartment and fell onto the pale blue sectional, clearly comfortable in Kage's apartment. *She's definitely been here before.* I sat awkwardly on the sectional as far from her as I could get, because the last thing I needed was to get an MMA fighter jealous by sitting next to his girl. Apparently Vanessa didn't understand that concept, because she scooted right over next to me, kicked off her strappy sandals, and pulled her legs into the seat Indian style. She sat sideways facing me, but I faced straight forward, looking about as geeky and nervous as a guy possibly could.

A supermodel, I thought. *Sitting right next to me.* And then on the heels of that thought… *Kage's girlfriend.*

That really put things into perspective. I glanced around for Kage, who had disappeared as soon as we'd entered the apartment. I wondered what he was doing, and when he was going to come back.

"Mikey and I are just friends," Vanessa said, as if reading my mind.

I whipped around to face her, wishing it wasn't so obvious that her comment had affected me. "Doesn't matter to me one way or the other," I said. "That's your business."

She smiled, revealing teeth that had a slight gap between them. Rather than being unattractive, the imperfection had the opposite effect, amping her sex appeal tenfold.

Like Kage, she had the kind of face you couldn't get enough of looking at, each glance revealing a new facet of attractiveness. Her kohl-rimmed eyes were unnaturally large, her nose slim, lips full and slicked with a clear balm. My eyes kept wanting to drop to the swell of her breasts and the trim waist beneath, just to see what society's ideal looked like in person.

Her dress was shoved up around the tops of her thighs, barely covering the important stuff. In her little sun dress and loose curls, I thought she would look right at home in a sunny meadow on a spring day. A light sprinkle of freckles across her nose added to the illusion.

A melodic rap song suddenly started playing over a central sound system, and Vanessa started bobbing her head to the music.

"So Mikey tells me you're a journalism major. What made you choose that?" Her tone was light and friendly like her expression.

"Yeah, I guess I just like writing, and I like sports. That led me to the communications field, and eventually to where I am now. Interning for Kage. Uh… Mikey."

She laughed at my obvious confusion over what to call him when I was talking to her. "Mikey and I go way back," she said. "We went to high school together."

"Really?" That got my attention. Talking with his childhood friends was a great way to get to know my client. "Has he always been… the way he is?"

Okay, I'm not going to win any Pulitzer prizes in journalism with that vague question.

"He's always been unique, if that's what you mean. But don't let the hard edges fool you. He's a big, soft Teddy bear inside. I'm telling you right now, if anyone ever hurt him, you'd have to pull me off the sonofabitch. I'd go to jail for Michael Kage in a heartbeat, no questions asked. I would do anything for him. Kill, maim…" She narrowed her eyes menacingly at me. "In other words, watch your step."

She was so earnest. I laughed when I tried to picture her being Kage's bodyguard. "That's so sweet. The big bad MMA fighter needs the protection of a size-three lingerie model."

"Size zero," she corrected, raising a delicate brow. "And I see my reputation precedes me. Or have you seen my pics?"

Why did that sound like an accusation?

I blushed, imagining looking at images of a scantily clad Vanessa in a lingerie catalog. I'm sure Mark Gladstone would not agree, but it seemed like it would have been an invasion of privacy to know what this girl looked like almost naked before I'd even met her.

"No," I practically whispered. "I've never seen your pictures." I rubbed my sweaty palms nervously against my knees and looked around for Kage. "I need to go to the restroom. Can you point me in the right direction?"

I had gone when Mark and I had arrived at the last bar, but now I just needed to get away for a moment.

Maybe see where Kage was.

Vanessa inclined her head toward a door at the back of the living area. "Right over there. Just go on in and the bathroom will be on your right. I'll grab a beer while you're gone."

The room on the other side of the door was not a restroom. It was a bedroom with a huge king size bed in the center. It had the same style picture window as the one in the living area, the urban glow of Vegas providing subtle illumination in the darkened room.

Kage sat on the unmade bed, leaning up against the headboard, dressed in nothing but a pair of boxers. A halo of smoke billowed up around his head. I froze in my tracks when I saw him, and that's when the smell hit me.

Weed.

Kage tilted his head back and blew a thick stream of smoke up into the air. His expression was a mystery in the low light, but the way the interplay of light and shadow accentuated every curve and dip of his muscled body made me feel uncomfortable in a way I didn't want to examine.

Without a word, he held out a blunt toward me in offering. I approached the bed on nervous legs. It wasn't that I'd never smoked weed. I'd done that plenty, especially when Braden was going through his dealer phase. My nerves tonight had more to do with the person who was doing the offering rather than what he was offering. Kage jangled my nerves, made me feel like a stupid kid. I thought it would get better as we got to know each other, but if anything I was becoming more awkward around him with every day that passed.

I hesitated. "What if I have a piss test or something?" I was genuinely concerned, having recently entered the workforce.

"Who's your boss?" he asked simply, an amused expression on his face.

"Oh, yeah." I felt my cheeks color slightly, but I wasn't about to let him get away with that comment. "Actually, I think you're more like a client than a boss."

He didn't say anything. Just kept looking at me like I amused him somehow.

I took the blunt from him and sucked in a hit. The smoke tickled going down, expanding too much in my chest, forcing me to turn away and cough into my hand.

Kage chuckled quietly and took the blunt from me, sucked in another hit, and gave it back. It was the familiar back-and-forth of getting high— an intimate exchange like fighting, or dancing, or fucking. It felt nice. I took a deeper hit this time, filling my lungs to capacity and holding it as long as I could.

I tried unsuccessfully to ignore Kage's state of undress. He'd worked out in front of me in nothing but a pair of shorts, but this was different. This was underwear, and it was really freaking me out.

He pulled one knee up and draped his arm over it, and I caught a glimpse of something I shouldn't have seen as his boxer fly gaped and settled back closed. Against my will, desire sparked down low in my gut.

Don't think about it, Jamie.

I tore my eyes away, already feeling lightheaded, and crashed down onto my back on the bed near Kage's bare feet. The ceiling was very far away, at least ten feet above me, the dark wood rafters beginning to shift when they should have been still.

"You boys starting the party without me?" Vanessa entered the room with a beer in her hand.

"Never," Kage said, his deep voice vibrating through me. "Come here, Nessy."

Kage got up onto his knees on the bed, and Vanessa walked over to stand right in front of him. He slipped the lit end of the blunt expertly between his lips, the fire disappearing within his mouth. Vanessa leaned in, and Kage put his hands on her shoulders, held her as she closed her eyes and parted her lips. Then he positioned the end of the blunt right at the edge of her waiting lips and shotgunned the smoke straight into her mouth.

It was a shockingly sensual act, and I licked my lips as I watched, unable to look away as Kage shared his high with Vanessa in the most intimate way possible. Then he crawled across the bed and leaned down over me, the blunt still wedged between his lips. I could tell by the urgent look on his face that the fire was getting hot inside his mouth, but he wanted to give me a shotgun before he removed it.

I parted my lips like I'd seen Vanessa do, my heart fluttering as Kage's face came close to mine and he blew smoke down into my lungs. I couldn't help thinking how intimate the act was, him blowing into my mouth, our lips nearly close enough to touch.

Then he was gone, sitting up and pulling the blunt gingerly from his mouth, being careful not to burn his lips. He took a deep breath and handed it to Vanessa, who hit it a couple of times before dousing the fiery tip and setting it in a hotel ashtray on the bedside table.

By this time, I was flying, no doubt about it. The rafters were really starting to move, seeming to breathe with a life of their own, casting blurry trails against the white expanse of ceiling. I shook my head, realizing with alarm that I was hallucinating.

"I haven't felt like this in a long time," I mumbled. "This is some good shit."

"Mmm hmm," Kage agreed, dropping down onto his back right beside me, his hip nearly touching mine. "Very nice."

Vanessa climbed onto the bed with us, lying down beside Kage, sandwiching him between us. "What do you think?" she asked him. "About what I suggested earlier?"

"No," he replied flatly.

"Hey, it's not like it would be the first time, you know?"

Kage grunted and spoke slowly, sounding very stoned. "That doesn't count. We were in high school. We were stupid."

"God, Kage, why won't you let me do something for you? How long has it been?" Then Vanessa started crying. Not like an authentic cry, but the whiny kind you do when you're fucked up and everything strikes you as emotional. The kind of cry you're ashamed of when you think back on it from a sober vantage point. "You can't go through life with nothing but fighting, Michael. I can tell it's wearing on you. Please let me help you. Let somebody help you."

Kage lay there in silence for a moment, and my mind began to float up into the rafters. I have no idea how long it was before he spoke again.

"He's not down for it," he said quietly, calling me back to earth.

Whoa… I am truly fucked up. Where was my mind just then?

I kept expecting the two of them to start making out, but they just lay there staring at the ceiling. Talking with each other like I wasn't even there. I kept trying to make sense of what they were saying. It seemed like they were talking about me, but in my blitzed state I couldn't quite grasp the meaning of their words.

"How do you know he's not down for it? Did you ask him?"

"Don't have to." Kage swallowed. "He's got a girlfriend."

"Ex-girlfriend," I corrected, my voice shocking even to myself. I hadn't known I was going to speak. Was I actually taking part in the conversation? Hell, I didn't even know what they were talking about, did I?

"See?" Vanessa said, swiping at her tears. "Ex-girlfriend. I know a single guy when I see one."

Kage didn't respond.

"Tell you what," she slurred. "I'm gonna get up and party by myself. You boys just stay here and sulk, or whatever. Could you give me some better music, Mikey? How am I supposed to dance to this crap?"

Kage sat up and grabbed a remote off his bedside table. He pressed some buttons, and then a pop song I'd never heard started playing through the central stereo system.

Why is it that everything sounds good when you're high?

"Here we go," Kage groaned. "Nessy dances when she's drunk. Just ignore her and she'll pass out soon."

I sat up and watched in undisguised fascination as she danced by herself in the middle of Kage's bedroom, twisting and smiling and occasionally shaking her trim hips. After a moment, she beckoned me with the crook of a finger. "Don't worry, I won't bite," she said when I hesitated. "I just don't wanna dance by myself."

It had been a while since I'd danced, but the kind of moves she was doing didn't require much technical know-how. She wrapped her arms around my neck and spun me with her. I looked back at Kage, rolling my eyes in an attempt to seem innocent of all blame in the situation. It was a little embarrassing dancing with him in the room.

Watching us. Why does that turn me on so much?

The fact that he was watching made my already-burgeoning erection stiffen up even more. I could feel the blood rushing to my dick as his eyes tracked our movements across the floor. I kept stealing glances at him, making sure he was still watching.

After a moment, Kage spoke up. "Don't think you're gonna seduce my intern, Vanessa."

She laughed. "If you won't, I will. Somebody's got to do it. Can't have the poor boy going around Vegas with this neon *Virgin* sign on his forehead."

"I am not a virgin," I grated, so appalled by the idea that they would think I was a virgin that I glossed right over the part where she said *if you won't*.

"Relax." She placed one of her small hands on my chest. "I'm just fucking with Kage. I don't really think you're a virgin, and I'm not seducing you, either. Contrary to popular belief, I'm not easy. Mikey, on the other hand, is very easy tonight. Isn't that right, Mikey?"

"Vanessa..." Kage growled menacingly. I turned to look at him and nearly choked at the sight of the monster erection tenting his boxers. My eyes locked in on it. It was the first time I'd purposely looked at another guy's hard dick like that, and the imposing outline of flesh behind the thin veil of diamond-patterned fabric made the bottom drop out of my stomach.

Was he turned on by watching us together?

I felt my eyes widen, and I looked back up at Kage's face, searching for the answer.

He rolled over on the bed and climbed under the covers. A not-so-subtle move to hide his arousal. "Vanessa is sleeping over tonight, Jamie. You're welcome to stay, too. If you want."

"Um, yeah, sure," I said, trying not to sound too excited at being invited to the slumber party. "Where should I sleep?"

Instead of pointing me toward a guest room or the couch, he lifted his own covers, opening up a cozy-looking spot right next to him. All I could think of was being that close to Kage's enormous erection. Would it accidentally touch me? Had it abated by now?

As if sensing my hesitation, Vanessa climbed in behind Kage on the other side of the bed, setting the example. It worked to make me feel more comfortable about accepting Kage's offer, and I quickly stripped down to my boxer briefs and climbed into the bed. He settled the covers in over me, tucking me in.

"Well, this is great," he said. "In bed between the two hottest people in Vegas, and I'm not even getting laid."

I blushed in the dark. Vanessa was clearly one of the hottest people in Vegas, but I was sure he was just including me so that I wouldn't feel left out. It was a nice gesture just the same, and it made me feel all warm and fuzzy inside.

"So what do you have planned for us tomorrow?" I asked, trying to make small talk. I truly didn't care about anything outside of that bed at the moment, much less anything to do with work.

"I figured we'd just do the afternoon training session tomorrow so that we can sleep in a little. I never like to train early after I smoke."

"Do you smoke often?" I asked the question cautiously, nonchalantly, not wanting to seem judgmental.

"No. Just every now and then when I need to take the edge off, or if I have an injury it helps with the pain. But when I finally get a pro fight scheduled, I'll have to make sure it won't show up in a drug test just before or just after the fight. The Nevada Athletic Commission doesn't outlaw pot exactly, but you just can't have over a certain amount of THC in your system 12 hours before or after a fight."

"I see you've done your homework," I said with a laugh.

"Well, I needed to know if it's something I had to cut out completely. I would, of course. It's no big deal."

Vanessa huffed in the dark. "Are you guys going to talk business all night? You're harshing my mellow."

We both ignored her comment and continued to talk business.

"You don't do any kind of steroids or anything, do you?"

"Hell, no." He sounded genuinely offended.

"Well, a lot of publicists are hired to clean up the mess after an athlete has tested positive for PED's. I'm just doing *my* homework."

"You must really be high if you think I'd do that shit." He pushed the covers down to the tops of his thighs, exposing his upper body to me. "Feel this." He flexed his arm, and I reached out and squeezed. "All natural, baby. And this…" He indicated his torso. Even in the dark, I could tell he had his muscles tensed for me. "You wanna see what a real man feels like? Feel that," he coaxed. Vanessa giggled from the other side of him, and I think he elbowed her, which made her giggle even more.

I dropped a hand onto his chest, soft rasp of hair beneath my fingertips. His pecs were like the plates on a suit of armor, but warm and silky to the touch. The little hollow in the center of his chest beckoned to me. I dipped a finger into it and then ran the backs of my knuckles down the bumpy terrain of his eight-pack, marveling at the perfection of his form. Before I knew it, the pads of my fingers had begun to idly explore the crisp texture of his happy trail.

I could blame the weed or the alcohol, but the truth was I liked the feel of his body. It sent a lightning bolt of need all the way from my fingertips to my dick, and all I could do was turn my brain off and feel. God, did I ever want to feel… I was in the zone, where all was sensation, and there were no consequences— only actions. My fingertips just barely grazed the band of his boxers, running along the edge, slipping under the fabric just enough to separate it from his skin.

"Where you going with the hand there, chief?" Kage's voice was low and breathy, with a seductive undertone that sent my need soaring right off the charts. But his words brought me to my senses. Reminded me of where I was and what I was doing, and to whom I was doing it.

"Sorry," I muttered, snatching my hand back. "I'm really stoned. I don't think I know what I'm doing." I thought I ought to change the subject before he figured out I liked it. "Uh, back to the steroid question… I didn't mean any offense, Kage. Professionally speaking, I just need to know what I'm dealing with at all times so I don't get blindsided. I need to know you inside and out in order to do my job properly. I won't judge you no matter what."

"Professionally speaking?" He sighed, and I thought I detected a hint of disappointment. "Because that's your job? To not judge me?"

"Exactly. It's my job."

"That's what I thought." Kage definitely sounded disappointed. Possibly even a little pissed off. "You know what they say about all work and no play?"

"It makes Jack a dull boy?"

"Who the hell is Jack?" he slurred. "I was talking about you. All work and no play makes Jamie boring as fuck."

That smarted a little; I won't lie. But Kage was high— we all were— and things were being said and done that might not seem the same once we sobered up.

"Well, work is all I have right now. I'm in a strange place with absolutely no one to talk to, no friends, no social life. What do you expect? I had hoped to get to spend a little more time with you. Maybe you could tell me a little bit about yourself. As it is, I have to pick up bits and pieces from the grapevine, and I don't know what the hell to believe. And you've got me stuck down there in that cubicle half the time, or sitting on the sidelines watching you sweat. Then the other half I'm in my room working on your social media presence, or getting kidnapped and taken out to be someone's jailbait… uh… bait."

He gave me a puzzled look.

"I'm talking about Mark Gladstone. I think he wants me with him to attract younger girls."

"Yeah, you keep thinking that and you'll be in a world of shit before you can say *no thank you, sir.*"

"What's that supposed to mean?"

Kage shrugged, and a muscle in his jaw twitched.

"Mr. Cryptic strikes again," I mumbled. "Can you even say anything without talking in code?"

"Yeah. When you're ready to pull your head out of your ass and stop acting like a little boy. You are so goddamn naïve."

"There you go again with the riddles and code. Why don't you just say what you mean?"

He growled and ran a hand through his hair. "You don't even know what you're asking, Jamie. You say you want to get to know me? You'll know everything soon enough, because you'll do whatever it takes to get the job done. It's your nature. You'll know my deep, dark secrets. My fears. All of the ugly things that you will struggle to keep the public from catching wind of. Because I assure you— if you never listen to another word I say, listen to this— I am ugly. I am dark, and I'm bad, and I'm rotten to the core. And if you think being my publicist is going to be a walk in the park, you might want to go home to mama. Because it's about to get rough."

"Yeah, you keep threatening I'm going to get to know you, but I'm not seeing it." I looked hard at him. Tried to see his eyes in the gloom. "It seems like you have this security system that I can't breach, and every time I get close, a silent alarm goes off and you batten down the hatches."

He dropped back down onto the bed and stared at the ceiling. "You've got some pretty serious hatches yourself."

"That's bullshit," I said. "I'm an open book."

"Yeah? Like you lied to me about having a girlfriend? Real open book, Jamie."

I covered my face with my hands, wishing I could go back in time and take back the lie. "It wasn't exactly a lie, okay? I just… I forgot."

Kage barked out a laugh. "You're fucking lying right now. I'm not stupid, Jamie. I can tell when I'm being lied to. I could tell it over lunch that day when you took the phone call, and I can tell it now. I don't know if I can trust you. I need to be able to trust you."

"Okay," I sighed. "Jesus, you really know how to obliterate a guy's ego. The truth is, I forgot for a second and called her my girlfriend out of habit. We'd only broken up a few days before I came here. Then when I realized my mistake, I didn't want to admit it to you. Getting dumped is not something to brag about. It's… humiliating. And there you were being all Mr. Perfect, and I didn't want you to think I was lame or something."

He didn't respond, so I turned back over, putting my back to him. Then Kage turned over in bed and moved toward Vanessa, away from me. It was like we were a couple having an argument.

"Kage…" Vanessa said slowly. "Please tell me you brought your baseball bat to bed."

"I don't play baseball," he said.

"Then could you scoot over a bit? We're supposed to be going to sleep."

"Dammit!" Kage laughed and moved toward the center of the bed. "Okay, if you want to be that way. But I didn't figure Jamie would let me cuddle with him."

I laughed and turned halfway over, meeting his gaze in the dark. "I don't care. Vanessa did say you were a big teddy bear."

"Yeah?" He laughed darkly. "Don't believe anything she says about me. She has ulterior motives."

She laughed, but she didn't refute what he'd said.

Even though I'd basically invited him to cuddle with me, I never actually expected it to happen. I was just trying to act cool and to make up for the little quarrel we'd just had. So when he scooted up behind me and slipped an arm around my waist, I took a deep breath and held it. His warmth surrounded me, soothed me.

"You can breathe, Jamie," Kage said near my ear. "I'm not going to eat you."

"I know." I let the breath out and felt instantly better. Then I shifted around a bit to get comfortable. Something firm brushed my ass, and I settled against it, feeling a sense of euphoria wash over me.

This was okay, right? If Kage and Vanessa thought it was okay, then it must be okay.

Okay to feel this way.

After a few minutes of silence, Kage said in a gravelly voice, "Don't ever fucking lie to me again."

"I won't," I whispered. At that moment, I thought I'd rather die than ever lie to Michael Kage again.

I lay there feeling him pressed against me in the dark, listening to the sound of his breathing. I didn't dare move, because I was afraid he might let go of me.

Chapter 9

THE morning light did not sneak into Kage's bedroom. It laid siege to it, sending us cowering for cover beneath the down blankets and sheets. All three of us came fully awake there, one by one, stifled by the echoes of our own breath.

Kage was the first to brave the day. He threw the cover down the bed, revealing not only himself, but Vanessa and me as well. Vanessa giggled in her husky morning voice, and I yelled in protest.

"No lazy people in my bed," Kage announced as he ran for the bathroom, dragging the covers along with him so that we couldn't burrow back down. He dropped them outside the bathroom door and disappeared inside.

"Is there another bathroom?" I asked Vanessa, turning away so that she wouldn't see my morning wood.

"There are two more bathrooms out there. One off the living room, and one in the other bedroom."

"There's another bedroom? Why did we all pile up in here?"

"It was a slumber party." She laughed. "And because Kage would have lost his mind if you and I were wandering around unsupervised out there while he was in here. He's very jealous, you know. Maybe you're figuring that out by now."

"But I thought you two were just friends." I tried to sound nonchalant when I felt anything but.

"We are. Well, we are now, anyway. Things used to be different back in school. Mikey was my first love. I thought we would get married one day, you know? Have babies. Do the whole family thing."

My face colored at the thought, and at the personal sentiment behind the words. I wanted to get to know Kage, but this was definitely not what I had in mind. It embarrassed me, and even worse, it made me feel somehow desperate. Telling me she'd been Kage's first love… well, hell. Vanessa may as well have sunk a knife into my belly. It was ripping me up inside, and I didn't even know why.

I just knew I didn't want it to be true.

I wanted Kage to have never loved before. Wanted to keep him on that pedestal I'd put him on the first time we'd met. He was larger than life— beyond all of that. He wasn't supposed to love someone.

Not like that.

Kage chose that moment when I was seething in silence to come out of the bathroom, his eyes slightly puffy from sleep. The bruise beneath his left eye was clearly visible in the light of day. He rubbed his belly lackadaisically, splaying his fingers over the taut ripples of his abs.

My eyes slid shut, and my tongue snaked out to wet my lips, and heat washed over me. For an instant I was back in that bed with Kage pressed against my back, gripping me with his powerful arm.

"Isn't that right, Mikey?" Vanessa asked him, as if he'd been in on the conversation all along. Her voice jolted me out of my little fantasy.

"Isn't what right?"

"That we were each other's first love. I was just telling Jamie."

Kage pulled a pair of running shorts out of his walnut dresser and watched himself in the mirror as he put them on. "That's right," he said, and his confirmation twisted the knife in my gut.

"We were going to get married and have babies," she said again.

"Yep." Kage walked over to her and folded her into his arms. "Then things changed. And now I love you even more."

I cleared my throat. "Well, I'd love to try to figure you two out and all, but I've got to go to the restroom before we have an accident in here."

With that, I left the room, not waiting for either of them to respond. All of that stuff was none of my business, really. Well, actually it was my business in a way. If there was any chance it could affect Kage's public image, then it was by definition my business. But right now I just wanted to get as far away from that piece of information as I could.

Hell, I'd never even been in love myself. And then to find out that the unstoppable Michael Kage— *The fucking Machine, for Christ's sake!*— had loved a girl. I suppose it humanized him in a way I wasn't prepared to accept. And whether I wanted to admit it or not, it pissed me off badly.

When I returned to the room, Vanessa and Kage were lying on the bed again with their phones in their hands. "Selfie time," Vanessa told me. "Grab your phone and jump in here. I haven't seen my BFF in ages, and I want to have something to remember in case it's another year and a half before he decides to call."

I did as I was told, and we all started snapping selfies, jockeying for position, laughing, dropping our phones. First I got one of just me and Vanessa, because hey… supermodel. Then I got some of all of us, with Kage pushing his handsome face in from the side.

"Okay, switch," Vanessa called, and she flipped agilely over the top of me, leaving me in the middle between her and Kage.

I inched closer, he inched closer, and soon we were practically cuddling again. It felt different doing it when I was sober. But once I got going, I was snapping shots like crazy. Smiley shots, serious shots, blurry blooper shots. At one point, we all started making the goofiest faces we could come up with. I wondered fleetingly if these pictures would be worth something someday, because even though I was the epitome of mediocrity myself, I was flanked by two people who were destined to be stars.

I was thinking maybe this publicist gig wasn't going to be so bad, when Vanessa reached right across my face and hauled Kage to her, nearly scrubbing my lips off with her arm. Then she planted a sloppy kiss on his cheek. "I love seeing you this way," she crooned. "It's about damn time."

Kage gave her a castigating glare and wiped the kiss from his cheek. Then he stood up and stalked away from the bed, bringing our selfie love fest to an uncomfortable close.

"You know..." I spoke to Kage's back while he stared out the window at Vegas. "This makes me think we should do a more personal style photo shoot for you, Kage. I've got lots of pictures of you training, and lots of video, but none of you just hanging out in your apartment."

"You really think that would be a good idea?" His voice was flat, but at least he was speaking.

"I do. We need to get more eyeballs on you, right?" I got up and joined him at the window, staring out over the city and seeing none of it. "I think it would really humanize you for your fans. It would make you relatable. We're doing really well already with the social media accounts I've started. I post pics of you in different places, and it's already getting you some followers and web hits. But some personal stuff? Yeah, I think that could be really good for us."

Kage ran his index finger back and forth along his lips as he mulled it over in his mind. "All right, how about tomorrow? Never mind, what am I saying? Tomorrow is Sunday. That's like slave labor, isn't it? Making you work on Sunday."

"I don't mind. What else do I have to do around here? What time tomorrow?"

"I don't want to take advantage of you, Jamie."

"No problem. Like I said, I've got nothing else to do. You'll save me from two-thousand calories of straight carbs and fat out of the snack machine."

"Why are you eating out of the snack machine?" Kage finally looked at me, and his expression was horrified. "I'm going to start having your meals sent up. You obviously can't be left to your own devices when it comes to choosing food."

"Hey, I've done okay on my own for twenty years. It's not like I'm a lard-ass or anything."

He took a moment to assess my body. Slowly, carefully. With his eyes on me like that, I almost came to regret the fact that I hadn't yet put my clothes back on. I was standing in front of him in nothing but boxer briefs, and they were in danger of becoming too tight.

Kage took a deep breath. "You're definitely no lard-ass." He reached out and pinched my slight love handle with a smirk. "But you could stand to cut a carb or two."

I wanted to huff and stomp, maybe even punch something. Because dammit, I wanted him to think I looked good. Then I compared my body to his and relented. The guy clearly knew what he was talking about.

"Okay, you're the boss. I'll eat whatever you tell me to eat. But I'd better end up with a body like yours, or I'm gonna be pissed."

Kage's face stretched into an evil grin. "Guess you'd better start participating in my morning workouts, then. Starting Monday, you're no longer observing. You're breaking a sweat."

"Bring it on," I said with more confidence than I felt. My muscles were already protesting at the mere thought of Kage's workout.

"I have to say, I love your choice of intern, Mikey," Vanessa said, lounging like a cat on the bed. "He's very *eager*." Her emphasis on the last word gave me the distinct impression that she was fucking with me. Or maybe with Kage. I wasn't sure which.

It ticked me off, but Kage grabbed a balled-up dirty sock off the floor near his bed and threw it at her. "Shut up or I'll tell Jamie what you do for a living when you're not modeling."

Her mouth dropped open. "You wouldn't dare."

"Don't mess with me, Nessy. I'm serious."

"Fine. No more teasing." She wrapped her arms around her midsection and gave him an exaggerated pout. It was all very flippant, but I thought she looked genuinely cowed.

"I'll pick you up at your place Monday morning," Kage told me. "In the meantime, eat what I send up. If you want a snack, make it high protein, low carb, okay?"

"Your wish is my command." I aimed a smug look in Vanessa's direction and felt vindicated when it hit the mark. "Guess I'll get dressed and head out now. I need to go call my mom."

I SAW where you called yesterday," I told my mom when she answered the phone. "Sorry, I was in the middle of a business call, and then things went kinda haywire last night."

"Haywire?" she asked. "Are you behaving yourself?"

"Mom, I'm almost twenty-one now."

"My baby's growing up," she said, a mix of joy and sadness in her voice.

"I'm not your baby. That would be Paul."

"You're one of my babies. All three of you are equally my babies. Even after Jennifer gets married in August, she'll still be my baby. Then I'll just have one more."

"Oh, God. Don't start calling Chase your baby, too. That douchebag doesn't deserve you."

"Watch your language, young man. I'm still your mother, and I will put a strap across your back when you come home."

I laughed. "Since when do you *strap* people, mom?"

"Since they've gotten too big for their britches."

"Okay. Well, I can assure you I don't need a strap. I'm a working man now. I think you'd be proud of me."

She covered the mouthpiece and yelled at Paul to put the jelly back in the fridge and rinse the knife, then resumed our conversation. "I've always been proud of you, Jamie. Always. I'm glad you're doing well." She paused. "I sense there's something wrong, though. What is it?"

"Nothing."

"Don't nothing me. A mom can tell."

"It's just… love life issues."

What am I saying to my mom? I don't even have a love life.

"Problems between you and Layla?"

Layla who?

"Something like that."

Actually, nothing like that.

"Anything I can help you with? She's not pregnant, is she?"

"Mom! No, of course not."

"Well, you're not being very forthcoming, son. I just figured I'd head you off at the pass with the most difficult news I could think of. You know I'll understand, right? Whatever it is, I'll understand. In fact, I have some difficult news of my own to share."

My heart leapt up into my throat. "What is it?"

"I got the test results back. I have breast cancer."

"What?" I nearly dropped the phone. My face flushed hot, and I couldn't think straight. My mom. This was my mom. Cancer? Was she going to die? Jesus, here I was worrying about petty little conflicting feelings I was having over some guy, and my mom had cancer.

Way to put things into perspective, God.

"It's okay," she said calmly, though I could barely hear her through the pounding of blood in my ears. "The prognosis is excellent because they caught it early. I'm opting for a radical double mastectomy. I'm not going to let the same thing happen to me that happened to your aunt. She kept thinking she could beat it without getting a mastectomy, and she lost the bet."

I started to cry before I even realized I was doing it.

"Don't cry, baby," my mom pleaded. "Your father and I have cried enough for everyone, and now it's time to be positive. I want the threat gone so that I can be sure I'll be around to be a grandmother to your children, okay?"

"Okay," I sniffed, wiping the tears away with the back of my hand.

"Really, it's fine, son. The doctors say it will be fine, and I believe them. They can work wonders with plastic surgery these days. It's not like it was in your grandma's day."

"I love you, Mom," I blubbered. "I'm sorry."

"Shhh, baby. Nothing to worry about. Go take care of your love life and forget about this. It's nothing but a blip on the radar of life."

SUNDAY morning, Kage started having my meals sent up. Talk about spoiling me. I was getting chicken, fish, seafood, fresh vegetables, and brown rice delivered to my door like clockwork. Possibly the coolest part was knowing that he was ordering two of everything, and that I always knew exactly when and what he was eating even though we weren't in the same room. We were sharing a diet.

By Monday, he'd even started making pre-workout shakes for me with creatine and protein to give me energy and build muscle.

We settled quickly into a routine. We shared morning workouts, then I observed and took pictures. I started using the machines some while he trained. After lunch, I would go to the office to work in my little cubicle. Kage had failed to find me an office, but I assured him that I was fine in the cubicle, and that I wasn't blasting any sensitive information around the office. One day I tried to work in my room, but I found I needed the office setting to keep me motivated and feeling legit. However, I did go to my room to make business calls or to talk to Dr. Washburn. Not only did it feel uncomfortable talking out in the quiet office, but Kage was right. There were certain things those people didn't need to hear.

I especially felt skittish about revealing anything to Catwoman Cathy or Mark Gladstone. They were altogether too nosy, giving me the third degree every time I walked through the door. They always wanted to know how Kage and I were getting along, and I always told them as little as possible. It was weird. I always wondered what they could possibly get out of knowing all of my business, but after a while I figured out that it was probably just the thrill of gossip that drove them. No doubt they discussed everything I told them amongst themselves and with anyone else who would stand still long enough to listen.

It got to the point it seemed like I was being felt up every time I entered the office. I know that sounds icky, but it's true.

Mark Gladstone still tried to chat me up in private, like we were buddies or something. I was polite, but I tried to limit our conversations with excuses and sudden bathroom urges. He thought he was God's gift to the universe, but he definitely wasn't the kind of guy I could ever consider a friend. If it hadn't been for needing to feel like a real professional, I would have stopped going into the office altogether.

On Tuesday afternoon, I'd used some of the photos I'd taken to create a press packet. Well, really it was a glorified flyer, but I used every ounce of creativity I had in me to make it appealing. I painted Kage to be this infamous underground fighter who was on the verge of becoming a superstar. It wasn't true exactly, more like a forward-looking statement, but it was based on fact.

Through snippets of conversations and a few comments Kage had made directly to me, I'd pieced together a picture of what was really going on in the Michael Kage camp. To be honest, I'd almost begun to believe he was just a rich guy with a hobby— that he'd probably never even been in a real fight. But the truth was more dramatic and bizarre than a publicist could have hoped for.

Kage had been training to be a fighter all his life, since he was around four years old. It's all he ever wanted to do. I wasn't clear on the specifics of how his uncle ended up being his guardian, or where his parents had gotten off to. But I did know that his uncle was just as serious as Kage about him getting a UFC contract and becoming a champion. He'd poured a lot of money into Kage's training, and then when he felt Kage was ready, he did the unthinkable.

He offered a reward to anyone who thought they could beat his nephew in a private MMA fight to the finish. The fights were broken up into typical three-minute rounds, but the difference was, there were no judges. The fight could only end with a submission, a KO or TKO, or a forfeit. Originally, the prize offered was ten-thousand dollars. Big bucks for a struggling lower-level fighter. But as Kage began to require stiffer competition, the amount went up.

By the time I came to the Alcazar, the prize for defeating Michael Kage was one-hundred-thousand dollars.

It was as yet unclaimed.

Now technically this was a rumor, or a legend if you will, because I had seen no real evidence that Kage had ever participated in a fight other than his sparring practice with Marco. But I believed it, just as I was coming to believe that Kage could walk on water or make a blind man see.

So I used the legend to our advantage on the flyers. I sent them to three large gyms within driving distance of Vegas, announcing that this mysterious undefeated fighter would be in their area soon if they'd like to have him stop by. I didn't attempt to charge for appearances. In my mind, this was just a way to get Kage used to the exposure while getting the word out about him. People associated with the MMA world needed to know the name of Michael Kage.

I didn't know what kind of response to expect, but I was thrilled when one of them called on Friday to book him.

"What did you do that for?" Kage asked when I told him what I'd done. "Am I gonna have to miss two workout days for that?"

"Yes. But it's a good idea. It's just one appearance, but we need to get used to this kind of thing, Kage. One of these days, people are going to be dying to get you in their gym. Think of it as a trial run."

He nodded. "Okay, I just don't know what to expect. Do other guys do this?"

"I think so," I told him. "I'm pretty sure they do."

He laughed and ruffled my hair. "Me and my rookie publicist. All right, if you want me to do it, I'll do it. It could be fun to take a road trip."

I didn't tell him, but I thought a road trip sounded fantastic. "Do we need to rent a car?"

"Actually, I have a car," he told me. "It's in the parking garage. I just hardly ever drive it."

I gave him a skeptical look.

"Don't worry. I'm a great driver. If I hadn't gone into fighting, I probably would have been a race car driver."

"Oh, that's reassuring."

Chapter 10

THE anticipation of our road trip was killing me. Before, I'd been sweating the actual appearance and trying to pretend I wasn't a stupid college kid from Stone Mountain, Georgia. But now that the trip was imminent, I was more worried about all of the time Kage and I would spend closed up in a car together. Plus, Kage had suggested that we get a hotel room the night of the appearance and drive back home the next day.

I was preoccupied all week, and it showed in my workouts.

"Focus," Marco would bark at me. "If I'm going to be training you, the least you can do is give me a hundred percent. That's what I'm giving you."

Kage would just smile or wink at me when I'd get into trouble with Marco, but he never interfered.

They had started teaching me punches and kicks, and I was trying to perfect my form. Sometimes I took Marco's place as Kage's punching bag, but I got the distinct feeling he was going a lot easier on me than he did Marco. Which was probably a good thing. I probably would have ended up in the hospital if Kage had opened up on me one good time.

After Tuesday's practice, three days before our scheduled appearance, we stayed in the gym after Marco had left.

"I want to learn some submissions," I said after the door closed behind Marco. I knew Kage was worn out, and it might not be the best time for a lesson, but I didn't want Marco to be around when I was trying to learn anything too serious or dangerous. The instructor had this way of looking at me like I wasn't shit. Like he didn't think I deserved to breathe the same air as Michael Kage.

Maybe I didn't.

Thank goodness Kage didn't seem to share that opinion. He doted on me, took the time to make sure I was comfortable and that I understood things. I didn't know why he did it or what exactly he saw in me, but I was grateful.

Even as tired as he was, worn out from hours of hardcore drills that would put a lesser man in the emergency room, Kage smiled that indulgent smile and held out a hand for me. I placed my hand in his and quickly found myself spun around with my back pressed up against his front, his arm like a steel band around my throat.

"Triangle choke," he said. "Now I drop the other arm in behind your neck, grab onto my bicep to lock my arms in place, and I've got you in a vice. Just try to get free."

I struggled, succeeding only at making the arm around my neck tighten. It didn't surprise me that I couldn't muscle out of the death grip of a professionally trained MMA fighter, but it did surprise me to discover I was ashamed of that fact. Logic assured me that I should not be able to escape, but pride said I wasn't much of a man if I couldn't. How must it feel for a seasoned professional fighter to get caught in such a grip and be unable to escape, knowing that defeat was only seconds away? Was it humiliating for them, or were they hardened to failure? Did they have a more realistic attitude, or were they slaves to pride just like I was?

"Struggle, Jamie." Kage leaned from side to side just enough to goad me into action. "Use your hands and your fingers. Try to claw your way out. I want you to feel how effective this hold is."

I wiggled and clawed, but to no avail. "Can't," I choked out in a strangled voice. "No way." He wasn't hurting me, but he was dominating me for sure.

Finally, Kage let me go and turned me around to face him. "Are you okay? I didn't hurt you, did I?" The concern in his eyes was real, and it made me feel safe.

"No, I'm fine." I rubbed absently at the side of my neck, feeling the film of sweat he had transferred from his arm to my throat.

"You sure?"

"Yeah. Show me some more. I want to learn."

"Okay. How about you try that move on me?" Kage turned his back toward me and showed great patience as I executed a ham-handed triangle choke on him, moving through the steps slowly and hesitantly, like a kid learning to tie his shoe. He indulged me by spreading his legs and bending his knees, striking a horse stance so I didn't have to stand on tip-toe to reach him. "Very good," he lied smoothly. "You're a natural. Now let's take it down to the mat, and I'll teach you a couple of armbar variations."

We rolled around on the mat for a few long minutes as I attempted to mimic Kage's armbar maneuvers. The guy made everything look so easy, it was surprising how difficult it was to actually attempt them myself. Several times, I nodded and assured him that I had a sequence of motions down, only to discover I actually had no clue what I was doing. It was excruciatingly embarrassing, and I decided this would probably be the last time I asked Kage to show me any moves.

Maybe a trivia night was in order, or an online IQ test showdown. Anything to show my own worth after this crash course in humility.

"How do you know when to do these things on someone?" I asked. "I can see how a person could memorize the moves and execute them on command in practice, but in a real fight your opponent isn't going to get into the perfect position and just let you armbar him."

"You're right about that." Kage laughed. "He's not going to let you get away with anything if he can help it. The key is drilling these things over and over again in practice to the point that you feel it when the setup is right. Sometimes you don't even have to think about it. Your body knows it's time to get the bastard into an armbar, and it does it without any help from your brain."

"Muscle memory, right?" I asked, marveling that I'd actually gotten the chance to use a piece of information that I already knew.

"Exactly. Your mind may not know what to do, or even have time to process what's going on in a fight. But if you've trained right, your body will know. Which is a beautiful thing if you're like me, because my brain turns off as soon as the fight begins and doesn't turn back on until an hour or two later."

"I'll never get to that point." I frowned, surprised that I even cared. "This job is going to be over in a couple of months, and it'll be back to school for me. I'll be lucky if I can even retain a quarter of what you and Marco have shown me."

Kage didn't comment on that. Instead, he leaned back onto his hands and spread his legs into a vee. Then he patted the mat between his legs.

I tried to follow his unspoken order, crawling up between his legs and turning in a confused circle like a dog trying to settle into a bed. Finally I got turned in the right direction, and Kage pulled me down into a seated position, my back pressed to his chest.

He put his powerful legs around my waist. Then he draped his left arm over my left shoulder, slid his right hand under my right arm, and grabbed onto his left wrist, securing his arms diagonally across my chest.

"This is the rear mount position," he said. "And what I'm doing with my arms is called the over-under grip. Some people call it the seatbelt grip."

I didn't figure I'd forget the seatbelt grip any time soon, because the name actually described the position perfectly. But then he changed positions suddenly, and his left arm was around my throat again, just like in the triangle choke we had worked on. He didn't squeeze, though.

"I'm going to show you how to do a Rear Naked Choke."

I couldn't help it. I laughed.

"What's so funny?" He loosened his grip slightly.

"I'm sorry. It's just that every time I hear Rear Naked Choke… Well, it just sounds dirty."

"You just have a filthy fucking mind," he teased.

I made a sound of protest. "You've gotta admit it sounds dirty."

"Nah," he said, his voice low and seductive right beside my ear. "It's only dirty if you do this."

He dropped his right hand onto my thigh and ran his fingers deliberately up under the fabric of my shorts. His fingertips caressed the front of my underwear, skimming over my dick, and my entire body tensed.

But just as quickly as it had happened, it was over, and Kage was laughing quietly at my ear. The warmth of his breath on my cheek added to the chill that was spreading over my entire body, and I tried to ignore the tightening in my groin and the fact that I was getting hard. I struggled to get away, terrified that he'd discover my reaction, but he tightened his arm around my neck just enough to calm me back down.

Then he was back to the business of showing me how to properly execute the submission, as if he hadn't just touched my dick. As if he hadn't made me hard. I couldn't focus on what he was saying. My mind was blown, and all it could do was replay the memory of that quick caress over and over.

"And this is how you finish it," Kage was saying, still against my ear, still in that same low tone that sounded almost seductive. He slid his right arm behind my head and secured it in the same way he had the Triangle Choke. "Do you want me to choke you out?"

He made it sound like a treat, like something you might sell your soul for. Then again, maybe I was just perceiving it that way. Except for the offhand grope, Kage been nothing but professional. I was the one who was affected— the one having unprofessional thoughts. He'd accidentally brushed my package during a joke, and I was freaking out.

"Um... Is it safe to choke someone out?" I heard myself asking.

"Not if you don't know what you're doing," he admitted. "But when it comes to something like this, you couldn't be in better hands."

And after today, I'll never think of those hands the same way again.

He hesitated. "If you don't feel comfortable, it's no big deal. I just thought you might be curious about what it feels like. You'd be surprised how many people have asked me if I would choke them out."

"Really? People actually ask for that?"

"Yeah. But if you don't want it..." He started to ease his hold on me.

"Do it," I blurted before I could change my mind. Because I *was* curious. And because I didn't want him to let go of me.

He tightened his grip on me again, putting gentle pressure not on my windpipe, but on the arteries to either side of it. I felt the damming of the blood flow there, and that same pressure I always got in my face when I strained way too hard to lift weights. The last thing I remember was a tingling sensation in my brain, like a thousand fireworks bursting in slow motion, and Kage whispering in my ear. "It's okay, Jamie. I promise I won't hurt you."

The next thing I knew, I was lying on my back, looking straight up into Kage's handsome face as the world came swimming back into focus. Only it seemed like I'd been watching him for a while, listening to the soft droning of his voice. How long had I been back?

"Hey, chief." He smoothed my hair back from my forehead. "How are you feeling? That shit is wild, huh?"

Wild, indeed.

It felt like I'd just been reborn into the world. How long had it been since Kage had whispered that he wouldn't hurt me? For all I knew, it could have been years. It seemed like years.

"How long was I gone?" I asked.

He smiled down at me. "Only a few seconds."

"Are you serious?" I sat up too fast, nearly crashing my head into his. The world wavered, and I was reminded of that overwhelming brain tingle I'd felt just before losing consciousness. "It felt like so long. I think I was dreaming."

"Oh, yeah? What did you dream about?"

"You." His eyebrows shot up, and I hurried to continue. "You and I were in this post-apocalyptic world, and we were trying to get away from zombies. This girl came to our house and tried to get us to let her in, and I was gonna open the door, but you stopped me and told me she'd been bitten. Somehow you knew. And then we had to go out on a late-night food run, and we ended up in the cafeteria of my old school, and all we could find was whole kernel corn, green beans, and corn dogs. You said the corn dogs were too fattening, so we didn't get them. And you'd only let me get skim milk."

Kage was grinning. "So, I was in charge, huh? You did everything I said."

I had one of those embarrassing moments when you realize you've babbled your dream out before you're completely awake.

Because if I'd had some time to think about it, I might have edited that dream before sharing it with Kage, if I'd ever shared it at all.

"I guess that is what it sounds like. I'm sure there was more, that's just all I remember."

"Damn, Jamie." Kage ruffled my hair. "That brain of yours must be busy as hell, because you were literally only out for a few seconds. How did you have time to dream all that?"

"I think you may be lying to me about the time frame."

He chuckled. "Maybe I should get a video of it next time so you'll see I'm telling the truth."

"Next time?"

"Or not." He shrugged. "But you were adorable when you were convulsing and drooling."

I felt the blood rush to my face. "Are you serious? I was drooling?"

"Nah, not really. I'm just fucking with you. You weren't drooling… but you did convulse a couple of times. And before you freak out, that's perfectly normal." He laughed and stood up, pulling me onto shaky legs. "Let's go get some grub. All that talk of zombies and bad school food has got me hungry."

"Yeah, I could use some food, too. But could we go to a burger place? Just this once?"

He shot a chastising look in my direction. "Jamie, have you looked in the mirror lately? Your abs are really starting to get ripped. You look too amazing for me to let you put garbage in that body."

And just like that, he had me puffed up with pride. If a guy like Michael Kage thought I looked amazing, there was no way I was eating a greasy hamburger. Ronald McDonald himself could not have talked me into it.

We ordered baked fish, brown rice and asparagus from room service, and we ate it on the glass dining room table in Kage's apartment. The food was delicious, and the conversation was easy, but I couldn't help thinking how surreal it was that getting groped and choked unconscious by a guy had actually become a part of my life. Even more puzzling was the fact that it really didn't bother me that much.

When we'd both scraped our plates clean, Kage leaned his chair back on two legs and rubbed a hand absently over his flat belly. "I think I should have ordered two pieces of fish. I'm still hungry."

My eyes instinctively followed the movement of his hand as it moved down his belly, and his fingers dipped into the waistband of his shorts and stayed there. When I looked back up, he was watching me with a half smile on his face.

I stammered. "Um, let me, uh… I'll just take these dishes out into the hall." I bustled around the table stacking the plates and silverware. Anything to take my mind off of Kage's hands and the memory of what it felt like to be touched by him. And the fact that the same hand he'd slipped into my shorts earlier was now in his shorts.

When I set the plates down on the floor in the hall, I glanced back through the open door at Kage, who was still watching me with that amused expression. That's when I knew that I could not go back into that room. Not that night. Maybe not ever. My mind was playing tricks on me, and I wasn't sure if it was because of what Kage had done during practice, or if it was because we were spending too much time together. Maybe I just wasn't used to this kind of friendship. I'd never been friends with a fighter, and never with someone like Michael Kage. He was unpredictable and flighty, he took chances, and he was consummately physical. The man was a superstar in the making. And gorgeous. God, was he gorgeous.

And it was time for me to go back to my room.

"Goodnight, Kage," I said just loudly enough for him to hear me.

"You're going already?" He looked surprised. "It's still so early. I thought maybe we'd catch a movie on TV or something."

I faked a yawn and felt guilty for it. "I'm tired. Not used to working out so much like you are. Maybe it was being choked unconscious that did me in, I don't know." My attempt at humor fell flat. "Anyway, I'll see you tomorrow. Thanks for dinner. It was much better than fast food. I don't know what the hell I was thinking suggesting burgers."

Kage lowered the front legs of his chair back down and smiled, but I could tell he was disappointed. It probably got lonely living in an ivory tower, but there was nothing I could do. I had to get away and regroup before I embarrassed both of us.

"Goodnight," he said. "See you tomorrow."

"Yeah, see you tomorrow." I closed the door and listened to the click. Then I made my way slowly back to my own room, knowing I wasn't going to sleep when I got there. It was his fault— Kage's fault for touching me like that. I just haven't been touched in a long time.

Once I was behind the locked door of my own room, I gave in. I stripped my clothes off, and my hand was around my stiffening cock before I even made it to the bed, stroking and pulling like I'd wanted to all night, easing that excruciating ache. I dropped onto my back on the bed and allowed myself to think the thoughts I'd been pushing away all night— unacceptable thoughts that I knew I'd try not to acknowledge ever again. Imagining it was Kage's hand stoking my cock, I came onto my own belly in less than a minute. It was the most forceful release I could remember having, like a million demons were flying out of me, and I had to throw my forearm across my mouth to stifle my lusty groan.

"Well, that was amazing," I said aloud, blinking up at the ceiling as I floated back to earth. "But it's out of my system now. When I wake up tomorrow, all of this will just seem like a really funny dream. I'll laugh, and I'll say, *Jamie, that was so stupid!* And then I'll never think of it again."

I went to sleep believing that. But when I woke up, the first image that flitted through my mind was of Kage's hand on my cock.

Chapter 11

WEDNESDAY night found me in my room brooding. I was feeling increasingly confident in my professional abilities, but not so confident in my social skills.

For one thing, Kage had been distant to me all day. I had a feeling it was because I had run out on his invitation to hang out after dinner the night before. It had definitely come off as rude. I knew that. But everything was getting too confusing for me, and I'd had to get away from him.

It hadn't helped much that I'd gone straight to my room and fantasized about him, but he didn't know that part. All he knew is that I said no.

Practice had been intense, like he was driving himself— and me in the process— even harder than usual. He'd barely spoken to me except to order me around. Hell, even Marco had noticed the difference in Kage's demeanor, and he kept giving me dirty looks like it was my fault.

I suppose it was.

After practice, he had slammed out of the gym without a word. Then Marco had followed suit, leaving me standing by myself in a place I barely belonged.

So now here I was. Another night with just me, the hand, and acres of free porn choices on the internet. I climbed out of the shower, dried off, and padded naked to the bed, where I already had my laptop setup and ready to go.

I knew the fact that I had showered and planned a night of porn was problematic. Next, I'd be having one of those inflatable dolls over for dinner in my kitchenette. But I'd worry about that after I came and was wallowing in post-wank shame. Right now, I had a hot date with the internet.

I pulled up my favorite free site and scrolled through all of the categories: *Big Boobs, Facials, Blow Jobs, Hand Jobs, Water Sports, BDSM, Blondes, Brunettes, Redheads…*

Of course, nothing seemed like it was going to hit the spot. It never did. The problem was, I had an itch that none of the videos on this particular site were going to scratch. I knew why, because it had been a long time coming, but that didn't make it any easier to accept.

There had been plenty of warning signs, plenty of vague urges tamped down with a swift efficiency that only the human mind had the power to pull off. We humans are masters of hiding from ourselves when we want to, carefully skirting those darker places in the corners of our imagination, chuckling to ourselves as we pass safely by. Closing our eyes and pulling the covers up over our heads, thinking *No way, buddy. There's no monster in my closet.*

But there *was* a monster in my closet. It had been okay as long as I could keep my head down and skirt those dark places, dodge those close bullets, go over to my girlfriend's place and fuck the ugly thoughts away. But the last few weeks had been different, because now the monster was right smack dab in my face.

He was a rough-hewn, muscular, hundred-ninety-pound monster, and he meant business. No way could I ignore the overwhelming presence that was Michael Kage.

No sense denying it now, cause porn don't lie.

You can lie to everyone. Your parents, your friends, your preacher, your girlfriend, even yourself… But when you click that play button, your heart rate doubles, your dick gets axe-handle hard, and you come like a freshly-tapped fire hydrant… that's truth right there.

And my truth was that I had been jerking off to advertisements for a long time. You know those rotating gifs that tease you with the best shots from the pay sites?

Well, one time I *accidentally* clicked on the gay portion of my go-to porn site. I'd clicked right back out again, but the damage had been done. Now the all-powerful advertising engine knew what I craved, and it was relentless. It showed me men sucking other men's dicks, hairy asses getting pounded bareback, twinks getting creamed in the face in group orgies. The fact that I had *favorite* ads was even more damning.

Yeah, I'm ashamed to say that I could sometimes hit pay dirt within ninety seconds simply by watching those gay banner ads.

Why the hell would a person do that, you ask? For me, it was simple.

As long as I didn't click, I was straight.

I dropped the towel from around my waist and fisted my hard cock, checking out the ads the website was so graciously serving up for me. I started to move my hand over my full erection, tentatively at first, barely skimming the surface of the flesh. I was a preteen again, exploring the joys of masturbation for the first time, and lord have mercy was it ever good. Brand new sensations flooded my system. Only they weren't new; they just felt new every time.

I knelt on the bed, got a full-access grip on my dick and squeezed. I looked at the largest ad on the page and groaned out loud as my favorite part flipped past— a little blond baseball player on his knees, his tongue snaking out and tasting the strands of white coming at him from both sides. *Str8 Turned Out*, it said. I wondered what the two other guys looked like— the ones unloading on him. Were they muscular? I hoped they were athletes, too. I always imagined they were big, hot, muscular baseball players who just caught this little guy in the showers. But you could tell by looking at him, he was definitely up for it. He wanted their big cocks, needed to feel them in his mouth.

Yesss, I thought with a groan. *He needs that so much.*

I leaned down and clicked on the ad for the first time. Suddenly my laptop screen was full of vaguely suggestive images of men and a huge button urging me to pay to come inside. *Thirty bucks a month, dammit!* And there was absolutely no satisfaction on this page. I needed to see the full video of that baseball twink sucking two monster dicks, and I was going to have to find my credit card to do it. Why the hell hadn't I done that ahead of time?

Because I'd never paid for internet porn before.

I rolled off the bed and went to grab my wallet off the bedside table, and that's when I saw that I had a text message and missed calls on my cell phone. I swiped the touch screen and discovered that it was none other than Kage who had been burning up my phone.

Oh, the irony.

I quickly returned his call, all too painfully aware that I was doing so naked— and with a raging boner.

"Hello?" he slurred happily into the phone. "Jamie. What a nice surprise. I was just thinking about you."

"Kage? Are you… Where are you? It sounds loud."

"I'm at a party," he said, his slurring making it all too clear that he'd had a few too many drinks. "In a hotel room. Been calling you. Need you."

My heart jumped up into my throat.

"You need me?"

"Yeah, I can't—" It sounded like he dropped the phone, and there was laughter. A woman's laughter that instantly raised my hackles.

"Who is with you, Kage?" I don't think I disguised my irritation in the least.

His laugh that came across the phone was deep and slow, and I felt it down to my toes. My still-hard dick twitched, and I stifled a groan.

"Focus, Kage." I said through clenched teeth. "Why did you call me? What do you need?"

"Ohh, fffuck," he slurred. "I called you?" He paused, as if in thought. "I think I wanted you to come get me."

"I'll be right there." *With fucking bells on, baby.* "Where are you? Which hotel?"

"Ummm… where are we?" he asked his female companion. She mumbled something I couldn't hear. "We're at the Alcazar, Jamie."

"You're here? I don't understand." He told me the room number, and I said, "I'll be right there. Let me get some clothes on."

"Are you naked?" he asked, his voice sounding high-pitched and playful. I couldn't help smiling.

"Uh, yeah. I just got out of the shower."

I tucked the phone between my shoulder and my ear, hopping from foot to foot as I pulled on my boxer briefs and a pair of shorts. Then I put on the first clean t-shirt I could get my hands on. I slid my feet into my sneakers without socks, stuffed my key card into my pocket, and hurried from the room. The elevator seemed to take forever as I listened to the irritating sounds of partying over the phone line. Laughter and music, the shuffling of Kage's phone as he moved, and that annoying woman's voice.

What the hell was he doing, anyway? How would he be when I found him? The thought of him being in a compromising position of some sort set my teeth on edge. I couldn't get to that hotel room fast enough.

"I'm here," I told Kage over the phone as I banged my fist on the door of the suite. "I'm knocking on the door right now. Let me in."

"Thass my boy," I heard him tell someone. "Open the door. No, it's not the cops."

When the door swung open, I was assaulted by the mingled scents of alcohol and weed. There was some cigarette smoke mixed in there, too, and I was hoping like hell Kage hadn't been smoking cigarettes. He'd probably never forgive himself for that.

"Jamie," he called from across the room. "I'm over here."

What I saw made me boiling mad. Most of the party guests were packed on the floor around the coffee table in various states of undress, and Kage was right in there with them.

"What the hell is this?" I couldn't help asking.

"Strip poker," the glassy-eyed woman next to Kage told me, scrunching up even closer to him to make room. "Wanna join in?"

"No, thank you." I glared at Kage, who had apparently lost everything but his boxers and his socks. "You. Get your clothes on and let's go home."

It was irrational of me to be so angry. Kage was a grown man, and he could get drunk and play strip poker if he damn well pleased. I knew it, and still I was acting like a pissed-off father.

Or boyfriend.

Kage just looked up at me through slitted eyes and grinned. I'd never seen him like that, and I had to wonder how much alcohol a guy his size would have had to consume to be that smashed.

"Why would you do this to yourself?" I asked rhetorically, as I searched for his clothes. I grabbed his shirt and shorts off of the sofa behind him, and his sneakers from beneath the coffee table. "Come on. I tucked his clothes under my arm and reached down with the other arm to help him up. Thankfully, he accepted my help and staggered to his feet.

"Thank you for coming," he slurred, draping his big body over me, his arms around my neck. I thought we'd both topple over, but I managed to remain standing long enough to get him to step into his shorts, trying to ignore the subtle dangling movement behind his boxers.

"Don't worry about the shirt and shoes," I told him. "Let's just get out of here."

The woman who had been sitting beside him threw me a pouty look. "You taking my sexy fighter? He was supposed to stay here tonight. He promised he'd show me how to wrestle."

I laughed humorlessly in her direction. "He's not gonna be showing anybody anything tonight."

I slammed out of the room with Kage still draped over me, but now he'd moved around to the side and had one arm around my shoulders. It was breaking my heart to see him so out of control, for more reasons than one. I could barely even look at him.

I took him to my room, because I couldn't locate his key card in his pants, and he couldn't seem tell me where it was. Hopefully, no one from the party would find it and break into his penthouse. That was too much of a disaster to contemplate.

"Go lie down on the bed," I told him as I went to the kitchen to fix him some water. If there was one thing I knew about hangovers, it was that water was the best way to avoid them. Fortunately, the refrigerator was stocked with bottles of filtered water. The last thing I needed was for Kage to start a drunken tirade about the horrors of drinking tap water.

"Ooh, someone's been a bad, bad, *bad* boy," Kage slurred from the bed, and as I rounded the corner, my heart stopped. He had woken my laptop from sleep and was staring at the gay porn website I'd been trying to join.

I pulled the laptop from in front of him, took a look at the sign-up page, and felt like the biggest asshole in the world when I dropped my jaw and acted like it was the first time I was seeing it. "What the hell is that? Guess it was one of those pop-ups. See, that's why I hate free porn sites. They inundate me with pop-ups for things I'm not even remotely interested in."

"Yeah?" Kage asked with a drunken smirk. "Like what?"

"Oh, I don't know… like what you saw." I couldn't even say the word *gay* in his presence. "And like underage girls and BDSM and stuff."

"So no handcuffs for Jamie. What *do* you like?" He seemed suddenly far too sober. I was about ready for him to pass out.

"Um, I like…" I faltered, unable to come up with a single thing that I liked.

Kage laughed. "That much stuff, huh? You're a wild man."

I huffed. "Well, what do you like, since you think I should be so forthcoming?"

"Forthcoming," he repeated with a laugh. "You crack me up, college boy. Okay, if you must know, I like dark hair." He smiled and closed his eyes, laid back on the bed, looking like he was conjuring an image in his imagination. "Big brown eyes that melt your soul every time you look into them."

I swallowed and suddenly had a little trouble breathing.

"Athletic body, long legs wrapped around my waist," he continued in his slurry voice. "Smart, funny, sexy… glasses. Where are your glasses?"

I cleared my throat. "I thought we were talking about porn."

"Oh yeah, porn." He smiled again without opening his eyes. "I imagine we probably like about the same things in that area. Pretty close, anyway." His voice trailed off, and he got quiet.

I didn't dare prompt him for any more conversation at that point, because I got the feeling he was trying to turn the focus back onto me. Best to avoid that at all costs. Instead, I removed the laptop from the bed and worked the covers down. Kage helped me a little by scooting around as needed.

"You want to get rid of those shorts and socks?" I asked—innocently, of course.

"Yeah, but I need your help." He peeked at me out of one eye before closing it again.

Trying to be as emotionally removed as a doctor examining a patient, I pulled off first one sock then the other and tossed them on the floor. Then I hooked my fingers into the band of his shorts and began to shimmy them down his hips. I had to work them over the bulge in the front of his underwear, noting in a very clinical manner that either he had the largest soft dick of anyone I'd ever seen, or he was at least partially hard. But then, he was drunk. He couldn't be held accountable for anything, including the state of his dick, right?

My fingers *accidentally* trailed down the outsides of his muscular thighs, the hair tickling my fingertips. I took a deep breath as I hovered over his prone body and caught the distinct scent of his manliness— a hint of sweat mixed with warm musk. Passion bloomed in my belly, unfurled and spread through me like wild vines. I had the ridiculous urge to bury my face in him and just breathe. His scent was driving me crazy.

I slid his shorts the rest of the way down his legs and threw the covers up over him before I did something to embarrass myself. Then I undressed down to my boxer briefs and burrowed down under the covers on my side of the bed. I stayed as far away from him as I could, afraid of what would happen if I caught his scent again. It took me forever to go to sleep. By that time, Kage had long since begun the labored breathing of a drunken slumber.

The next morning, I woke to the sounds of him getting dressed.

"Hey," he said apologetically, looking like the hell he must have been feeling. "Sorry to wake you. And sorry about last night. I have no idea what I might have done." He shrugged and offered a half hearted smile.

"You were fine. Don't worry." I laughed. "You didn't do anything embarrassing."

Unfortunately, I couldn't say the same for myself. Maybe he wouldn't remember the porn site, and maybe he had been too far gone to notice how long it had taken me to get his shorts off, or how I'd scented him like a bloodhound.

"Whose shirt is this, anyway?' he asked, pulling the plain white t-shirt over his head.

"It's not yours?" I giggled. "Oops. I have no idea."

"Well, I guess it's mine now. Meanwhile, someone has one of my favorite Under Armor shirts."

"I'm so sorry. I was just in a hurry to get you out of there. You were playing strip poker, and you were down to your underwear. It was an emergency situation."

"Emergency, huh?" He rounded the bed, coming to stand over me. Then he shocked me by leaning down and giving me a hug.

"Thank you for coming to get me. I'm really ashamed that I called you, and I promise it won't happen again, okay?"

"Have you lost your damn mind? If you get into a jam again, you'd better call me. I'm not mad, okay? I'm here for you." He was still hugging me, and I wrinkled my nose and pushed him away. "And you're right, that is definitely not your shirt. It doesn't smell like you at all. Take it off." As soon as I realized what I'd said, I started backpedaling. "I don't mean literally take it off. I just mean I wish I'd grabbed the right shirt. Now you smell like cigarette smoke and cheap cologne. And some other guy."

He raised a brow at me, looking as cocksure as he could through the haze of what had to have been a massive hangover, and pulled the shirt back over his head. Then he strutted over to the trash can in the kitchen, balled it up, and threw it in. "Happy now?"

He stalked back over to the bed, reminding me of a panther the way his muscles moved beneath the flesh of his increasingly tempting upper body. I wanted to close my eyes, but I couldn't. He climbed onto the bottom of my bed and crawled up toward me, sending my heartbeat skittering out of control. Then he climbed roughly on top of me and covered my face with his chest.

"Does that smell right? Huh? Do I smell like myself?" Knowing from our sparring that I couldn't handle being tickled on my sides, Kage went straight in for the kill. He tickled like he fought… one hundred percent invested.

"I can't breathe," I screamed in a voice muffled by the press of his chest. "Help! Marco!" I don't know why that was the first name that came to my lips, other than the fact that I thought if anyone in the hotel could drag Kage off of me, it would be him.

"You think Marco can help you? He wouldn't stand a chance against me. Nothing can save you now." He burrowed in even harder, tickling me until I was just a trembling heap unsure of whether I was laughing or crying. For a split second, I thought maybe I felt his lips brush the side of my throat in something like a kiss.

"Please… please…" I gasped, my thrashing limbs useless against his superior weight and strength. Even through the pleasure-pain, I felt the blood rushing to my cock, filling it out between my legs, making me all too aware of the slide of skin and the way my hips were bucking against his. Feeling his cock against my cock, and the rub and the friction. My legs wrapped themselves around his waist, my ankles locked together, and I rode his movements like a desperate bull rider just trying to make it through eight seconds. It was excruciating. Glorious. Shameful.

"Please…" I cried again, this time with a different meaning altogether. In that moment, I needed him so much it was scary. I felt like I would do anything.

Everything.

He laughed against my ear, his breath teasing the sensitive flesh there. "Please what, Jamie? Tell me I smell good."

"You smell good. You smell great."

"Yeah? You think so?" he asked, feigning surprise, as if my compliment hadn't been the least bit coerced. He finally stopped tickling me, and my whole body seemed to spiral down into the covers, tingling from the aftermath of Kage's sensual onslaught.

"Yes," I sighed, panting hard to catch my breath, relaxing by body, my arms and legs falling open and limp. I was too weak to wipe the tears from my cheeks. "You smell fucking awesome, Kage. Now get off of me."

He did as I asked and climbed off of me, but he still wore the smug expression of victory. He had every right to wear it. The guy had just broken me in every way I could think of, and he didn't even know it.

"Why don't you give me a couple of hours to get showered and feeling better, then we'll go grab some lunch."

"Yeah?" I grinned.

"Yeah. But give me time, because I'm pretty hung over right now. Gotta go get some of Marco's magical hangover cure."

"What's that?"

"Ancient secret recipe." He felt around in the pockets of his shorts. "Have you seen my key card?"

"Nope. You didn't have it on you when I picked you up."

I know, because I felt every inch of you.

"I must have dropped it at the party. Everything's a blur after I got there. I swear I didn't think I drank that much."

"You were definitely hammered," I told him with a straight face. "You really don't remember anything?"

"Not really. Funny, I don't even remember how I got there in the first place." He frowned and furrowed his brow. "Oh, well. No sense crying now. I just need to go get that key canceled and a new one programmed before someone figures it out and steals all of my shit."

After he left the room, I showered and got ready for our lunch date. Then I watched the clock for a couple of hours, swapping from the bed to the sofa, wishing I could skip all of the downtime and get to the good stuff already.

I chastised myself for trying to rush time. Hell, I was living on borrowed time as it was. School started back at the end of the summer whether I liked it or not, and this new life of mine here in Vegas with Kage was beginning to feel way too comfortable. Already, I was wondering how I would be able to say goodbye.

12

"WAKE up, sleepyhead," the text from Kage said. "It's time to go."

"Shit." I texted back. *"I'm not even packed."*

"Open your door for me," he replied.

I rolled out of bed and stumbled to the door of my suite. The day of our road trip had finally arrived, and I'd overslept. Kage was waiting outside with an energy shake in his hand.

"This will wake you up," he said as he handed it to me. Then he glanced down my nearly naked body and back up again, taking in the sight of my morning wood. "Something you need help with?"

"Very funny. I just need to go to the bathroom. You just dragged me out of bed."

His brows shot up and he laughed. "I meant like with packing or something, genius."

"Oh. I thought you were making a joke about… never mind. I'm just an idiot." I turned and went to the bathroom without another word.

Kage chuckled from behind me. "I'll just grab a few things out of your drawers. You don't need much. Two changes of clothes, I guess. I've got deodorant and stuff."

"Yeah, you definitely better not forget the deodorant."

He let out a grunt and moved up close behind me. "If I didn't know any better, I'd think you were trying to tell me I smell bad."

"Of course not." I turned around and found myself standing face-to-face with him. "I just meant that you'll probably be sparring or working out or something at the gym. And hell, I need deodorant, too. I don't want to smell. Do you want me to smell?"

"I don't care. Do you think I smell bad, though? You've got me paranoid."

"You smell fine." I had to look away. Not because I was lying, but because I was telling the truth, and I didn't want him to see how true that truth was.

"Would you check me just to make sure?"

"I guess, if you want." I leaned in close, my face hovering about an inch from his chest. At least he had a shirt on. I don't think I could have taken it if he hadn't. I took a deep breath, closed my eyes, and got a nose full of Michael Kage pheromones. Those pesky little things that were increasingly causing bad things to happen to my body and mind.

Just when I got my nose right next to his armpit, he raised his arm, grabbed the back of my head, and shoved my face into his armpit.

"Jesus Christ, Kage!"

The guy laughed harder than I'd ever seen him laugh— by far. I liked seeing him that delighted, even if it was at the expense of my pride. However, that didn't mean I was going to let him get away with it.

"Wow, I didn't think you actually had a sense of humor. Glad to see I was proven wrong."

His laughter slowed, and he rolled his eyes at me. "Keep it up and you just might lose your surprise."

"Surprise?" I couldn't help the goofy grin from taking over my face.

"Just go downstairs and get in the car. If we leave now, we may be able to get there early enough to check in somewhere."

"Do you really think it's necessary to get a hotel room? It's only a few hours' drive."

"I don't want to feel rushed," Kage said. "What fun is a road trip if you're in a hurry to get back home?"

I had to agree when I saw Kage's car. He had a killer black Corvette convertible with black and red interior, and I spent the first hour of our three hour drive admiring every inch of it. It was a beautiful day for riding with the top down, and we took full advantage of it. After a while, I took my shirt off.

"Make yourself comfortable," Kage yelled over the sound of the wind.

"Why thank you, I will." I reclined my seat back so that I could get sun on the entire front of my torso. I even rolled the band of my shorts down and pulled the legs up to expose as much skin as possible. Then I just laid back and closed my eyes, enjoying the feel of the heat and the movement of the air over my skin.

"You don't play fair," Kage yelled.

"Tell you what," I yelled back without opening my eyes. "Let me drive back tomorrow, and you can get a turn."

He laughed. "We'll see. I don't let just anybody drive my baby."

"Who has gotten to drive it?" I peeked at him out of one eye, noting that he'd stripped his own shirt off. He looked summery and free and unnaturally handsome, with his gleaming skin and his chocolate-and-caramel hair blowing in the wind. He was too perfect.

"No one but me has ever driven this car. Yet."

I closed my eye again and grinned. "You should let me be the first."

He didn't say anything more on the subject. In fact, the rest of the ride was so comfortable and quiet that I fell asleep. After a while, he reached over and shook me awake.

"You're getting a little pink, man. Your skin is fairer than mine, so I think you should put your shirt on. And you're gonna have a white mark in the hollow of your throat where your necklace is."

I sat up and pulled my t-shirt over my head, feeling disoriented. "Where are we?"

"About twenty-five miles away. We're supposed to be at the gym at one, so we'll go there first and do our thing, then check into a hotel later this afternoon."

"Whatever. Sounds like a plan to me." I checked my appearance in the mirror.

Kage laughed. "We are so fucking unprofessional."

My heart sank, and I think my entire job flashed before my eyes. "You think I'm unprofessional?"

"No. I said *we* are unprofessional. I happen to like it that way, don't you?"

"Yeah, not everybody gets to smoke weed with their boss, have slumber parties with them, or lay out in the seat of their convertible. I guess I'm pretty lucky."

"So I'm your boss now? What happened to client?"

I threw my hands up in the air. "I don't know. I give up trying to figure out our dynamic. It is what it is, no matter what we call it."

"True. Though technically my uncle hired you."

I pondered that for a moment. "Kage, do you find it odd that I've been here for over three weeks and still haven't met the guy who hired me?"

Kage's mouth pulled into a bleak line. "My uncle is not the kind of man you just pop in to meet. If he wants to meet with you, he'll make it happen. Otherwise, it won't."

"So you think there's a possibility I could work here all summer and never meet him?"

"I doubt it. You'll probably meet sometime. Do something he doesn't like, and I can almost guarantee he'll come find you."

I gulped. "That sounds terrifying. Why you gotta say shit like that?"

He chuckled, but he didn't say anything to try to put my mind at ease. That was not a good sign.

THE gym was a great success, if I do say so myself. I hadn't had a clue what to expect, so I was pleasantly surprised that we pulled it off without a hitch. Of course, some credit had to go to the gym owners and employees.

When we got there, the owners ushered us to a private sparring room where we briefly discussed what we wanted to happen. Kage conducted a mini class on MMA techniques and answered a lot of questions about his philosophies of fighting. I set up my camera and took tons of pictures and video.

In attendance were MMA students and gym regulars, many of whom had come in specifically to see Kage, and they all seemed to love him. The gym printed out copies of the front of my flyer, and Kage signed his autograph on the backs. I made a mental note to bring pictures for autographs next time. It was a rookie mistake, but as Kage said, we were winging it.

"I felt like a fraud," he said when we got back into the car.

I started laughing. "That is exactly what I told my professor after I posed as a reporter the night we met. But that was the first time I'd ever done anything of the sort. You are an expert on fighting, so I don't understand how you could possibly feel like a fraud."

His expression was unusually vulnerable. "You presented me as some sort of celebrity. Those people think they're going to see me fighting on TV or something. They have no idea that the only place I fight is a secret place, and it's by invitation only. They would never be welcome there."

"It's okay, Kage." I wrapped my fingers around his wrist and swung it back a forth a few times, a playful gesture to cheer him up. "Look, you hired me for a reason. I'm doing my job, and I'm going to get you on TV. It's only a matter of time before you're a legitimate celebrity. You've got the talent, now I'm getting you the exposure you need."

That seemed to appease him, thank goodness.

Chapter 13

HE DROVE up to a hotel that looked way too expensive, and a valet practically whisked the Corvette from under us.

"Come on, we don't have to stay in a place this nice," I told Kage as I hurried to keep up with his long-legged strides through the hotel lobby. "Except for your place, I've hardly ever stayed in a hotel that had the doors on the inside of the building. I'm used to cheap, you know? Wonder how much this place is. It's really not necessary."

Kage stopped abruptly, and I nearly fell over him. "Shut up, Jamie. Let me pick the hotel I want. It's my money."

"But taking this trip is my fault. You wouldn't even be here if it wasn't for me. It's nice of you, but—"

"But nothing." He turned and placed a hand on my shoulder. Bent down so that our eyes were even as he looked into mine. "I want to do this, okay? You shouldn't have to fight off roaches and bed bugs on your birthday." He smiled. "Besides, I don't want to sleep in a dump. Haven't you ever noticed I'm spoiled?"

A smile crept over my face. "You remembered my birthday?"

"Of course," he said, looking almost shy.

"Well, I appreciate the gesture. I think you're letting your imagination run away with you, though. Cheap motels aren't all that bad, for the most part."

Kage stopped smiling. "Jamie, I grew up in motels. You've lived in a house all your life. Between the two of us, I think I know what the fuck I'm talking about."

I swallowed and chose not to say anything more. Kage swaggered on up to the front desk, leaning casually against it with one elbow propped on its gleaming surface.

The female clerk was tall, brunette, and pretty. She knew her way around a makeup kit, that was for sure, and her teeth were freshly-lasered, glow-in-the-dark white.

"Can I help you boys?" she drawled, eyeing Kage like he was the main attraction at a bachelorette party. Then she cocked her head and narrowed her eyes suspiciously at him. "Hey, you seem familiar. Do I know you from somewhere?"

Yeah, from your dreams, bitch.

It had really started rubbing me wrong when women looked at him that way. He was a person, for heaven's sake, not an object. What right did they have? They didn't even know him. Certainly not like I did. He could have been a serial killer for all they knew.

Kage noticed the scowl on my face before I did. "What's the matter, Jamie?"

"Nothing," I huffed, crossing my arms across my chest like a bratty child. I made sure not to look at the desk clerk.

Kage's expression was puzzled as he turned his attention back to the woman. "No, ma'am. I don't think we've met." He gave her one of those signature Michael Kage smiles— the ones that break hearts and incinerate panties. "I'm sure I would remember if we had."

Oh, yeah, Kage. Go the extra mile and make sure she falls in love with you. As if you have to try.

She smiled back. "It's just— you do look awfully familiar. Are you sure you haven't come in here before? I never forget a face. It's one of the reasons I'm so good at my job."

Kage shrugged, already bored with the game. "Well, my friend and I just need a room for the night, if you don't mind. Can you hook us up?"

"Oh, right. Two full size beds? Smoking or non?" She had begun to tap keys on her computer. It was all business now, as it should have been from the start.

"What kind of suite do you have?" he asked. "Something with amenities. Maybe a mini-bar or Jacuzzi tub? What's the nicest thing you've got?"

"Kage…" My protest went unacknowledged, and I scowled as the clerk consulted her computer.

"We have a junior suite available with a fully stocked bar and whirlpool tub." She frowned. "Oh, but it's only got one king bed, and the sofa isn't a pull-out."

Kage pushed his credit card across the desk. "We'll take it."

"Are you sure?" The woman tapped around on her keyboard some more. "I could call our sister location. It's not far from here, and they may have some two-bedroom suites available."

I shocked everyone, including myself, when I said, "We like to cuddle, okay lady? Now just give us the key."

Kage raised his eyebrows at me, looking thoroughly amused. I was grateful when he didn't make any apologies for me. Just waited for the woman to finish the transaction and hand over the key cards to our room. When the papers were signed, we were dismissed with a curt "Have a nice stay."

Kage picked up both of our duffel bags and slung one over each shoulder. I tugged mine off of his arm and slipped it over my own shoulder. He gave me another of those amused looks, but he surrendered the bag easily enough.

"That was a bit reckless, don't you think Mr. Publicist? Spreading rumors about you and your client cuddling might not be the best idea you've had."

I glared at him. "It's not a rumor, Kage. Maybe if you're ashamed of it, you shouldn't have done it."

"How would I know if I was gonna be ashamed of it ahead of time?"

"Are you?" My voice echoed too loudly in the posh lobby, and a few people looked my way. I stretched my legs to keep up with Kage, lowered my voice. "Are you ashamed of it? There wasn't anything wrong with it. *Was there?* I mean, it wasn't anything… sexual."

"If I'd thought there was anything wrong with it, I wouldn't have done it," he said. "But I don't think that hotel clerk needed to know about it, either. Do you?"

"Probably not," I conceded. "I just don't like her."

"And not liking her is reason to tell her our personal shit? I didn't particularly like her, either."

"Hard to tell with the way you were flirting."

"You flirt way more than I do, Jamie."

"I don't flirt."

"You're shameless with it, dude. At least I pick and choose who I flirt with. You turn on that southern boy charm for everyone you meet." He stopped at a bank of elevators and pressed the call button. "Well, everyone but me." He gave me a pointed look, no doubt remembering every rude comment I'd ever made to him.

I sighed. "I don't do it like you, though. I'm just being friendly. Every time you talk to a girl, you're just oozing sex. You're giving off the wrong impression. Your public image needs to be an untouchable bad boy, not some indiscriminate man-whore."

His head whipped around, and he settled angry eyes on me. I saw in a flash that I'd gone too far. He was right, of course, and I was wrong. I'd lost. So why couldn't I stop arguing the point?

Before Kage could speak, the elevator bell dinged, and what seemed like about fourteen people filed out. He caught the door, and we both stepped in, followed by a giggling couple who looked like it was taking everything they had not to pounce on each other. The sexual energy was coming off of them in waves.

Apparently, Kage felt it too. He leaned back into a corner and winked in their direction, his recent anger fallen by the wayside. I stifled a laugh. What was it about elevators, anyway? If Kage and I had not been there, that couple would probably have been half naked by the time they reached their floor.

They were the stereotypical honeymoon couple found in every romantic comedy, and they made me jealous.

It seemed like ages since I'd had someone. I thought about Layla and tried to spin a fantasy in my mind, but it was hard to fit the two of us into the shoes of the couple on the elevator. She and I had been active enough, and horny enough, but I couldn't remember a time when I'd ever felt anything like what was emanating from this couple. Their desire was damn near palpable, the stuff love songs were made of. It was the first time I'd ever seen anything like it in real life.

The couple hurried off the elevator at the fourth floor, while Kage and I continued on to the fifth. He was quiet after they left, and I wondered if he was thinking wistful thoughts like I was. Had he ever had a relationship like theirs, or was he like me?

When the elevator stopped on our floor and the doors slid open, Kage grabbed the strap of my duffel bag where it settled against the front of my chest and pulled me roughly along behind him. I chuckled, wondering if he thought I couldn't find my way out of the elevator without his help.

Our room was large and tastefully decorated, if a little boring. There was a floral sofa, a wall-mounted LED, a small kitchen, a balcony, and a comfy-looking king bed. After several hours in a car, I was ready to fall into something soft.

I sighed and dropped my duffel right inside the door, taking in a lungful of frigid air. I had always loved the feel of an air-conditioned hotel room, like walking into a furnished meat locker. I slipped my shoes and socks off and left them by the door, enjoying the nubby feel of the carpet between my toes.

Kage grabbed the remote from a glass end table, turned on the TV, and flipped it to sports. He dropped down onto the floor, his back against the sofa, and stretched his arms languidly along the cushions behind him.

He looked right at home as he watched something about the NBA summer league. His brown skin gleamed with fresh color from our drive down, the contours of his muscles fascinating me as if I were seeing them for the first time. He had his knees bent, legs spread, with the soles of his sneakers planted on the carpet. The loose fabric of his gym shorts revealed too much at the tops of his thighs, that long, sharp groove leading up into his groin area clearly visible.

He remained intent on the television, oblivious to the fact that he was a god among men. I looked away. Went to the kitchen to check out the bar.

With the selection of alcohol I found on the counter and in the fridge, we could have easily hosted a party. There were tiny bottles of Canadian Mist, Jack Daniels, Johnny Walker Red, and several flavors of vodka. A fat bottle of red wine sat on the counter, while a wine chiller held white wines and a couple of bottles of champagne. Rounding out the offerings were six-packs of Budweiser and Guinness, along with a couple of plates of cheeses and fruits. A box of Ritz crackers sat on the counter, and I had to admit, crackers had never looked so good.

"Dude, I'm fucking starving," I said loudly. I turned around and smacked right into Kage, who had moved up behind me without making a sound.

"So am I," he said. "What do you want?"

"Whatever you need." I spoke to his throat rather than looking up into his eyes. My voice wavered. "Um… Fish, grilled chicken, greens… Anything is fine."

"We always eat my way. I want to take you out for your birthday tonight. Maybe to a club or something, but first I want to buy you whatever you want to eat. Pizza or cheeseburgers, something like that. How about a fudge cake or peach cobbler? I can handle the temptation. I'm strong."

Yeah, he was strong all right. He was also standing too damn close to me. It was hard to breathe with someone standing so close.

"Remember what you told me the first time we met?" I asked. I don't know what possessed me, but I reached out and flattened my palm against his abs. "You told me you don't get a body like this by eating fast food, and you're absolutely right. I don't want to bring you down to my level, Kage. I want you to bring me up."

He shifted. I felt the ripple of muscle through the fabric of his shirt, the heat of his skin, and I knew I'd made a terrible mistake. Something was happening in my shorts. That old familiar tingle and tighten, the purely physical reaction to skin on skin contact, made infinitely worse by the fact that I'd been celibate for way too long. I was getting hard.

If I didn't get a woman soon, I was going to have to keep a respectable distance from Michael Kage. Definitely no more sparring, because if he ever noticed what was happening to me every time he touched me, he might think—

Oh, God.

The touch was too personal. It wasn't just a friendly touch. There was a wave of desire rolling up behind it, and I think he felt it, too. How could he not?

I moved my hand, meaning only to let go of him, but my fingers skated delicately over his belly in the process. He shuddered and grabbed my wrist, yanking down and back, using a mini arm drag to pull me flush against him.

"What are you doing?" he grated, his voice low and dangerous.

"I— I don't—" Stuttering was not helping my case. I finally looked up into his eyes, impossibly green and glittering with some emotion I couldn't read. Whatever that emotion was, it terrified me.

He secured my hand behind him and used his hips to back me hard against the fridge. The glass liquor bottles jangled inside the door, and the cracker box fell over onto the counter with a thud.

Kage was either about to kiss me or beat the utter fuck out of me, and I was pretty sure I wanted the first but deserved the second. I squeezed my eyes shut, waiting for a reaction that never came. Instead, I heard the spinning roll of a glass bottle making its way across the counter, just before it crashed to the floor.

My eyes flew open. Red wine gushed up our legs, splashing onto Kage's white shirt and staining it. Sticky liquid puddled around my bare feet, and something stung the sensitive skin on the top of my left foot. I sucked in a breath.

"Fuck!" Kage yelled instinctively, glancing down at the carnage. "Your feet. Don't move, there's glass everywhere."

He squatted and wrapped an arm around my thighs, hoisted me up and cinched my legs against his ribs. I grabbed onto his broad shoulders, feeling the power there. He looked down and surveyed the floor, stepping gingerly back before tiptoeing across the kitchen floor like he was negotiating a minefield. He wiped his sneakers on the very edge of the carpet before making his way all the way across the room and lowering me to the bed.

"Don't move," he told me again. "I'll be right back."

I watched him disappear into the bathroom, still in shock from the bottle disaster, and even more from what had happened before.

Kage returned with a warm wet cloth and a folded tissue and dropped to one knee on the floor in front of me. He pulled my left foot onto his knee, and that's when I noticed the shard of glass sticking out of the top of my foot.

"Damn," I said. "I didn't even know that was there."

He snatched the glass out of my foot and set it on the bedside table, then used the cloth to soothe the spot. After a moment, he cleaned the wine from the rest of my foot and moved on to the other one. A tiny rivulet of blood trickled from the hole the glass had left in my foot, and he staunched it by pressing the square of tissue against it.

"Don't worry, it's not deep," he said. "It may sting a little, but it shouldn't bleed much."

"You don't have to do this," I told him, embarrassed. "I'm not a little kid."

"I don't mind. I'm used to taking care of boo-boos." He reached up to ruffle my hair, like I truly was a kid in need of nursing. "The difference is, they're usually my own."

He stood up and carried the rag and tissue to the bathroom, and I heard him washing his hands. I looked down at my foot and saw that he was right. It had already stopped bleeding, though the skin was a little red and swollen around the gouge.

Kage turned on the shower. "Call the front desk while I wash up, will you? Have them send someone up to clean the floor. You can shower after me, and then we'll head out to dinner. Maybe we'll find some trouble to get into, like a club."

Getting into trouble with Kage sounded a little too dangerous, but I didn't say so. Maybe I needed a little dose of dangerous. Or a little dose of Kage.

I pushed aside my increasingly inappropriate thoughts and called the front desk. Within minutes a man and a woman showed up and made quick work of tidying the kitchen. They vacuumed the glass and used some sort of magical solution to get the stain out of the carpet. I asked if I could borrow some of the stain remover for our clothes, and they looked at me like I'd asked for free money. "Never mind," I mumbled, and they hurried from the room.

Kage came out of the bathroom followed by a plume of steam. He was naked except for a white towel around his waist, and I tried not to notice his iliac furrows disappearing into the low-slung fabric, or the dark blush of his nipples.

"Did they get the kitchen clean?" he asked, pausing in front of the wide mirror over the vanity. He leaned in toward his reflection, checking his face, studying some imagined flaw there. From the back, his towel hugged his ass intimately, displaying those unreal dips in the sides of his muscled ass cheeks. I had never seen anyone in such amazing shape. He was truly a work of art, a walking statue of David.

And apparently oblivious to my inner turmoil. He looked like the last hour had never happened.

"Yeah, the kitchen's spotless, Kage. Unlike me." I pushed past him, needing to get into the shower, more concerned with washing away the confusion and dread rather than the wine. I reasoned that I was probably just exhausted from the trip. Freshening up ought to do the trick, set things back to the way they were before we walked into this place. It appeared to have worked for Kage.

The shower didn't help me much, though. Physically, I was restored, but I was more emotionally wrecked than when I'd gone in. For one thing, I couldn't stop thinking about jerking off. Several times, my hand had wandered down below and gotten my cock nice and slippery with hotel soap, only to fall away when I thought of the man in the next room. I just couldn't do it with him out there. Not today. Not after what had happened.

But what exactly had happened, anyway? I was leaning toward the conclusion that I'd made an ass of myself, and Kage was too nice to call me out on it.

I'd only touched him, and just barely at that. Just a simple graze of skin.

Yeah, while looking up at him with that lovestruck expression, Jamie. You fucking moron.

"Your mom called while you were in the shower," Kage told me when I finally emerged. I looked in the mirror and ran my fingers through my hair, noticing how long it was getting. How it was curling around my ears.

"Did you talk to her?"

"Yeah, I answered it. I wouldn't have, but I figured since it was her, maybe it was okay."

"I don't mind you answering my phone, Kage. What did she say?"

"She said she loves you, Happy Birthday, and that she's supposed to report for surgery at seven a.m. Monday week. What the hell is Monday week?"

"It means not next week, but the Monday after. Don't ask. It's something my grandmother always said."

"Jamie, why didn't you tell me your mom had breast cancer?"

"Because it's got nothing to do with my job. Why would I bother you with my personal sob stories?"

He gave me a reproachful look. "Because I care. Because I could talk to you about it. And because I'm going to take you down there to be with her for her surgery."

I whirled on him. "You can't do that. It's… please don't make me be a burden on you. This job means a lot to me, and I don't want to make you regret hiring me."

"Shut up," he said. "Don't say things like that. You make me seem like a tyrant or something. I thought we were—"

He didn't finish his sentence.

"What else did my mom say?" I asked, mainly to break the silence.

"I told her we would be flying down for it. She's fussing about it just like you are. She thinks it's a wasted trip, because she's going to be fine. But I told her that it didn't matter how minor the surgery was, because I wanted to bring you. A boy should be there for his mother. End of story."

That made me smile. "And what did she say to that?"

"She said to tell you she loves you, and that she's glad you have a friend like me." He chuckled. "That part was a little embarrassing."

"That's because you don't know how to take praise unless it's about fighting." I noticed Kage had set my toothbrush out on the counter for me. I picked it up, squirted toothpaste onto it, and started to brush, watching Kage in the mirror.

"Jennifer is bringing her boyfriend, too," he said, emphasizing the word *her*.

I paused and stared at him for a second, then started brushing again, hopefully before he noticed my reaction.

"Chase?" I mumbled through a cloud of toothpaste bubbles. I finished brushing, rinsed, and splashed my face with cold water.

"I guess that's his name. Does your family like him?"

I shrugged, turning to face him. "They're fine with him, I think. I personally think he's a bit of a tool. Why?"

"I've never met anyone's family before." Kage shuffled his feet, looking about as uncomfortable as I had ever seen him. "Do you think they'll mind that I'm a fighter? I know some people don't like fighters. They think we're mean or crazy or something."

I smiled. Maybe it was because it reminded me that he wasn't perfect, but his sudden show of vulnerability was touching.

"Don't sweat it," I told him. "My family is gonna love you. All you have to do is flash those dimples, and they'll be bitten by the Michael Kage love bug. I don't know what it is about you, but everybody adores you, even when you treat them like shit."

"Yeah?" He sat on the bed and started pulling one of his boots on, bunching his jeans down around the top in that casual, sexy way he seemed to do everything. His button-up shirt wasn't buttoned up yet, and the top snap on his jeans was still unfastened, revealing the caramel fuzz of his happy trail. "Do you?"

"What?" I startled and snapped my gaze away from his body. "Do I what?"

He watched me closely as he pulled on the other boot, and there was nothing on his face to give away what he was feeling. "Do you adore me? You say everyone else does. I want to know how *you* feel."

I stared at him, stunned into awkward silence. What exactly was he asking me? Did he want to know if I felt the way everyone else did about him? Because that one was easy to answer; I was just as enamored of Michael Kage as all of the fans he'd been racking up, and every person who got pulled into his gravity just by being near him. He was magnetic, irresistible, and special in a way I couldn't quite put my finger on.

But if he was asking something else, something *more*…

But he couldn't be. I was the one acting like I had a schoolgirl crush. The one whose knees got wobbly every time he got too close.

"Do you mean—" I took two faltering steps toward him on rubber legs, wondering what had happened to my muscles. They'd been there a moment ago. "I don't— I can't—I don't know—"

Oh, Jesus. This is… impossible. I can't tell him how I really feel.

"You don't know?" He tilted his head at me, like he was trying to read me from a different angle. "It's not exactly rocket science, Jamie. Stop over-thinking for once. It's either yes or no, simple as that. Yes. Or. No."

"Fuck you, Kage." I don't know why those were the words that came out of my mouth. They weren't at all what I was thinking, but the way he was pressing me had me ready to bolt. I wanted to escape, so that I didn't have to admit the uncomfortable truth that I felt more for Kage than I was supposed to. That I was some sort of freak.

"Hey, come here," he said, his eyes softening. But instead of waiting for me to come to him, he stood up and closed the distance between us himself. His open shirt fluttered at his sides, exposing those ungodly abs and those smooth flanks that always seemed to draw my eyes.

"Uh…" I made a sound, a helpless little squeak, and felt my face flood with shame.

Kage stopped directly in front of me. "I just want to know how you feel about me is all. I'm not sure how else to find out besides asking." He chose his next words carefully, slowly. "I know I'm reckless, at least when it comes to my life. But when it comes to something that really matters, I can't afford to be reckless. I have to be careful, you know?" He took a deep breath, ran a hand over his head. "I'm trying to say something here, if you'll let me. You know I have to be careful, but I'm asking—"

"Yes." I hadn't wanted to say the word, but it came out anyway. And there it was, on the air between us.

"Yeah?" He grinned, but there was something vulnerable in his eyes.

"Hell, yeah," I assured him, this time with more energy.

Kage nodded, still smiling, then turned away and finished getting dressed. And that was it.

He seemed awfully chipper as he buttoned his clothes up, but I was confused. I couldn't help wondering what I'd just confirmed. What exactly had we been talking about? Because for a minute there, it had seemed like—

No, I couldn't afford to think crazy thoughts like that. And there was Kage busy getting dressed like it was just any other day. Not like I'd just admitted—

Oh. My. God. I might as well walk out into the middle of traffic and kill myself.

I'd just admitted that I had feelings for Kage. Whether he'd meant it that way or not, that's what *I* had meant. No more pretending I was just horny, or that what I was feeling was a simple case of hero worship. Nope. The truth was I had a humdinger of a gay crush on my client. Like dicks and balls and ass and muscles and man kisses. Like gay as shit. Like… *ah, hell.*

I ran to the bathroom and splashed cold water on my face as a wave of nausea crashed over me.

Chapter 14

KAGE and I got out the door in 20 minutes, and somehow we managed not to speak another word to each other until we were out of the hotel room. He still seemed to be in his chipper mood, while I was still brooding over what happened. I really needed to get past the ridiculous idea that somehow things had changed between me and him. If he had indeed meant what I thought he had meant, he wouldn't be acting like there was nothing amiss.

ince we were in the middle of the shopping district of sorts, there were plenty of restaurants to choose from. There was a little Italian eatery on the corner near our hotel, an Ethiopian place in the next shopping center over, and the requisite Asian buffet took up what looked to be a whole city block. But the thing that caught Kage's eye was a little 1950s style diner with a checkerboard sign and about 10 booths in total. It had an old-fashioned soda fountain at the front with red vinyl barstools, and the workers wore white aprons and black and white striped paper hats. The tables were made of that old-fashioned gray Formica that I remember seeing in my grandmother's kitchen before she remodeled.

I wasn't so sure this would have been my first choice, but the gleeful expression on Kage's face won me over. The guy wanted to buy me a burger. Who was I to say no?

"You sit right there, and I'll go order." He gestured me toward a booth near the door. I really wanted to order for myself, but I sat down to humor him and watched as he strutted up to the counter with a spring in his step that made me chuckle to myself. He really was enjoying this. A few minutes later, he returned to the table with a big smile on his face and a tray loaded down with food.

"There's a lot of grease on that tray," I said, eyeing the two enormous burgers piled so high with fixings they were in danger of toppling over. A boat of fries sat between them, and they were flanked by monstrous 42 ounce cups of soda— the old red and white paper cups that collapse if you let them get too soggy. Kage was so utterly pleased with himself, even my grease comment couldn't dislodge his smile. The glitter of excitement in his eyes was contagious, and soon we were both smiling like jackasses. "This looks delicious," I told him, licking my chops at the sight of the strips of bacon dripping down the sides of the burgers. "What all did you order on these, everything they had in the kitchen?"

"Not quite." He picked up his soda and took a sip. "I left off the chili and onions, and I ordered no tomatoes on yours."

I raised a brow. "How did you know I don't like tomatoes?"

Kage didn't bat an eye. "It's no mystery, Jamie. I've watched you choke them down for me, but I know you don't like them. I never said anything before because they're really good for you. I had hoped you would like them if you ate them enough times."

"I'm afraid not. I tried, but there's something about them I just can't like."

"Yeah, that's how I feel about asparagus." He took another sip of his soda, and indicated mine. "Have you tried your soda? It's vanilla root beer." I picked it up and sipped absently at it.

"But you eat asparagus all the time."

"That's because it's good for me."

I shook my head. "It never ceases to amaze me how much self-control you have. You push yourself to the limit in training day after day, pushing so hard for a goal that hasn't even begun to materialize. But you keep the faith. And you eat things you don't like because they're good for you, and you resist the temptation for things that are bad for you, even though you love them. Case in point, that vanilla root beer. I swear your eyes roll back in your head every time you take a swallow."

Kage chuckled. "We both know I have my vices. One of them in particular is becoming impossible to resist." He braced his feet on the edge of my seat, his boots just brushing my thighs. "But then you're well aware of that, aren't you?"

I felt the room closing in on me. Why did he have to say things that sounded so much like innuendo? And he was so damn *good* at it, aiming that sexy half smirk across the table at me. It was getting to the point that every time he looked at me with an ounce of intent, my dick started getting hard— like it was right there in the old-fashioned hamburger joint beneath the gray Formica table top.

I need to get to the bathroom. Get myself under control.

I made a move to get up, but Kage was a step ahead of me as usual. Before I could do much more than twitch, he'd secured my forearm to the table with his strong grip. "Eat your burger. It's getting cold."

He wasn't so much forceful as he was resolute, and I couldn't help thinking that he knew. That he was well aware of why I was trying to escape to the bathroom, and he didn't care. He just wanted me to eat, so that's what I would do.

My hard-on and I stayed in the booth, and I ate half of my burger like a good boy. The other half went into a Styrofoam doggy box that I carried under my arm as we strolled languidly back to our hotel. The idea of finding a club was forgotten for the moment, and we were just two guys walking along without a care, breathing in the air of a strange city. Funny how being in an unfamiliar place can make you brave— make you do things you wouldn't normally do— things you just might regret when you get back to the real world.

That's what my whole summer with Kage was like. One long string of things I *might* regret.

Chapter 15

THAT night in the hotel was the first time I ever thought of Kage and me as… *us*. It was the first time I felt like something more than Kage's satellite.

We were laughing at some stupid joke I'd made about the lady at the front desk, but as soon as the door to our room opened, we both got quiet, marching solemnly forward like we were walking to the electric chair. The door clicked loudly behind us, effectively shutting us off from the rest of the world.

I think maybe we both knew that this was it. That something was about to happen.

Kage crossed to the TV and clicked it on with the remote, but he didn't sit down on the sofa. Instead, he turned toward me and shoved his hands into the pockets of his jeans. He looked almost nervous. "Wanna watch a movie or something?"

I was hovering around the kitchen area, remembering the spilled wine and the way he'd backed me against the counter. I wondered what might have happened if the bottle hadn't fallen.

"A movie would be good," I said. "Something with action maybe." I rummaged in the fridge. "Want a beer? I think I'm gonna have a beer."

"Yeah, bring me one." He scrolled through the movie menu while I popped the tops and crossed the room to join him.

We finally agreed on one of the *Fast and the Furious* movies, though I couldn't say which one. I was too preoccupied with trying not to look at Kage. Trying to seem casual.

I kicked my shoes and socks off and sat down on one end of the sofa, started swilling beer like it was going out of style.

Kage was sitting on the other end of the sofa unlacing his boots. He took them off, stuffed his socks inside them, and pulled his feet up onto the seat. He took a long, slow pull off of his beer and cut his eyes over at me. The movie was just starting.

"Are you trying to get drunk?" he asked me.

"No, why?"

"Because you're chugging the hell out of that beer. You want another one?"

I gave him a tight smile. "No, thanks."

"Damn, Jamie. You've got to loosen up. Come here."

"Huh?" I took another swallow of beer and stared unseeing at the TV screen.

"I said get your ass over here."

I tipped my beer up and found it empty. "Oops, gotta get another beer."

Kage arched a brow. "You said you didn't need another one."

I looked at the beer and back at him. "Well, I've got to go to the bathroom anyway, so might as well grab one."

"Bathroom, huh?" He shook his head, but he smiled. "Okay. I'll see you when you get back."

I hurried to the bathroom and locked the door behind me. *Fuck.* What was I doing? What was going on here? My mind was a whirling dervish as I glanced frantically around the bathroom. This was definitely not one of those movie motel bathrooms with the little escape window. Didn't matter. The bad guy was always waiting outside anyway.

But there was no bad guy here. What was I thinking? It was just me and Kage and the inevitable. My stomach was so tight it was folding in on itself. And quivering. God, was it ever quivering. I was fucked.

So incredibly fucked.

I undid my pants and took a gratuitous piss. Then I washed my hands, took a deep breath, and opened the bathroom door. Kage was still on the couch where I left him, and I skirted the living area by way of the kitchen, grabbing a beer from the fridge.

"Want a beer?" I asked, willing my voice not to squeak.

"Nope."

When I got back to the sofa, I hesitated before sitting down, taking a swallow of beer.

"Got your bathroom break out of the way?" Kage asked.

I nodded.

"Then set that beer down on the coffee table and get your ass over here."

I did as he asked— no, as he commanded— and set the beer on the table.

He was lying back on the arm of the sofa with his legs stretched down the length of the seat cushion. When I didn't make a move toward him, he spread his legs and put one foot on the floor. Then he patted the seat between his legs.

Instead of stepping forward, I stepped backward. "God, Kage—" I took another step backward, shaking my head. "I want you so, so much."

"Then where are you going?"

That's when I took off like a spooked horse, stumbling backward. I only got about three steps away before he was on me, taking me down and pinning me on the carpet. In the shuffle, my nearly-full beer got knocked off the table, and all I could hear was the glug-glug-fizz of the stuff spurting out onto the floor.

"My beer," I gasped.

"Fuck the beer, Jamie." He brought his mouth down onto mine and took my lips in a hungry kiss. He wasn't rough exactly, but he was needy, and he definitely did not kiss like a girl. He didn't let me be the aggressor or let me lead. He pressed in and took what he wanted, leaving me breathless.

All I could do was kiss him back, let him explore and taste. I was just along for the ride, and what an amazing ride it was.

"We shouldn't be doing this," I said when he pulled back and looked into my eyes.

He gave me that amused look he always seemed to save just for me. "Yeah? What do you think we should be doing?"

His lips were full, sexy, and right in front of me. I couldn't resist lifting my head and taking a kiss for myself. The feel of his beard stubble was something new and unexpected, and I liked it. Like the way it scrubbed my lips and face, made them more sensitive.

I noticed I had a death grip on his shoulders, and I loosened my arms and let my hands wander tentatively across the expanse of his shoulders. Even the feel of the t-shirt with the hard muscle beneath was delightful. It was as if I'd never felt a t-shirt before. In fact, it was as if I'd never felt *anything* before. Like my nerve endings had just been woken from a lifelong state of dormancy.

"We should be doing something work related."

His eyebrows shot up in surprise. "Like what? You wanna work out?"

"No." I rolled my eyes, feeling my face go all goofy and hot just imaging what kind of workout he might have in mind. "What about that photo shoot I asked you about? The more personal one."

He seemed to consider it for a moment, then shrugged and said, "Okay." He hopped up off of me just like that and pulled me up with one hand.

I straightened myself up. Smoothed my clothes. Tried to brush the lust off of me.

"I'll get the camera ready," I told him. "You just… get however you want to be, I guess."

He retired to the bedroom area while I readied the camera, trying to remember all of the tricks the camera guy had told me about nighttime indoor shots.

I had hoped Kage would be fully dressed when he returned, since it would have theoretically made things less complicated for me and my increasingly confusing emotions, but no such luck. His boxers were the only barrier between me and the body I didn't want to think about.

My brain illogically suggested that maybe if I worked out really hard and got a body like that of my own, I wouldn't be so interested in his anymore.

Yeah, right. Because that makes total sense.

"How do you want me?" he asked, running a hand through his hair. We were standing so close I could smell the shampoo.

"Well, put some damn clothes on, first of all," I said irritably.

He laughed. "Wow. Okay. I wasn't sure how you wanted me, so I figured I'd start from scratch and let you dictate. Do I need to put on a full-body Eskimo suit, or will shorts and a t-shirt be fine?"

"Very fucking funny. Just dress like you normally do."

He looked pointedly down at his boxers.

"Normally when you have company," I added. "Your fans don't want to see you sitting around in your underwear scratching your balls."

"You sure about that?" He smiled. "I'll bet there's one or two out there who wouldn't mind seeing that. Besides, who are these elusive fans you keep talking about? The few people I signed autographs for tonight? No one knows who I am, Jamie."

That made me chuckle. "Who do you think I am, some kind of amateur? I've got this covered. Let me show you something."

I set up my laptop on his coffee table and sat down on the sofa while Kage went and got dressed again. Then he joined me on the sofa looking very patriotic in a pair of dark blue shorts with white piping, a faded red t-shirt, and no shoes.

I used my finger on the touchscreen to navigate to Kage's website, but he wasn't paying my computer any attention. "Where are your glasses?" he asked.

"In my laptop case. But I'm fine without them."

"You're squinting at the screen. Put them on."

I let out a groaning sigh and reached over to retrieve them out of my case. Then I slipped them on and tried to avoid looking directly at Kage.

"Has someone teased you about your glasses, Jamie?"

"People always tease about glasses."

"Well, I think they're sexy."

"You do?" I still didn't look at him.

"Very."

I cleared my throat. "Well, let's get back to work." I directed his attention away from my face and to the computer screen where his website was displayed. Then I spent the next hour showing him the extensive social media presence I'd been building for him.

"Jesus Christ, Jamie. When have you had time to do all of this?" His expression was one of true amazement.

"That's what happens when you move to a new town and don't have a social life." It sounded like a complaint, but I knew my words were tinged with pride. I had worked hard for Kage, not because I had to, but because I wanted to. I'd never even seen the guy fight, but I believed in him. Believed he would be a star.

"You see here?" I pointed to an action shot I'd taken of him doing a high kick into the air. It was one of my favorites, and it had gotten hundreds of comments. "People love you, Kage. Every time I post a picture, it gets shared like crazy. And your website is already getting a good amount of hits."

His eyes widened. "I have a website?"

"Of course. *MichaelKage.com.* I told you that already. Probably went in one ear and out the other, just like half the shit I tell you. I've been working on it, and I've got it ranked for a bunch of good keywords."

"Yeah, like what?"

I navigated to the click-through data. "Let's see... *MMA fighter, best MMA fighter,* that's a good one. *Michael Kage,* of course. People are actually googling your name now, which is a really good sign." I cleared my throat. "Um... *hot MMA fighter, sexy MMA fighter.*"

Kage started laughing. "Really? How the hell did I get in there for that?"

I thought I was going to implode with embarrassment. "Well, I put them in myself. I purposely optimized your site for all of those keywords."

"So you said I was sexy?"

"Let me explain how this works," I said in my best business presentation voice, removing my glasses and tucking them neatly back into my computer case. "I thought a lot of people might be looking for a sexy MMA fighter, so I optimized for the term. It just has to do with knowing what your audience is looking for, and knowing that when people get to your site with those search terms, they won't be disappointed in what they find."

Kage's chest clearly puffed up at that. "Well, let's give them some sexy pictures, then. I saw where one woman said she liked my thick arms. Let's get some shots that show them off."

"There are many people saying they like every single part of you, Kage. But yeah, we can show off your arms. Stay there on the sofa and kind of prop your arm on the back. Yeah, like that." I centered him in my camera frame and took a picture. "Now bend your elbow and lean your head on your hand. Oh, yeah. That shows off the swell of the bicep right there. Very nice." Kage smiled at the compliment, and I got a few shots of him showing the boyish dimples I had come to know and love.

After I'd gotten a bunch of seated shots, I suggested he remove his shirt.

"I thought you wanted me in clothes. Make up your mind, fickle boy." He was clearly amused as he pulled his t-shirt over his head and cast it aside.

Just the way he did it, the way his muscles rippled with that simple movement, made my heart rate pick up. It wasn't fair, because it was artless. Surely he had no intention of tempting me, and yet that's exactly what he was doing. Tempting just like he had hours ago in my suite, and every day in the gym, and just generally every second of the day if I was breathing.

"I thought maybe we could gradually unveil you," I explained. "And don't fuck with me, Kage. Stop trying to embarrass me. This is business. Let the master do his job."

"Sure thing, chief. How's this? Sexy enough?" He stretched onto his side, lengthening out and showing off the leanness of his flank. For some reason that expanse of smooth, hairless skin always drew my eye, made me want to reach out and run my hand along it. My fingers itched to touch him there, and to follow the curve all the way to his hip.

I gulped and somehow turned my brain off enough to get through a few shirtless photos. "Smile for me," I practically whispered, and he did. "Now pull your shorts down a little on your hip there." He gave me a funny look, but he did as I asked.

"Like this?" He teased the waistband down over his hip bone, revealing the deep iliac furrow that angled down into his shorts.

"Perfect," I breathed, snapping a group of photos in that pose. "People do really go for that *V* of yours."

"People, huh?" He smiled and stuck the tip of his tongue playfully between his teeth.

The tongue I just tasted. Don't think about it.

"Adorable. How about a sexy wink?" I asked unselfconsciously. He fired off a few winks for me as I tried to catch it at just the right second. "Wow, that's gonna be hot. I can't wait to get these posted." By this time I was in the zone, feeling like a real photographer. Like in my mind, I may have been slightly considering a career change.

"I'm curious," Kage said nonchalantly, rolling onto his stomach as I continued to snap pictures. "Which do you think is sexier? Choice A…" He pulled his shorts down just enough to show the top swell of his muscled glutes and the beginning of his ass crack. I sucked in a breath and continued snapping, willing my heartbeat to slow down. This was good stuff. See? I could separate my personal feelings from my profession. My finger was shaking as I pressed the button. "Or do you prefer choice B?" he asked.

Without warning, he flipped onto his back and hooked his thumb in the waistband of his shorts, yanking down enough to reveal a bed of dark pubic hair and about two inches of the top of his very thick, very hard cock. He used his fingers to hold down his massive erection, which remained covered by the fabric of his shorts, but not hidden. There was no disguising the outline of that beast of a body part.

I let out a strangled sound and fumbled the sinfully expensive camera. It landed on the carpet a safe distance from the spilled beer and was forgotten. My logical mind went on vacation, and all I could think was that I wanted to put my mouth on that spot he was showing me, to see what it tasted like. Find out what it smelled like and if it was as warm as it looked.

"Definitely a B," Kage growled. Then he lowered the front of his shorts even further, hooking the band under his balls and releasing his cock. It sprang up and bounced off of his tight belly, leaving a sticky trail of precum on his tanned skin, and in that moment, as every molecule of my being seemed to converge into a throbbing mass at the base of my scrotum, I realized I was officially and utterly fucked.

My own dick had swelled to the point of pain, and my mouth was watering with the need to lick every inch of Kage's body from head to toe. He was so goddamn gorgeous. It didn't seem quite possible that he wanted me, and yet every move he made said that he did.

I tore my eyes away from his hard cock and met his gaze, which was amused and trained right on me.

"Don't look so worried," he said. "It likes you. Can't you tell?" He stood up in front of me and dropped his shorts to the floor, kicking them out of the way. He wasn't wearing any underwear.

"I don't... I can't..." I found myself stuttering, though what I was trying to say was a complete mystery even to myself. "Kage—"

"Shhh," he whispered, lowering his head until his lips were right next to my ear. "It's okay to want me, Jamie. I want you, too. Stop making excuses and just let go."

I whimpered embarrassingly, but he didn't seem to mind. He cupped my cheek in his palm and pressed his lips softly against mine. The kiss wasn't demanding. It was the opposite of the first kiss we'd shared— reverent, gentle, exploratory.

At first I couldn't get my lips to move, but Kage moved his ever so slowly against mine, coaxing me into action. I parted my lips and felt the tip of his tongue slip between them. When my knees buckled, he was there to catch me, wrapping his strong arm around the small of my back and cinching me tightly against him. The knowledge that he was naked against my fully clothed body made me weak with anticipation.

Kage pushed his tongue deeper into my mouth, and suddenly I was sucking hungrily at his tongue, winding my arms around his neck, and pressing my lower body against his. I was desperate to get closer, to feel through the barrier of my clothing what he had pressed against me. My hunger knew no bounds, growing exponentially with each passing second as it became clearer that this was not some fevered fantasy. This was actually happening.

And I was going to let it.

He unwound my arms from his neck and reached down to pull my t-shirt over my head so that we were skin to skin. The scrub of chest hair against my nipples was exquisite torture, and I moaned, pulling back to catch my breath.

"Fuck no, you're not going anywhere!" Kage yanked me back against him. "I've waited too long for this. Been patient enough." He covered my mouth and face with kisses, moved down to my throat, and bit the sensitive skin there until I cried out. I was overcome with passion, my breath coming in quick gasps as I fought to keep it together. I had always thought of myself as a player and a skilled lover, but I swear Kage made me feel like a virgin all over again.

"Take off your pants," he said.

"What are you planning on doing to me?" I asked, my voice distant to my own ears as I worked my shorts down my legs, leaving my boxer briefs on.

"What I should have done when you first got here. And if it hadn't been for you lying to me about having a girlfriend, I would have."

"How did you know I'd let you?"

He chuckled. "I could tell by the way you look at me. Like you're eating me alive with your eyes."

"I don't do that," I protested. "I don't even like guys."

"Liar." Kage shook his head and took a step back. "Get on your knees, Jamie."

"Pardon me?"

"Don't give me that look. I said get on your knees."

I wanted to tell him no, that this was insanity, and that I wasn't gay. I wanted to point out that I'd just recently had a girlfriend whom I'd fucked soundly on a regular basis. But instead I sank to my knees in front of him and waited, looking up at his unbelievably perfect body, all muscles and planes and smooth skin. The boyish face with the five-o'clock shadow, the dark locks of hair that fell loosely around his face… and that's when I felt it. He was right. I was devouring him with my eyes, because God help me I could not get enough.

I took in a deep breath, let it out, and finally gave in— to him, to me, and to the desire that had been chipping away at my sanity. Kage saw it the moment I submitted, and his mouth tipped into a salacious grin as he stepped toward me. He held that intimidating cock in his hand, the fat head mushrooming obscenely out from his fist.

"Tell me what you want, Jamie. I'm not going to let you blame me after this is all over. You tell me what you want, or you don't get it."

I was so ashamed, so scared. I tried to tell myself it was okay to be weak, because Kage was strong enough for both of us.

"I want it in my mouth," I whispered, feeling ridiculous.

Did I really just say those words?

He took a step closer, the head of his dick nearly touching my lips. I caught the scent I'd been dying for, and it took every ounce of restraint I had not to dart my tongue out and steal a little taste of him. I needed for this to begin, for him to put me out of my misery, but something told me he wasn't ready. He wasn't satisfied with my answer yet. I wanted to please him, though. Wanted to please us both. That was my one coherent thought as I knelt there like a beggar, with carpet fibers digging into my knees and shame threatening to suffocate me.

"I want you, Kage," I admitted, trading shame for candor. Hell, if I was actually going to take another man's pipe in my mouth, I ought to be man enough to at least say the words. "I want to suck you off. I want you to fuck my mouth. I want… everything. You want me to beg? I will. I'll do—"

He pushed the swollen head of his cock between my lips, cutting off my words. I felt the curve of smooth flesh slide in, and he shuddered hard and threw his head back for one blissed-out second, then looked down at me again.

"You don't have to beg, baby." He wrapped a large hand around the back of my head, holding me in place. "I just need you to realize that you want this as much as I do." Then he began to move, incrementally at first.

I stretched my lips to accommodate his size, feeling the ridge on the underside of his cock head running along my tongue. He tickled the roof of my mouth, bounced lightly off the soft spot at the back of my throat.

"Relax your throat," Kage said. It was the same thing I always told the girls when I rammed my cock down their throats. And now he was saying it to me.

I relaxed, felt a slight urge to gag, but nothing like I would have expected. My mouth settled around him, and I applied an ever-so-slight amount of suction for him to sink into and pull against. I didn't know how it felt to him, but it felt amazing to me. God, how had I ever lived without the feel of his cock in my mouth? It was as if every moment I'd lived so far had been building up to this very moment, when I would discover a need like I'd never known before.

"You feel so good, Jamie. So goddamn good…" His hips pistoned his cock slowly in and out of my mouth, and I moaned around him. "I swear I've wanted to fuck this mouth ever since the first night we met. This fucking smart mouth. Fucking liar's mouth. God, you're so sexy."

I tried to pull away at that, to argue that I wasn't a liar, but he wouldn't let me. He held tight to the back of my head with impossibly strong fingers, keeping my mouth stuffed full of his cock. He guided every movement, pushing in and pulling out at a slow, even pace. Jerking the lower half of his cock with his hand while the upper half copulated with my mouth. His hand never let up on the back of my head. It was all very restrained, as if he was afraid of losing his rhythm and spinning out of control. I loved it. The discipline of it, the predictability, it all seemed to amp up the anticipation for what was to come.

"Your mouth was made for my cock, Jamie. I want you on your knees like this for me all the time. Fuck. So beautiful down there." He babbled on, sometimes making sense, sometimes not. I didn't care. Every word was the hottest thing I'd ever heard. His always-sexy voice was laced with a darker edge— the edge of profound lust— and I found myself wishing with every ounce of want I had inside me that I was the only one who had ever inspired him to sound like that. That his past would just be gone in a puff of smoke, and there would be only me.

I would be his. His Jamie. His boy.

I waited patiently for his release, hypnotized by his voice, dreaming of belonging to him, loving every second of every slide of skin. My mouth learned the shape of his cock by heart— every swell, every vein, every ridge. I sucked it like it was my only source of sustenance.

"I'm not ready to come, but I can't stop it," he groaned. "Love you so much down there."

His cock thickened noticeably in my mouth as he spoke, veins plumping, flesh growing impossibly turgid. His controlled movements never sped up, never changed, but he let out a long, agonized grunt as he erupted. I felt his load shooting down the underside of his cock, pulsing through the channel like a freshly unfurled firehose and filling my mouth with wicked hot spurts of cum.

I'd never felt anything so erotic, so carnal… I wanted it, loved it, needed it like I'd never known I needed anything in my life.

It seemed his orgasm would never stop, and still I took it and swallowed hungrily. I slurped it up and begged and whimpered for more as I felt my own cock spilling into my boxers, rhythmically echoing the warm jets of cum that Kage was shooting down my throat.

It was by far the sweetest release I'd ever known. Far better than any girl I'd ever been with, far better than any desperate, pent-up porn jerk I'd ever had. I suppose it was inevitable after so many days of watching Kage and thinking about him, needing to touch him, and of stuffing down the desire.

When Kage had finally stopped coming, and his aftershocks had all ceased, he looked down at me and shook his head as if to clear the lingering fog of lust. "Holy shit, that was amazing." He reached down under my armpits, hoisting me easily off the floor, and I was just weak and shaky enough that I didn't balk at being picked up like a child. He pushed me down onto the sofa and kissed my stretched and swollen lips. "Your turn," he said.

My face went bright red, and I glanced down at my cum-soaked boxer briefs. "No need for that," I admitted. "I'm good."

"Oh, wow," Kage said in a soft voice. "Baby, that's hot. You just came like that?"

Now it was his turn to get on his knees, only I didn't have to tell him to. He did it all on his own. He leaned in and pressed his open mouth to the fabric of my boxers, enclosing my waning erection within his warm mouth. What he was doing felt amazing, mouthing me through my wet shorts. Then he pulled them down and all the way off my legs, tossing them to the side like he had his own.

Ever so gently, he used his tongue and lips to clean me, mindful of the post-ejaculation sensitivity of the head of my dick. I shuddered at the sensation of his warm tongue dragging along my softening flesh, and of his lips nipping playfully at my inner thighs. The sheer intimacy of it all was staggering.

Once, he looked up and smiled at me as he worked. "So sweet," he said quietly, sounding unlike himself, and my heart squeezed so hard in my chest I thought it would stop beating.

When it was all over, and we were both floating around the suite on endorphins, Kage fixed us each a protein shake. Then he got dressed for a night run.

I had no clean underwear, so Kage tossed me a pair of his boxers. They were large, and I had to roll the waistband down once. He chuckled when he saw me doing it. "Do I need to run to the store and get you some underwear?"

"No, I'll wear these." In truth, he would've had to pry them from my cold, dead fingers. Wearing his underwear gave me a sense of being close to him, of belonging to him. In that moment, I think I understood exactly why my girlfriends had always wanted to wear my jerseys.

And why I hadn't let them.

Kage shrugged noncommittally, but there was pride in his expression that he couldn't disguise. He wanted it, too. Wanted to run alongside me through the streets, knowing that I was wearing his underwear, and that we'd just been in each other's mouths.

After our run, we settled into bed together, both of us exhausted and ready to go to sleep. Kage rolled over and spooned me like he had at the infamous slumber party. Just like then, it felt so safe and comfortable in his arms, like I was meant to be there. That scared me more than I wanted to admit.

Chapter 16

THE drive home the next day was laid back and relaxing. Kage wore his boots and a pair of loose, faded jeans that hung from his hipbones and showed his striped purple boxer shorts. He pulled on a plain V-neck tee and drew his hair into that cute topknot.

He caught me staring at him about ten times before we even made it to the car.

"What is it?" he asked finally.

"I don't know. You look… good."

"Better than usual?" He glanced down at his attire. "What do you like? I'll wear it every day."

I laughed. "Those jeans and boxers for one. But I think it's just maybe, I don't know."

We were on our way to the front desk to check out, and he stopped at the elevators and pushed the button for the lobby. "Out with it, college boy. Use your words."

"I guess I feel sort of like I can look at you now. Like I couldn't really before, but now I can."

"Oh, I get it." He raised a brow and gave me one of his devilish grins. "You mean since you've had my cock in your mouth, now you can admit that you find me irresistibly attractive."

"Something like that."

The empty elevator arrived, and we stepped on. The doors slid closed behind us.

Kage immediately set our luggage down, crowded me, and backed me into a corner. He pulled his t-shirt up to reveal his abs and boxers. "You like that?"

I looked down and took in the sight of that body I was becoming addicted to. "Yes."

He kissed me softly on the lips and put his hand on my dick, cupping my balls and rubbing me through my shorts. Through his boxers I was still wearing.

"You like this?" he asked between kisses.

I sighed and leaned into his touch. "Yes."

He shoved his hand down under my sac and stretched his fingers back between my legs, pressing his fingertips up into the crack of my ass and putting the barest of pressure on my hole.

I gasped and went up on my toes.

"I'm going to fuck you. You know that, right?" He dropped his mouth to the side of my throat and pressed warm, soft kisses there. "I'm so hard right now just thinking about it." He groaned and bit into me, not enough to break the skin, but enough to hurt in a good way.

Suddenly the elevator stopped, and a family filed on. A husband, wife, and teenage son and daughter. Perfect American family. My face went scarlet, and Kage stepped away from me and smiled.

I couldn't help it. I let out what I think was the goofiest laugh to ever cross my lips. I could still feel Kage's saliva on my throat, and the memory of his fingertip pressing against the entrance to my hole, and I just broke down. The mother and father tried not to look in our direction, but the son and daughter stared unapologetically. I think they all knew what was going on, and that made it even more hysterical to me.

To Kage's credit, he held it together. He nodded politely at the family and stood there with his hands clasped in front of his boner. I, on the other hand, couldn't cover mine now without drawing attention to it. I was already being watched like a hawk by the two teens. Finally, I couldn't take it anymore, and I just turned and buried my face in the corner and shook with near-silent laughter.

I didn't turn around until the elevator stopped, and the family had disembarked into the lobby. I heard the mother say, "Should we complain?" And the father mumbled something I couldn't hear. The teens just giggled.

Kage held the door for me as I got myself under control and was finally able to step out.

"Remind me to never play poker with you," he said. "You cannot keep a straight face."

The same lady was working the desk when we checked out as when we arrived. She recognized us and gave Kage that same blinding smile. "Did you enjoy your stay?" she asked.

Apparently she thought my comment about cuddling had been a joke, because it hadn't discouraged her interest in Kage one bit. I felt like she needed reminding. But I had barely taken a hesitant step toward Kage when he reached over and hauled me to him, pulling me into a one-armed embrace and turning my body to face his.

"You have no idea how much," he told her, settling his mouth on mine for a quick kiss. Not enough to get us kicked out of the hotel, but enough to let anyone who might have been looking know that we were together. "Thank you for choosing such a romantic room for us, ma'am."

She smiled. "My pleasure. You two take care."

"See?" Kage said when we were out of earshot. "A little friendliness goes a long way. Yesterday you came at her with that, *We like to cuddle, bitch!* That's why she got an attitude."

"No, I think the difference today was that you weren't flirting with her."

He smiled indulgently at me. "Okay, you win. No more flirting."

I frowned. "I didn't say you couldn't flirt. I'm not your boss or anything."

"Or jealous?"

"Fuck no, I'm not jealous. Even if I did have a right to be, which I don't, I'm not really the jealous type."

"So I can flirt with anybody, male or female, and you'd be fine with it?"

"Well, I don't think you should be flirting with guys, for obvious reasons. You're trying to get a UFC contract. The last thing you need is for anything to cause problems with that."

"And you think it would definitely be a problem? You think people would care?"

I laughed harshly and stared at him. "Dude, people always care about shit like that. At the very least, it would overshadow your talent and reduce you to a novelty act."

"And at worst?"

"You know the answer to that. No contract."

"I think you're being a little negative. But, you're the expert."

I didn't mention the fact that I was far from an expert, because I didn't think it took an expert to figure out that making out with guys in public was the last thing a UFC hopeful ought to be doing. I also didn't think Kage was that naïve, either. He knew I was right, but for some reason he was playing devil's advocate. Sometimes it seemed like the more I got to know him, the less I actually knew him.

"Kage, you do understand that we can't be open like that in front of people, right? I mean that was a one-time thing. Just because no one knows us here. We'll have to be extra careful when you get more well-known. And around people we know."

I saw his lips tighten, and I knew something about what I had said didn't sit well with him. He did let me drive his Vette, but he slept almost the entire trip. Or at least he stuck his sunglasses on his face, crossed his arms, and lay still the whole time. I enjoyed the drive as much as I could while worrying that Kage was pissed at me.

Once we arrived back at the Alcazar, he seemed to have a fresh outlook. There were no remnants of the attitude he'd had when we got in the car, so I breathed easier.

"I'm starving," he said as soon as I parked the car in his space in the parking garage.

"Yeah, I could definitely use something to eat," I agreed.

We dropped our things off in our respective apartments, then Kage came and picked me up. We headed down to the Grotto together. The whole way there, I couldn't shake the feeling that we looked different now. That everyone could see what we'd done—what we were to each other.

Steve accosted us when we were walking through the empty lobby. As if pulling the words straight out of my head, he said, "Hey, you two look different!"

We both stopped mid-stride and made a detour to the front desk, where Steve stood alone. I gave him a nervous smile. "What do you mean, different?"

"You look nice and tan, like you've been to the beach. I need to lay out before I disappear with this white-ass skin of mine. Where have you guys been going, up on the roof?"

"Oh," I said, hoping I didn't sound as relieved as I felt. "Our tans."

Kage smirked at me and took over. "We went out of town for a couple of days on business, and we took my car with the top down."

"Lucky!" Steve said with a pout. "You still got that black Corvette?"

Kage nodded.

"He let me drive it," I said, instantly realizing how bratty I sounded.

"No need to rub it in, Jamie." Steve crossed his arms and fixed me with a mock glare. "We can't all be as hot as you, coming in here with those big brown fuck-me eyes and wrapping the boss man around your little wee-wee."

"That is ridiculous!" My mouth fell open. Kage just laughed, and I stared helplessly at him. I looked around behind us to make sure we were still alone. "Do you just let your employees say shit like that? What if someone heard him and believed that?"

Kage stopped laughing and smiled at me. "You want me to set him straight?"

I nodded emphatically. "Yes."

Kage put on his serious face and took a deep breath. "Steve, just so you know, Jamie's wee-wee is not little."

"I knew it. I fucking knew it." A huge grin overtook Steve's face, and he covered his mouth with the fingers of one hand, his glitter nail polish sparkling under the fluorescents. Then he did a little hip shake behind the counter and pumped his hands in the air. "The minute Aldo brought this beautiful boy through the front door and said he was your intern, I said, *Mmm hmm. I see where this is going.* And then the way you've been acting? So obvious."

I was still shocked and pissed about the whole direction of the conversation. We were supposed to be keeping a low profile, and here Kage was encouraging lewd comments from big-mouth Steve. Hell, he had basically just admitted that we'd been intimate.

"Remember what we talked about earlier, Kage?" I grated under my breath. "Career on the line."

Kage reached out and touched my face, cupping my cheek in his palm and running the pad of his thumb across my bottom lip. "Chill, baby. Steve and I are friends. He won't say anything, and there's nobody else around."

I glanced behind me again at the empty lobby, then into the darkened casino, where a couple of elderly ladies were playing slots with their backs to us.

Steve winked and pointed discreetly at a security camera. "Just don't forget about those," he warned in a sing-song voice.

Kage balked. "I don't give a fuck. I can touch his face if I want. Fuck the cameras. Fuck my uncle, fuck the public..." His voice got louder and louder, until he was nearly yelling. "I'm a grown man."

"Uh-oh," Steve said. "I feel a Kage rage coming on. Jamie, you need to get your man in there and get him some food in his belly. Then take him upstairs and give him some good loving. We don't need him going all ragey on us."

"Shut up, Steve," Kage said. "Come on, Jamie. Let's get to the Grotto and see what Enzo's got on special today."

When Enzo heard we were in the restaurant, he bustled out, wiping his meaty fingers on his apron. "Kage, Jamie… So glad to see you today. I have something extra special. You like lobster?"

I nodded, licking my lips. "With butter sauce?"

"Of course with butter sauce. My special herb butter sauce will have you begging for more."

"I think I already want more," I told him. "Bring it on."

Kage just sat back and watched me with one of his smug cat smiles. His eyelids were at half mast, and I couldn't shake the feeling that he was imagining me naked. Enzo took one look at him and beamed, so I was pretty sure he saw it, too.

"Anything special today, Kage?" he asked. "How about some white wine, and a tiny little itty-bitty piece of cake for dessert?"

"Sounds good, Enzo," he said.

I nearly dropped my teeth. Michael Kage was ordering cake?

After we'd done away with four glasses of good white wine and six mouthwatering lobster tails, Enzo ordered our table cleared and brought out a large piece of cake and two forks, placing it in the middle for us to share.

"This is our White Wedding Cake," Enzo said with a grin. "We don't even put it on the menu. It's for special guests only."

Kage and I each picked up a fork and took a small bite of the dessert.

"This is delicious, Enzo," Kage groaned. "If I'm going to blow my diet, this is definitely the way to do it."

Enzo smiled and slipped his hands into his apron pockets. "I just like to see you happy, my dear. Things are going good for you, yes?" He turned to me. "You are helping him to get his contract?"

"I certainly hope so." I smiled across the table at Kage, who dragged another bite of cake off of his fork with his teeth. "I think we're making some real progress. He's definitely more well-known than he was a month ago."

"And well-liked," Kage added. "Thanks to Jamie pimping me out like a porn star."

My eyes widened in surprise, and Enzo started waving his hands in front of his face. "I'm out of here," he said, smiling. "This conversation is getting too weird for me. Enjoy your cake, boys."

"Hey, I'm just giving your fans what they want," I told Kage after Enzo was gone. "More skin. You work hard for that body, so you might as well show it off." I took a bite of cake and licked the icing from my lip. "Besides, it's not like I have any fight footage to share. Hell, I've never even seen you fight. For all I know you never have."

"Don't even think about taunting me," he said dangerously. "You have no idea how many people I've hurt. I sent a guy to the hospital the night you flew in. I broke his arm in an armbar. Stupid fucker wouldn't tap out."

"What? You've fought since I've been here?" I dropped my fork and scowled at him. "Why didn't you invite me? I want to see you fight."

"Are you sure about that?" He reached over and touched my hand where it lay on the table, teasing it open with his index finger. Suddenly he looked vulnerable, seemed to be searching for the right thing to say.

"What? Do you not want me to see you fight? That doesn't make any sense. It's not like I haven't watched you train almost daily for the last month."

"That's different." He traced a figure eight into my palm over and over, staring at it all the while.

"Why don't you want me to see you fight, Kage? I don't understand. Are you afraid you'll lose?"

He huffed out a breath. "I'm never afraid of losing a fight."

Apparently, I was going to have to drag whatever this was out of him, because he wasn't going to give it up easily.

"What is it that you don't want me to see?"

"I guess I just don't want you to see me differently." He didn't look me in the eye as he spoke, just kept watching his finger tracing that figure eight, which seemed to have literally become an infinity sign. "You don't know how brutal it can get in there, Jamie. How brutal *I* can get. I kinda like the way you look at me now."

"Like I want to eat you alive? You like how I've got the cannibal thing going on, huh?"

He laughed quietly. "Yeah, I like that."

"So what makes you think that will change?"

"Fighting is different when it's someone you know." He finally met my eyes, and there was a haunted look in his. "You want to see me get punched in the face so hard my knees buckle? Or kicked in the kidney so hard I can't stand up straight?"

I stared at him, my eyes wide, imagining the things he was describing. He was right. I wasn't sure if I could sit on the other side of a chain link fence and watch Kage get hurt.

"What, no comment?" he asked.

There was a change in his voice, and in his demeanor. That little light his eyes had when he looked at me— the one that made me believe he might see something special— was gone. Snuffed out and replaced by a cold darkness. Then the barest hint of a sneer tipped one corner of his lips, and I pulled away.

"Think you can handle watching me bend a gown man's arm backward, hearing the bone snap before he has a chance to tap out? How about punching a man in the face until there's blood spewing everywhere and he's lying there limp like a rag doll, head flopping as I bash his fucking head into the mat? Have you ever seen a guy kicked in the face so hard you think his neck snapped? How about seeing me choke a man unconscious and wondering for the next sixty seconds if he's ever going to wake up again?"

"Kage—"

"That's what I do, Jamie. I hurt people. Do you know what they call me in there?" He gave me a smile that was one part sarcastic, two parts cruel. "They call me the Machine. Do you think you can have feelings for a machine?"

Feelings? Did he want me to have feelings for him? Because I was pretty sure I already did.

"Michael…" I don't know why I called him by his first name. It just came out, and in the moment it felt right. "You're not a machine, okay? You're human. And on top of that, I believe you're a good person."

"You don't know that for sure. What if I'm not?" It sounded more like a threat than a question. "What if I'm a bad person, and you just haven't gotten to know the real me yet?"

"Why are you trying to scare me?" I asked, leaning toward him and looking into his eyes. Searching for that spark, silently begging for it.

Then he blinked and gave me a weak smile, and there it was again. The old Kage. The one I'd spent the last weeks trying to get to know.

He shrugged. "Not trying to scare you. I just need you to know."

"Know what?" I pressed.

"Can we get out of here?" he asked, avoiding the question. "Let's go to my apartment."

Kage threw down a tip for our server, and we made our way to the elevators across from the front desk. While we waited, Steve called out. "Hey, guys, something I forgot to mention."

We walked over to the desk again, and Steve looked around before speaking. "You know Aldo said he was on babysitting duty when he brought Jamie in. I didn't think anything about it then, but..."

"Yeah?" Kage narrowed his eyes. "You think he's still babysitting?"

Steve shrugged. "Yeah, I do. I've seen him watching a lot."

"How often?"

Steve looked over his shoulder, then back at us. "Enough to make me wonder. In fact, I actually entertained the notion that Aldo had switched teams and was crushing on our Jamie. I mean, everyone around here is. But it's not that, of course."

Kage ran a hand through his hair and took a deep breath. "Alright. Thanks, Steve." He took me by the elbow and guided me back to the elevators. "Just text me when you're ready for me to hook you up with that other thing," he called over his shoulder.

"I will," Steve said. "Bye, Jamie."

"Bye," I called, stumbling over my own feet as Kage pulled me roughly into the closing elevator. "So what the hell was that all about?"

"Steve wants me to hook him up with some of that stuff we had the other night."

"No, I mean the other. About the babysitting."

"Oh. My uncle's goons. Apparently you're part of their job description now."

"Really?" That little tidbit of information threw me for a loop. "What, are they following me?"

"Probably. I didn't mean to get you mixed up in all of this. I just wanted... Hang on." Kage slipped his key card into the penthouse slot, and the elevator climbed all the way to the top of the building.

The door slid open, revealing the long hallway with a large door on either end— one for Kage's apartment, the other for his uncle's. He stuck his key card into the lock on his door and didn't speak again until we were safely inside his apartment.

"You just wanted what?" I prompted.

"I just wanted you. My uncle thought I needed a publicist, and he was interviewing a couple of guys with big name clients: pro ball players, Olympic gold medalists, stuff like that."

"And you wanted me?" I sat down on the sofa and stared at him. "Why?"

"I don't know. It was like fate, right? What are the chances that I'd be at that show to see some dude I trained with a couple of times, and then here comes this hot little college guy making up shit like he's some kind of expert publicist? It was unreal, man. Blew my mind."

"So you hired me because you thought it was fate?"

He climbed onto the sofa, but not beside me. He got right on my lap, straddling me with his big thighs, and leaned in to kiss me. His mouth engulfed mine, and he sucked hungrily at my lips before pushing his tongue inside. I met him with a hunger of my own, and we licked and tasted and sucked until I couldn't breathe. Finally, he pulled back, even as I was moving in for another kiss.

"I hired you because you were the best man for the job," he said. "Because you were fearless."

"Fearless? I was scared shitless."

He laughed. "Everybody's scared, Jamie. Even me."

"Yeah, right. Earlier you said you weren't scared."

"I said I wasn't afraid of losing a fight."

I groaned. "There you go with the riddles again. One of these days, I'm gonna get a decoder ring so that I can carry on a conversation with you."

He took my face in his hands. "Look, all you need to know is that I hired you because you were a sexy little liar, and you were willing to say whatever it took to get my attention. What better qualifications should a publicist have?"

"I was not trying to get your attention."

He laughed. "Yes, you were. You were trying to get in my pants."

"Oh. My. God. I was not." My face turned fourteen shades of crimson.

Kage slid his tongue between my lips and pulled away again. "You would have gotten on your knees right there in the backstage area of Phillips Arena. You would have bent over that buffet table and let me take your ass right there in front of those reporters. They couldn't stand you, by the way."

"I know very well how much they hated me. However, I think you must be confusing me with someone else who would have let you bend them over. That was definitely not me."

"Yes, it was. You may not want to admit it, but even then you were looking at me like you wanted to eat me. You would have swallowed my cock right then and begged for seconds."

And then reality hit me right in the face. "You hired me because you wanted to fuck me."

One of those sexy cat grins stretched across his handsome face. "It may have crossed my mind."

"I feel so used. So cheap." I was only teasing. I *think* he knew that, but maybe he didn't.

"Tell you what," he said, hopping off my lap and leaving me with an unsatisfied boner I'd hoped he would help me take care of. "I don't want you to feel like I hired you for sex, because I assure you that is far from the truth. So I'm gonna let you do your job during working hours, and then you can choose whether or not you want to spend personal time with me during off hours. Okay?"

I groaned and made an obvious adjustment to my pants. "Damn, I need to learn to think before I speak. I really don't think that's necessary, do you? I mean, we're both big boys. We can handle it."

Kage smiled indulgently. "I want to, believe me. But I think you need to at least go to your apartment and sleep on it. I'm the one with something to lose here, so…"

His weighted words hit home, and suddenly I thought I understood. Kage was in a precarious position where a potential sexual relationship with me was concerned. For one thing, he was paying me. And for another, he was on his way to becoming a celebrity. If things went sour, or if I changed my mind because I felt pressured, it was his reputation on the line. He wanted me, but he was being careful, and I had to respect that.

On my way out the door, something occurred to me, and I looked back over my shoulder. "Hey, I thought your uncle was supposed to be some hard-ass businessman. How did you talk him into hiring an intern with no experience?"

He grinned. "I told him I wouldn't fight anymore."

17

IT WAS nearly impossible to get settled into my room that night. For one thing, I was a little bit angry. What was this business Kage had come up with about sleeping on it? I was also still shaken by the way he'd acted in the restaurant.

For a few minutes, it was as if he'd flipped into a different personality. His alter-ego. His Bizarro self.

I tried to busy myself with uploading the pictures I'd taken of him over the last several days. I put them on his website, then shared them on his social profiles. While I was messing around with his online presence, I noticed there were messages for him on a couple of sites.

Crap. I hadn't thought of that. Who was going to answer his messages? Me?

I downloaded the corresponding apps to my phone so that I could receive notifications when he got private messages. That was at least a start. But that got me thinking about the scope of the job I was carving out for myself, in essence creating from scratch. It was becoming much larger than I'd anticipated, and I wasn't sure how it was going to be possible to cleanly extract myself from it at the end of the summer.

Then of course that made me think of leaving Kage. *Fuck.* How had this all gotten so complicated so fast? And why was Kage waffling when it came to our personal relationship? I mean, he'd basically seduced me then sent me away to second-guess things. Or maybe he was the one who was second-guessing.

The more I thought about it, the angrier I got.

Yeah, I understood that he had to be careful, but he had been the one pawing all over me at the front desk, kissing me at yet another front desk, and discussing my penis size with a very talkative Alcazar employee. He was contradicting himself.

But there was really nothing I could do about it, so I did what I normally did when I felt helpless. I called my mom.

"It's good to hear from you, sweetheart." Her voice was tired like she'd been asleep. Or maybe she was ill. It was only nine-thirty in her time zone.

"Yeah, I was just hanging around here in my room with nothing to do, so I thought I'd call."

She laughed. "Oh, you have to be bored these days to call your mother."

"I've been really busy, Mom. I'm a working man now."

She coughed, and I couldn't help wondering if it had anything to do with the cancer. Funny how a diagnosis could make even a common cold or a sleepy voice sound terrifying.

"Oh, I know. I talked to your boss. Such a sweet guy. Is he really letting you fly down for my surgery?"

"Actually, uh… I think he's coming with me."

"Wow. I thought that's what he said, but then when I told your father, he said I must have misunderstood. He didn't think an employer would be that hands-on, he said. But I told him that you were doing a different kind of job, and that you and this man had become friends. Is that right?"

I lay back on the bed and stared at the ceiling, feeling a tiny tug in my heart, then closed my eyes. "Yeah, that's right. Did Kage tell you about what I do for him? About who he is and all that?"

"Not exactly. But he did tell me that the secrecy contract you signed did not extend to mothers, and that you could tell me anything you wanted about him."

My eyes flew open at that. "Really? Were those his actual words? That I could tell you anything?"

"Yes, honey. I wouldn't make that up. He said anything."

"He's an MMA fighter," I blurted. "Supposed to be really good, but I haven't seen him fight yet. You can check him out on *MichaelKage.com*. I made that website myself, Mom. I've been taking pictures of him, building his website, establishing a social media presence, and I got him an appearance at a gym over the weekend. He's rich, or his uncle is, and we live in this really fancy hotel."

She laughed. "Slow down, honey," she said. "Sounds like you're doing a fantastic job, but... He's a fighter? He didn't sound like a fighter. He sounded like a very nice person, and well-spoken."

That made me laugh. "Fighters aren't mean and illiterate, Mom. I mean, they could be, I suppose. But I think for the most part they're just normal guys who happen to beat each other up for a living. For our entertainment."

"Hmmm. I hadn't thought about it that way. Maybe it says more about us than them, that they do it for our entertainment."

"Maybe..." I wondered if Kage had ever thought of it that way.

"You seem different, son. What's going on?"

"Different?" My voice squeaked. That was the second time someone had accused me of seeming different in one day. Of course, the first had only concerned my skin color. This one was real. This was my mom, who knew me better than anyone on the entire planet and could always guess my mood or tell when something was bothering me. What made me think I could hide from her?

"I guess I'm growing up," I told her, which was partially true. "This working for a living thing really makes you look at things in a different way. Plus, all this stuff about you having... surgery." I couldn't bring myself to say the word *cancer* to her. Not while she still had it in her body.

"Don't worry about me," she said. "Everything is going to be fine. I'm doing the right thing to get rid of it for good."

"I know. I just don't like thinking about it."

She gasped on the other end of the phone. "Is this him, Jamie? *Michael "The Machine" Kage*, it says. I'm on his website. My goodness, he's... Well, he's something else. Look at this, Jennifer. This is the man— er, boy— your brother is working for. Somehow, I thought he'd be older, being your boss and all."

"Oh my God," I heard Jennifer squeal in the background. "Is he single?" Then she snatched the phone from Mom and asked me directly, "Is he single?"

"Nooo," I lied, jealousy prickling all along the back of my neck. "And neither are you. Aren't you supposed to be getting married soon?"

But she was gone, replaced by my mom again. "Let me put this thing on speaker phone. There we go." Her voice took on a tinny, distant quality. "Son, did you say you took these pictures yourself?"

"Yep," I said. "Kage bought me a really nice digital camera. It cost thousands of dollars, Mom. They look pretty professional, huh? I'm thinking about advertising my services when I get back to school, to make some extra money. Don't you think they look professional?"

"Well, yes, but some of them are sort of racy, aren't they? Is this what fighters are doing these days? Posing with their behinds sticking out of their pants? I can see his *crack*, for heaven's sake." She whispered the word *crack*.

"Oh." I had forgotten about the sexy shots I'd taken over the weekend. What the hell was I showing my mother? I thought of what had happened right after that photo had been snapped, and my face went hot.

"Can I volunteer to be your photography assistant?" Jennifer yelled. "Oh my God, Mom, look at that one."

A knock at the door startled me, and I sat upright in bed. "Hang on, Mom. Let me see who that is at my door."

When I peered through the peephole, Kage was looking back at me. My heart sped up, and I opened the door.

Before I could even say anything, he grabbed my head and leaned in, stealing a quick kiss. "Have you thought about things long enough? I can't wait anymore." He kicked the door shut behind him.

"Get on the bed, Jamie. I need you naked. I am so fucking hard right now."

I swallowed and held up the phone, feeling the color draining from my face. When his eyes stretched wide, I mouthed "*It's my mom!*"

"Oh. Fuck." He covered his mouth with his hand.

I brought the phone back to my ear. "Mom? Are you still there?"

"Yes, baby. Who is it? Is that the fighter?"

I let out the loudest, most obvious sigh of relief. "Yeah, Mom. It's the fighter. He's having a hard time with something, and he needs my help."

I could have sworn I heard my sister laughing in the background.

"Oh, well tell him I said hello, honey," my mom said.

I put her on speaker phone.

"Kage, my mom said hello. She and my sister are on your website looking at your crack right now."

"Jamie!" my mom admonished from the other end of the line. Then I heard my sister howling with laughter for sure.

Kage narrowed his eyes and shook his head at me. "Hello, Mrs. Atwood. Nice to talk to you again."

"Oh, hello Michael. I didn't know you could hear me. Please disregard my son's rudeness, and you have my blessing to take it out of his paycheck."

"Mom, no fair!" I yelled.

Kage leaned close to my ear and said, "I'll just take it out of your ass." To illustrate, he reached around and squeezed my ass cheek with one large hand, his fingers spreading me and bruising my flesh.

It gave me chills, and I groaned out loud.

"Mom, I've gotta go."

"Okay, honey. Goodnight."

I'd clicked off before the last word was completely out of her mouth. Then Kage was on me. He brought his other hand around to grab my other ass cheek, squeezing until I groaned again.

"I love that sound," he said before he claimed my mouth with his. My lips were already parted, and he just slid his tongue right between them, squeezing my ass again until I moaned into his mouth. Then he lost it.

He pulled me close and rutted against me, cock to cock through our shorts, kissing my throat so thoroughly I had to throw my head back to give him access. I'd never felt so ravished. I tangled my fingers in his hair and pulled, encouraging as much contact as I could get.

Fuck, I needed to get closer.

"Get rid of this," he growled, pulling my shirt so hard he ripped it. I didn't even care that it was one of my favorite shirts. I helped him pull it the rest of the way off without completely destroying it. That's when I noticed he had come to my room barefoot.

"You're not wearing shoes," I pointed out breathlessly.

"Or underwear." He pulled his shorts off and kicked them away, revealing his entire amazing body, and that gorgeous cock reaching out for me.

I grabbed hold of it without thinking, bit my lip and looked into his eyes, started stroking. I loved the way his mouth went slack and his eyelids fell halfway shut. I leaned in and sucked his bottom lip into my mouth, thrilling at the taste of him, the feel of his soft but masculine lips. The sandpaper scrape of his stubble against my bottom lip as I sucked on his.

He pulled away. "You ever jerked a guy off before?"

I shook my head. "No."

"Ever fucked a guy?"

I shook my head again and swallowed hard at the mere thought of it.

"Ever sucked a guy's dick?"

"Only yours."

He smiled. "Good. Let's keep it that way." He turned me around and walked me toward the bed, holding onto my biceps, sticking close behind me, talking softly to me. "I'm going to make you mine now. If that's what you want."

"Yes." I whispered, letting him herd me toward the bed and push me down face first. My feet were still on the floor, keeping me grounded. My only link with the real world.

He pulled my shorts and boxer briefs down over my ass, over my calves, and I stepped out of them. Then we were both naked, and I was bent over the bed, at his mercy. His hand caressed over my calf muscle, over my thigh, all the way back up to my ass. He rubbed it with a calloused palm.

I couldn't see him, only feel.

"You have a beautiful body, Jamie. I could look at you all day long, every day, and never get tired of looking."

"Thank you," I whispered. It was lame, but my head was reeling from his words. He thought my body was beautiful? It was almost unbelievable.

He kept moving his rough hands over my skin, caressing and exploring as if it were his first time seeing me. "Every time I look at you, I want to do this." He dropped his hard cock onto the track of my ass crack and ran it slowly up and down.

The drag of skin on skin and the thought of what he was doing had me making little noises that I didn't necessarily want to be making. Kage chuckled in his sexy, low voice. He grabbed me by the back of the neck and put just enough pressure there to thrill me, to hold me still. Then I felt the head of his cock as he slapped it against the sensitive skin nestled between my ass and balls. The spot I loved to press the tip of my finger against when I was close to coming.

I nearly flew off the bed. Went up on my toes. Buried my face in the mattress to mute my involuntary cry.

"Mmmm…" Kage hummed quietly. "Jamie's got a magic button?"

I felt him moving behind me. He went down on his knees, then grabbed me around the ankles and forced my legs farther apart. I turned my face to the side, my cheek flat on the bed, and curved my neck to look back at him— see what he was doing. When he caught me looking, he smiled at me and slid just the tip of his tongue out to tease me. Then he leaned forward and licked and sucked an agonizing trail from my balls all the way to my asshole.

If I'd ever heard such a sound come out of my mouth, I certainly don't remember it. It was somewhere between a growl and a squeal, and I quickly swallowed it back and held my breath against the overwhelming sensations.

"My God," I groaned when he pulled my ass cheeks apart with his fingers and used the tip of his tongue to prod at my hole, alternately pressing just inside the opening and pulling back with a gentle sucking action. It was like French kissing, but… *there.*

I had honestly never felt anything more stimulating, had never been more turned on in my life. Especially when he reached down with two fingers and pressed my taint. The sounds started back up, but this time I couldn't stifle them. I just let it roll. My knees were quivering, and I was all feeling, no brain, rubbing my cock against the edge of the mattress for relief.

"Kage… Can't take it. Jesus, Kage…" He wouldn't let up on the unholy stimulation, using his tongue and lips in ways I had never even considered before. I could feel the tell-tale rhythmic movements that let me know he was jerking himself off. Maybe he was close. "I'm gonna come, Kage. I can't take it."

Then he stopped, stood up and slapped my ass cheek hard. "Turn over," he ordered.

I flipped over immediately, presenting him with my very hard, very ready erection. He climbed onto the bed and stretched his body out over mine, hovering above me in perfect push-up form, and lowered himself to kiss my lips. Softly, thoroughly he kissed me before moving down to my jaw, my neck, the hollow at the base of my throat where my necklace lay. Then he shifted down and took my nipple between his lips, first sucking, then biting, until I was moaning again.

"You're gonna kill me," I whispered.

He laughed, then moved down until his face was even with my cock. I realized it was the first time he'd ever seen me fully hard, and suddenly I was shy. The way he was looking at me, admiring me, took my breath away.

"Just as pretty as every other inch of you," he said reverently as he bent to take it into his mouth.

He was rough with it from the beginning, having recently given an aggressive tongue lashing to my other side, and I sucked in a sharp breath. He groaned around me, sending vibrations through my entire body. Bridging my hips up off the bed, I pushed up into his throat without an ounce of restraint, over and over and over, feeling his throat spasm deliciously around the head of my cock every time it bottomed out.

I fucked his throat hard, and he took it like a champ, stroking his own dick with a fiery passion that rivaled my own. The level of heat between us was staggering. Never during sex had I felt so equal, so balanced, so complete— like matching halves of a whole.

When I couldn't watch him swallow my cock and stroke himself anymore, when the sensations finally became too damn much and I had to blow, I threw my head back and bridged my hips in one final thrust, digging my heels into the mattress and unloading everything I had into the depths of his throat.

Wave after wave of delicious pleasure washed through me until I thought my leg muscles would cramp from holding myself frozen in that position. Finally I relaxed my legs and lowered my weight back down onto the bed.

I was empty and limp, smiling and sated, when Kage climbed up the bed and knelt on both knees beside my head. His face was flushed with passion, with wanting me, and I thought it was the most beautiful thing I'd ever seen. He worshiped my face through hooded lids, biting his full bottom lip between his teeth hard enough to leave marks. As I watched, he pulled on his cock with the unstudied ease of one who knows his own equipment by heart— two fingers under, thumb on top, just the right torque— and shot ropes of hot cum all over my eager face.

Afterward, we lay on my bed and cuddled. I was spooned into his lap, his soft cock niched into the cleft of my ass. It reminded me of the first time I had let him cuddle me in bed, so in denial of how much I had wanted him. That night seemed ages ago.

"I can't believe this is happening," I admitted as his hands roamed my body.

He laughed quietly and planted a little kiss in my hair. "I can't believe it took so long."

I turned over in his arms and faced him, draping my leg over his hip. "I'm just so… I don't know." I touched his face, hoping he could feel what I couldn't find words to express.

He smiled back. Rolled my necklace between his thumb and forefinger. "What is this?"

"A necklace," I said.

"I know that, smart-ass. What does it mean?"

"My mom gave it to me. It's an Irish symbol, like a love thing. Like a code. You see it's a crowned heart being held between two hands?"

"Really?" He squinted at it. "Oh, I see it now. It would be easier to tell if you weren't wearing it upside-down."

I smiled. "That's the code part. Usually it's on a ring, but I figure it works the same way on a necklace. When you're single, you wear the point of the heart facing away from your heart. Then, when you meet your soulmate, you're supposed to turn it around." I laughed self-consciously. "I know, it's girly shit. I just wanted it because my sister got one for her sixteenth birthday, so my mom had one made that was a little more my style."

Suddenly there was a huge lump in my throat.

"You thinking about your mom?" he asked.

I nodded, trying to will the tears not to come. God, that was the last thing I needed to do. Have the most amazing sexual experience of my entire life, then break down in tears. My eyes were stinging, and the way Kage was looking at me was not helping.

"Here, turn back over," he suggested, as if he knew. Once I was spooned against him again, he said, "There's nothing wrong with crying for someone you love."

18

WHEN I woke up the next morning, Kage was gone. There was no note, no text message, nothing.

I drafted a text to him. *"Morning, sexy. Where did you disappear to?"*

I read it at least ten times. Was it too much calling him sexy? Should I play it cool and not text at all? I deleted the word *sexy*, typed it back in, then deleted the entire text.

I pulled on a pair of boxer briefs, then some shorts on over them. My reflection looked surprisingly sad after the glorious night we'd had. It was because I'd woken up without Kage beside me, and that was messed up. I'd never even spent the night with Layla, and we had dated for months.

Kage takes off the morning after, and I'm freaking out.

There was a knock at the door, and I almost came out of my skin. For a moment, I thought for sure it was Kage. But a glance through the peephole revealed the room service guy.

I pulled open the door and offered him a lukewarm smile. "Thanks." I ran to the kitchen and grabbed the three dollar bills on the counter. Then I took my food and tipped him.

Beneath the silver dome lid of the tray was my feast. Egg whites. Proatmeal. Dry wheat toast. Black coffee. *Fucking tomatoes.* I pulled my water jug out of the fridge and started chugging it. Where the hell was Kage?

Finally, I couldn't take it anymore. I grabbed my phone and texted, *"Where are you?"* This time I actually hit send.

"My apartment," he texted back. *"Had to take care of something. Come up after breakfast?"*

Relief washed over me. *"Sure."*

I was so screwed.

But now that I'd solved the mystery of the missing fighter, I had an appetite. I ate every bite on the tray, even the tomatoes. Then I took a shower, so that I didn't seem too eager. Plus, I thought it might be uncouth to show up wearing the remnants of his cum from the night before.

Kage answered the door to his apartment dressed only in boxers. He appeared freshly showered as well, his hair wet and slicked back, his skin scented with body wash.

Instead of inviting me in and engaging in conversation like he normally would have, Kage pulled my t-shirt over my head and had me in his arms before the door had even snapped closed behind me.

He clung to me, his face buried in the curve between my neck and shoulder, breathing heavily. He pawed ineffectually at my shorts until I pulled them down myself. But he didn't attack me like he had the night before. We just stood there in front of the door, holding each other. When I tried to pull back to get a look at his face, he held tight and wouldn't let me see him.

"Kage, are you okay? You're scaring me. Is everything all right?"

"I'm fine. Let's just watch TV or something." He let go of me, went into the living room, and used the remote to turn on the classic movie channel. Some black and white thing was playing, but I wasn't going to argue about his choice of movie.

We sat down on the sofa, looking straight ahead at the TV with only our thighs touching. This lasted for about sixty seconds, then Kage was up again. He went into the kitchen and refilled his jug with filtered water. He seemed severely agitated. I'm ashamed to admit it now, but my first thought was that he was on drugs— like cocaine or PCP or something. He was so damn jumpy.

Then he just stopped in the middle of the kitchen holding that jug of water.

"I can't breathe," he said. The words came out a soft gasp, his hand flattened over his chest. "I knew it. Fuuuck… not now. God, here it comes. I can't breathe. I can't breathe."

My whole body went white hot.

"Kage, what is it?" I was at his side in an instant.

He leaned against the counter and slammed his half full jug of water down, mangling it and sending water gushing all over the granite. It trickled from the far end of the counter and puddled onto the floor, but cleaning it up was the least of my concerns.

Kage sucked in a deep breath through his nose and blew it out slowly through lips stretched into a tight line so that only a thin stream could escape. He repeated the process over and over, not speaking, while I stood impotently beside him. I was afraid to touch him.

"Are you okay?" I asked, already knowing the answer to the question. "Should I call 911? You say you can't breathe, but you're breathing, Kage. You *are* breathing."

"Get my cell," he groaned, dropping his head to the counter, heedless of the water puddled there. He was still dragging in those labored breaths and pushing out thin ribbons of carbon dioxide. I realized he was purposely hypoventilating— the equivalent to breathing into a paper bag— and that meant he felt like he was close to passing out.

I ran as fast as I could to the sofa and grabbed his cell phone from the cushion. I wished I could take time to turn the TV off. It was loud and distracting, but I had to get back to Kage before he lost consciousness and banged his head or something.

Absurdly, it occurred to me that I was worrying about a fighter who had been slammed and punched and kicked and choked relentlessly his entire life.

"There's a number on there. It says Julie. Call it, tell her to meet me."

I fumbled with the phone and got the number dialed.

"Put it on speaker," he said at the last second. I did.

"Kage, what is it?" a female voice asked, sounding alarmed.

"I can't breathe," he told her simply.

"I'm on my way," she said. "Headed out the door right now. Are you at your place?"

"Yeah." He slowed his breathing even more. "Jamie's with me."

"Can he hear me?" Her voice seemed to carry a note of caution.

He nodded, then gasped. "Yes. You're on speaker."

"Jamie," she said firmly, surprising me. "Get Michael to the bed. Make him lie down, okay?"

"Okay," I said, hating the panic in my voice. I needed to pull it together, be strong for Kage.

"He's going to be fine," she told me. Even thinned out over a cell phone line, her voice was convincing. Commanding. "He's having a panic attack, that's all. It feels very scary to him, but he's not in any real physical danger. Just get him to the bed and comfort him the best you can. I'm already in the car, and I'll be there in less than fifteen minutes."

"All right," I said, my voice warbling with my own wave of panic.

"Jamie," she called, and I had to pull the phone back to my ear. "Don't let him out of your sight."

After I hung up the phone, I took Kage by the arm and led him slowly to the bed. He seemed weak, like the energy to move had been stripped from him. I got the feeling that if I let go of him, he'd sink down and not try to get back up— which is exactly what he did when we reached the bed.

I left him there lying sideways on the bed long enough to run to the front door and unlock it. Then I was at his side again.

I picked his legs up and got them onto the bed while he continued to hypoventilate and stare at the ceiling. His breathing was chillingly similar to my grandfather's on his final emergency room visit. A longtime emphysema sufferer, he'd lived with us for the final years of his life. During that time, we made frequent trips to the ER. On that last night, I'd held his frail, grasping hand as he fought for breath. The tube blowing oxygen into his nose did little to comfort him.

His words had been desperate, punctuated by labored breaths.

"Don't want." *breath.* "To do it." *breath.* "Anymore." *breath.*

He was tired. So tired. His chest heaved with exertion.

The nurse had explained what he was going through. How the work of breathing had become too much for him, how he was physically and emotionally exhausted, how he would give up if only his body would let him. But the instinct to survive is strong— much stronger than the will.

My grandfather had given up, but his body would not. *Could not.*

We'd stood watch over him for hours, me on one side, my mom on the other, and the rest of the family at the foot of the bed. I cried and swiped at my tears with the back of my left hand, because my right hand was wound in his gnarled and discolored fingers. I held on because it was all I could do. In my mind I felt shame, because I prayed for him to get relief. I prayed for him to die.

That night they put my grandfather on a ventilator, and he never came off of it. Not until they put the sheet over his head.

I blinked away the memory and looked at Kage lying there on his bed— fit and fine and in the prime of his life— gasping for air and looking so damn tired.

How could this be happening to him?

"I'm sorry, Jamie," he whispered. As if he had any reason to apologize to me when he was the one suffering.

I climbed into bed beside him and took his hand in mine, cuddling close, careful not to put any pressure on his chest or impede his breathing in any way. I laid a kiss on his shoulder and waited, mildly concerned that some strange woman was going to find us like that— cuddled in his bed in nothing but our boxers. Would it be obvious that we were lovers? When Kage had told her I was with him, it seemed as though she already knew who I was. They had talked about me before. Maybe she already knew about us.

Kage obviously trusted her. It seemed I had to trust her, too.

When the door clicked open and I heard her approaching the bedroom, I closed my eyes and braced myself for the worst. But she came in and introduced herself in a businesslike manner.

"Hi, Jamie. I'm Dr. Julie Tanner." Her dark hair was smoothed back into a conservative bun at the nape of her slender neck, revealing a beautiful face that was fresh and free of makeup. There was concern in her brown eyes.

A doctor. Now things were starting to make sense. She reached a hand out to shake mine.

"Uh… nice to meet you," I said quietly, glancing down at my thin boxer briefs and then at Kage's boxers, always in danger of gaping open. I suddenly felt very under-dressed, more so than I thought I would now that she was actually here, her keen eyes roving over Kage's body. A blush crept onto my cheeks. "I need to throw some clothes on. I just didn't want to leave him until you got here."

I crawled down the bed and got a t-shirt and shorts out of Kage's dresser and put them on. They hung loosely from my smaller frame, but I didn't care. I wanted to wear his clothes, because it made me feel like I belonged to him.

When I returned to the doctor's side, she was injecting something into Kage's upper arm.

"What's that?" I asked, unable to help myself.

"Librium." She capped the syringe and pressed a wadded up gauze square to the injection site, then secured it with a bandage. "It's to calm him down and help with the anxiety. He'll be out of it for a while. Why don't you go on back to your room and let me take care of him?"

"You sure? I don't mind staying."

She smiled, but it wasn't an altogether friendly look. More like a mask for barely-reined-in irritation. "I'm sure you wouldn't. But I've been treating Michael for a long time. We have a system we've developed over the years for dealing with these things."

"He can stay," Kage said, and his voice was so bland it scared me. For once, he truly did sound like a machine.

"I understand you want to keep your friend close by." Dr. Tanner rested her hand on his abdomen and spoke softly, her words barely reaching my ears. "But you know it's not for the best. Do you really want him to see you this way?"

I opened my mouth to protest. She was making it sound horrible, and her hand on his belly was really bothering me. I wanted to climb into bed with him, wrap myself around him, and tell that lady to back off. Who the hell did she think she was?

But I knew the answer to that. She was his doctor. His long-time doctor. I had known him for less than two months and had been intimate with him for three days. So the real question was probably who the hell did I think I was?

I took a deep breath and made up my mind. "She's right, Kage. I'm going to go for a run and work for a bit. See if I can get you some more appearances. I'll drop by later when you're feeling better."

He didn't answer, and the doctor acted like I hadn't spoken. It was as if I'd already gone. So I let myself out of his apartment, sparing a glance backward and cringing at the sight of that woman sitting on his bed.

OVER the next few days, I saw little of Kage. When I'd stopped back by his apartment to see how he was doing the night of the anxiety attack, no one had answered the door. I called and left a text message, but both had gone unanswered.

He was conspicuously absent from his training sessions, but Marco graciously, and surprisingly, offered to work me out. So I worked out, pouring everything I had into wearing myself out so badly that I didn't have the energy to think about Kage and wonder where he was.

Marco said he didn't know anything, but I suspected he wasn't being completely truthful with me.

In his absence, I changed his ringtone to a loop of *Mama Said Knock You Out*. It was cheesy, but I needed something to recognize him by when he called. On Wednesday afternoon, I heard it for the first time and nearly broke my neck trying to get to the phone.

"Hello?" I tried to sound nonchalant.

"You working hard for me?" That voice. I hadn't even realized how much I had needed to hear it.

"Yes."

"Good. I like to get my money's worth."

My mouth went dry.

"Trust me. You're getting a bargain."

He laughed, and even through the phone it gave me chills. "I know I am." He paused for a few seconds, and dead air stretched conspicuously between us. "You want to see me fight?"

"Yes!" No hesitation on my part. This is what I'd been waiting for.

"It will be this Friday night. I won't see you before then, so… Well, I'll see you then." He clicked off, leaving me to wonder what he'd been about to say. And where I needed to go to see him fight. There were too many questions, and too much excitement.

I was going to see Kage fight. The thought of it had butterflies already dancing in my stomach. No way I could concentrate for the next two days.

His ringtone blared from my phone again, and I answered it.

"I forgot to ask," he said. "How do you want me to finish this guy?"

I chuckled, amused by his bravado. "Something fancy. How about a flying knee?"

"When?"

"What do you mean, when?"

"I mean when in the fight? Should I take him out immediately or toy with him a bit?"

I laughed. "Jesus, your ego knows no bounds. Okay, hotshot. I think you should wait until the second round. It's the first time I've seen you fight, so you need to put on a show for me."

"Done. And Jamie… If I finish him with a flying knee in Round Two, I get your ass as the prize."

19

AT FOUR o'clock on Friday afternoon, a courier showed up at the desk of the office and handed Catwoman Cathy a gray metallic envelope with *Mr. James Atwood* printed on the front. There was an invitation inside— one of those expensive-looking ones they sent out for weddings. It said simply:

Alcazar entrance, 6pm sharp.

The white Range Rover was waiting at the curb when I stepped through the front doors of the Alcazar at six o'clock. Aldo begrudgingly opened the door for me, and I climbed inside.

As on the ride in from the airport, I marveled at the supple beauty of the tobacco-colored leather interior and giggled yet again when the seatbelt hugged me without being prompted. This time, however, I tried to remember all of the features Kage had described to me during one of our random conversations. I found the control to lounge back and bring the leg rest up, opened the center console refrigerator and pulled out a chilled bottle of water, and brought the lap desk up and down. All the while, I wished I had someone with whom to share the amazing experience.

I was in the belly of a great white shark, cruising out to God knows where on the outskirts of Sin City, leaving the lights and bustle behind. It was terrifying in a way to leave the oddly comforting artifice behind— the commercials, the casinos, the bachelor parties, the *What happens in Vegas stays in Vegas.* It was all a big, expensive facade, wasn't it? A tourist attraction built around darker business.

And sometimes you had to be driven out to the desert.

I shivered at the thought and tried to shove away the montage of gangster movie scenes that assaulted me. Surely that wasn't what this was. Kage's uncle couldn't possibly be that unsavory a character. Look at the boy he had raised.

A boy with issues. That much was becoming clearer.

The drive out was quiet— almost too quiet. Whatever it was that Aldo and Aaron normally talked about, they weren't talking about it with me in the vehicle. Then again, I'd never actually heard Aaron speak. Maybe he was mute.

"Could we have some music?" I asked.

Aldo touched the dashboard computer screen, and some opera song came blaring out of the undeniably good speakers. I sighed and leaned back in my seat, closed my eyes, and wished like hell I hadn't asked for music. Because *damn.* Couldn't he have turned on some rap or pop? Even country would have been better than this, mainly because now I felt even more like I was in a gangster movie. Didn't they always play opera when they were slitting someone's throat?

Fortunately I made it to our destination in one piece, despite the creepy opera music.

Aldo shut off the Land Rover and opened my door for me. The uncomfortable look on his face had me almost feeling sorry for him. He clearly hated my guts, and though I couldn't fathom why, the fact that he was forced to serve me had to have been humiliating for him.

When I stepped out of the SUV, I was greeted by the sight of a warehouse surrounded by cars. That was all. No lights, no fanfare, no valet parking. Just a warehouse that looked like it had seen better days, and a parking lot full of cars that ranged from broken-down to luxurious. Most of them were of the luxurious type.

Aldo and Aaron approached the warehouse, and I followed. The lack of conversation with these two was always a little disconcerting, making me feel more like a prisoner than a guest.

Aldo pulled the door open, and the loud squeal of metal on metal announced our arrival. About fifty men and women were inside the building, dressed in much better clothing than I was wearing. In my mind, I had imagined an underground fight would be a bunch of guys in torn flannel with dirty fingernails, shaggy hair, and prison tattoos crowded around a makeshift ring surrounded by chicken wire. The scene before me could have easily been intermission at a Broadway show.

I scanned the room for any sign of Kage. The sight of his handsome face and imposing body would have instantly put me at ease, especially since I hadn't seen it for days, but he wasn't anywhere in the crowd. He was probably in some back room meditating or sparring with Marco.

Meanwhile, I was sweating bullets.

As I was studying a man whom I could have sworn was famous, I felt the presence of someone very close behind me. My heart immediately jumped, and I spun around expecting to see Kage. Instead, I came face-to-face with a dapper, dark-haired man of about fifty. He was thin and tall in a ridiculously well-cut suit, and he practically sparkled, as if he'd been buffed and polished. I knew who he was instantly. He had the same vague Latin look as Kage, with the perfect perma-tan and five-o'clock shadow, but his eyes were a deep brown rather than green like his nephew's.

"Jamie," he said in a smooth, deep voice. "I'm Peter Santori."

I swallowed and tried to find my own voice. "Mr. Santori? I can't believe I'm finally meeting you."

He shrugged, but his eyes were shrewd. "I stay busy. It's not a simple affair to set up meetings with employees these days."

Employees. Yikes.

The guy was good at maintaining distance and superiority. I wondered how superior he'd feel if he knew about the intimacy his nephew and I shared. If he knew I'd wrapped my lips around his cock and swallowed his cum. Would he welcome me into his inner circle then, or would he have me taken out into the desert and dismembered to a soundtrack of opera music?

Looking into his calculating eyes, I'd have to say I was leaning toward the latter.

"Interesting place you have here," I said. When he didn't reply, I continued. "So this is where Kage fights. I can't wait to see him in action. So far I've only seen him train."

"Marco tells me you've been present at a lot of training sessions, and that you've even taken to utilizing his services for yourself."

Funny, when Mr. Santori said it, it sounded like I was stealing from the company. Like I was swiping staplers and post-it notes from the supply closet.

"Um, well, Kage invited me to participate in the workouts. Of course, I don't do anything major. None of that advanced stuff they work on."

He nodded slowly. "Well, I need to speak to some colleagues of mine before the fight begins, so I suppose we'll say goodbye for now." He shook my hand, and somehow he made it feel like a great honor was being bestowed upon me. I disliked him for that— for making me feel truly inferior.

I stood by myself in the center of that small sea of glitterati, watching Mr. Santori make his way deliberately through the crowd, occasionally stopping to speak to someone.

This was his place. In this warehouse, he was the man. That much was crystal clear.

There were folding chairs set up all around the octagon, and I found one near the front, plopped down in it and stayed there. Long minutes of boredom stretched into even longer minutes of awkwardness, until finally there was a commotion near the entrance of the cage. A stocky middle-aged man in a red t-shirt stepped into the ring, and people began moving in and claiming all of the seats around me. Soon, it was standing room only.

An announcer stood behind a corner podium and spoke into his microphone, his voice booming over the sound system. "Good evening, ladies and gentlemen. Welcome to another exciting fight night. As always, if the fighter in the blue corner can best the as-yet-undefeated Michael "The Machine" Kage, he will walk out of here with a hundred-thousand-dollars in cash. Let's wish both men good luck as they embark on this virtually no-holds-barred evening of fun and games."

The small crowd cheered for a moment, and then the challenger came trotting through a door at the back of the room. He had a small entourage of his people with him. It was nothing like the dramatic entrance of the fighters on UFC pay-per-view. It was somber and a little scary, with no music to dress it up. No theatrics. This was going to be nothing more than a fight, plain and simple.

After the first fighter, who remained nameless and was referred to only as *the challenger,* entered the octagon, Kage appeared at the door. My breath caught in my chest when I saw him.

That's my guy, I thought. *My lover.*

He stalked intimidatingly into the ring wearing nothing but a pair of red trunks, his hair pulled into that cute little queue atop his head. But that was where the cute ended. This Michael Kage looked alarmingly unlike the guy I was falling for. His green eyes appeared darker and more calculating than I'd ever seen them, even that day in the restaurant. I hated to admit it, but he looked frighteningly like his uncle— whom I had no problem believing would have me assassinated and dumped in the desert.

Kage walked into the ring looking neither hyper nor plodding. He had an air of confidence about him that made posturing unnecessary. I waited for him to notice me, but he seemed oblivious to the fact that I was even present. Probably a good thing. It meant he was focused, and according to Marco, that was half of winning.

The referee called the two men out to the center of the ring, had them touch gloves, and sent them to their respective corners. Then the announcer rang a bell, and the fighters were on the move.

The contender was aggressive, pressing in on Kage even before the echo of the bell had died. He released a combination of powerful if predictable punches— jab, cross, left hook to the body—presumably to get Kage off balance and on the defensive, but Kage was light on his feet. He easily sidestepped the guy's attack before catching him with a right cross to the side of his head. It rocked the guy good, but he recovered quickly, and smacked Kage with a leg kick before moving out of reach. Kage didn't flinch, though I saw an ugly red mark spreading on the outside of his thigh.

He glanced at the mark, then looked up at the guy, raised his eyebrows and smiled. I couldn't believe it. He looked perfectly delighted that the guy had finally landed something.

There was a flash of panic across the other guy's face, but he masked it quickly and moved back in for another rapid-fire combo. He was fast, but he was no match for Kage's unorthodox footwork or his ability to anticipate movements. With smooth efficiency, Kage either dodged or blocked everything his opponent threw at him. Then he spun around and took the guy's back.

Wrapping his arms around him from behind, Kage lifted the man into the air, thrust his hips forward and bent his knees, and slammed the man backward over his shoulder in the smoothest suplex I'd ever seen. Before the man could get his bearings, Kage was on top of him.

He was able to pull a half guard on Kage before being pounded nearly senseless by Kage's brutal hammer fists and elbows. Over and over he struck the fighter, until I was afraid he might kill him. Still the ref didn't stop the fight. Then when the guy was nearly done, had almost stopped fighting back completely, Kage jumped to his feet and let him up.

It almost looked like mercy, but I knew. It was exactly the opposite.

The entire round was a game of cat and mouse, with the cat looking like he was ready to eat the mouse at any second. Kage wasn't playful exactly, but he was enjoying the chase, getting off on toying with his opponent.

I wondered if the other spectators could see that, or if it was just because I was coming to know him so intimately. Of course, there was always the possibility that I was imagining it.

I didn't have to wait long for my suspicion to be verified.

In the final seconds of the first round, the challenger, who looked frighteningly banged up in the face, caught Kage with a hard right cross to the temple, splitting the skin next to his eye. My throat tightened and my heart skipped a beat. The thought of him getting hurt— really hurt— and of me having to watch it happen had not really hit home until then. It was the first time I'd ever seen a wound like that on his face, and I hoped it would be the last.

I saw the change in Kage's demeanor when it happened. A blank mask dropped over his face, and he looked like he was officially not playing anymore. If the bell hadn't sounded when it did, I imagine he would have unleashed his full fury on the guy. Instead, they separated to their corners, and the challenger got patched up while his coach yammered nonstop at him.

Kage kept his eyes locked on his opponent the entire time, looking strangely like he'd never experienced an emotion in his life. Cold, calculating, the antithesis of the guy who had held me while I cried for my mother, and then let me fall asleep in his arms.

I couldn't hear what Marco was telling him, but Kage smiled and jumped up ready to go when the bell sounded for Round Two.

Kage came in with a couple of sly jabs, bounced lithely out of the way when his opponent attempted a flailing counterattack. The guy's face looked like he'd been in a car accident. His left eye was swollen, and blood ran from his eye socket to his throat. He was done already at that point. I don't think there was a doubt in anyone's mind. But somehow he summoned a burst of energy— or more accurately desperation— and attempted to take it back to the ground, presumably to try for a last ditch submission. But Kage, with his lightning fast reflexes and talent for anticipating moves, saw it coming. The second the man changed levels and ducked down to shoot his legs for the takedown, Kage caught him with a vicious flying knee to the face.

The guy dropped like a sack of potatoes. Knocked out cold.

I sat there in my chair, my breath coming way too fast. Kage had finished the guy in exactly the way I had requested. How could that be? My mind spun, trying to seize on anything that made sense other than the fact that he had been in control the entire fight. That he had orchestrated it.

Inside the octagon, the referee, a doctor, and several other men were examining the fallen fighter and trying to rouse him. Kage glanced back at him once, saw him move, and then strutted right over to the edge of the cage where I was sitting. As he passed by me, he tapped his fist against his chest once, right over his heart, then looked directly into my eyes just long enough to give me a secret wink that sent shivers down my spine.

That's when I realized he was peacocking for me. The entire fight had been nothing more than my lover proving himself to me, and his message was clear: *I just smashed that guy's face for you. Just like you asked.*

For a moment, I thought I might be sick. With no more thought than ordering from a takeout menu, I'd just ordered a man knocked unconscious with a brutal knee to the face. And what's worse, I got my wish.

Kage left the octagon with no fanfare or theatrics. This was a private show, not one of the pay-per-view extravaganzas I was used to watching. I sat quietly, studying the injured fighter as he got to his feet, sensing the crowd moving out of the seats and away from me. Then Aldo was standing beside me, pulling something from inside his jacket, and handing me a sealed envelope with my name scrawled across the front in a messy hand.

Did Kage write this? After all we'd done, I still didn't know what his handwriting looked like.

I tore open the very end, careful not to damage the writing. Inside was a sheet of notebook paper with one sentence written on it.

"That ass is mine."

With my heart pounding like a war drum, I reached into the envelope and pulled out the key card to Kage's apartment.

Aldo waited beside me, looking respectfully away as I read my message. When I stood up, he led me back to the Land Rover without a word and drove me home, with Aaron riding shotgun as always. This time I barely noticed the opera music. I was too busy fretting over what was about to happen when Kage came home.

20

I THINK I can safely say I'd never experienced true anticipation before that night. Time was a taunting beast in the room with me as I sat naked on Kage's sectional.

Had I ever been so naked in my entire life?

My skin was hyper-sensitive to the velvety feel of the sofa's upholstery. In fact, I was hyper-sensitive to everything. The light, which I'd intentionally kept low, still seemed too bright. The air felt much cooler than normal, causing me to shiver a little, and the subtle sounds of Kage's empty apartment that normally went undetected were unnaturally loud. In the kitchen, the ice maker churned out a few filtered cubes. The Xbox hummed from its shelf in the media cabinet. Once, I thought I may have heard the elevator making its way to the penthouse floor, and that little tease in particular was tough to handle.

After an hour of waiting, my nerves were shot. How long would I have to wait? What would he do to me when he got there? Did he have a key card, or had he given me his only one? What if someone else came to the door, and I answered it in my birthday suit? Because I didn't dare answer it any other way. Didn't want there to be any question about whether or not I wanted Kage. I was ready.

By the time I finally heard the elevator arrive for real, my hands were a little shaky. I thought I would pass out listening to his footsteps approach the door and stop in front of it. I waited for a knock, but instead I heard a card slide through the electronic lock. It clicked, and the door swung open.

Kage strode in wearing his faded red t-shirt, and a pair of threadbare jeans that hung low enough to reveal his boxers. His hair was still knotted at the top of his head, though a few strands had worked their way loose. Without a word, he stepped out of his shoes at the door, pulled his t-shirt over his head and dropped it on the floor. The jeans came next. He worked the sexy button fly with nimble fingers as he approached.

He came to a stop directly in front of me where I sat on the sofa, and I looked up at him, waiting.

"Open your mouth," he said, pushing his pants to his hips and bringing out his cock. It was already hard, the head swollen and flushed.

I did as he said. Opened my mouth wide, anticipating the taste of his cock— a taste I already knew by heart. My own dick had waxed and waned through varying degrees of hardness ever since I'd received his note. Hell, since before that if I was honest. When I really thought about it, it seemed it had been that way since I'd gotten my first glimpse of Michael Kage.

He bent over the sofa, grasping the back with one hand and leaning on it for support, and fed his cock impatiently into my waiting mouth. He wasn't gentle. He shoved it down my throat until I choked and pulled back, only to shove it in again just as hard.

It reminded me of his performance in the ring, only now I was the mouse. The barbaric look in his eyes was still there, though now it was tinged with desire— and something else. Something that gave me hope and made my heart seize in my chest.

Kage was relentless, needy, leaning even farther in as I instinctively pulled back for breath. But I didn't want him to stop. I loved it. Loved it when he was rough. Because I was learning that the more he needed me, the rougher he got. And tonight he needed me bad.

He pushed me down onto my back on the sofa, then stripped off his jeans and underwear. When he was naked, he climbed on top of me and straddled my chest, pinning my shoulders to the sofa. Then he knelt up over me and forced his cock rudely into my mouth. All I could do was take it and suck it, looking up at him with watering eyes as he loomed over me and labored.

His face was tight with lust, as if he might lose control at any moment. But he was strong, and I knew he wasn't about to let go until he was good and ready. If he could choreograph a fight against a skilled opponent with a hundred grand on the line, he could damn sure control himself in bed.

He fucked my mouth with long strokes, not giving me a chance to speak. All I could do was grunt and whimper around him as he watched me closely with his shrewd, calculating eyes.

"My sweet college boy," he said in a reverent voice, reaching down with one hand and running his fingers through my hair.

He was choking me with his cock, but loving me with his touch and his words. It was the most cherished I'd ever felt, being used and loved at the same time, being needed so fiercely.

After a moment, he slipped his hand under my neck and cupped the back of my skull with his large hand. He lifted my head off the sofa so that it was at nearly a ninety-degree angle, and fucked my mouth deep and slow, using his hand to keep my head still. It was a lot like dirty boxing. I would have told him so if I could have spoken.

He didn't keep me that way for long, though. He sensed the very moment when I'd had enough, and he released my head back down to the sofa and pulled out. My mouth and his cock were both over-wet with saliva, and he rubbed the slicked head against my battered lips. Back and forth he dragged it over my mouth, watching me with those lust-filled eyes.

"Get to the bed," Kage said finally, and he stood and let me up. I knew what was about to happen. Knew what that look in his eyes meant. I had to get my bearings as I made my way to his room and climbed onto the bed with shaky legs.

I laid back on the bed and spread my legs, reaching down to pump my cock as I watched him approach. Then I bit my lip, gave him my best come hither look, and surprised myself with my first words of the evening. "You didn't shower. I can smell you on me."

"And that gets you off?"

"Yes," I whispered, still working myself, knowing I needed to stop soon. I was dangerously close to hitting that point when coming was too much of a temptation to stop. "I didn't shower, either," I said.

The more time I spent around Kage, the more his scent aroused me. I wondered if it was the same for him.

"You always smell sweet." He laughed darkly. "I smell like sweat, blood and fear. But I wanted you to smell it on me, Jamie. I wanted you to smell it on me the first time I fuck you. So you'll know who I really am. I need you to know me."

"I do know you," I said. "And you're perfect."

"Baby, don't be naïve. I'm a killing machine. The only things that separate me from the inside of a jail cell are a referee and a bell."

I dropped onto my back, staring up at those same rafters that had shifted and danced in hallucinations that seemed so long ago. "All I know is I want to be with you."

Kage climbed on top of me, planking up onto his elbows and lowering his body so that we were touching from hip to toe. Our cocks aligned against each other, and nothing had ever felt so good or so right.

His stubble scrubbed against my cheek as he lowered his head to whisper in my ear, "Last chance to run."

I smiled and wound my arms around his neck. "Why would I want to run?"

He peeled my arms from around his neck and secured them above my head with one strong hand gripping my wrists. "Because I want to hurt you."

At the sound of his words, my eyelids fluttered shut, and a dark need began to unfurl in my belly like an infinitely-repeating fractal. It was fear and desire all mangled together, because I knew in an instant that I would do anything for him. Anything he asked of me. And what he was asking was to let him work his aggression out on me.

He kissed me, licking along my lips, teasing my tongue with his, and finally biting my bottom lip hard enough to make me yelp.

Still holding my wrists just above my head, he slid off to the side of my body and took my nipple into his mouth, sucking on it and scraping his teeth along the sensitive sides of the tiny bud until I was breathing heavily. Then he spit into his hand and reached down between my legs, bypassing my dick and my balls and going straight for my hole.

His prize.

He lubed me up, rubbing his fingers around the outside and just on the inside, barely breaking the surface. I started to contract the muscle, loving the stimulation of the tip of his finger barely moving in and out. I knew there was going to be pain, but this didn't hurt at all. Not this part.

All the while, he continued to worry my nipple with his lips and his teeth. It was as if there was an electric wire that stretched from my nipple to my asshole, and every time he scraped his teeth along my flesh, my muscles would tighten around his finger in response.

"Christ… Kage. That feels so good." I couldn't hold the words back. He had said he wanted to hurt me, but everything he'd done had brought me nothing but pleasure.

My head rolled loosely on my shoulders, the only part of my body that was relaxed. The rest of me was coiled tightly around the epicenter of my desire— right at the base of my straining cock. Tingling waves of heat and tension radiated out from that one spot, and all I could think was *more, more, more.*

"This is mine now," Kage said.

"Yes."

"I don't share."

"Me, neither."

That made him smile.

Getting up onto his knees, he rolled on a condom, and grabbed a bottle of lube from the bedside table. He poured a pool of it into his cupped palm and then very slowly fucked his own fist, coating every inch from the tip to the root. All I could think was, *That's about to be inside me.* It made me nervous, because my ass was virgin territory, and his wasn't exactly a beginner-level-sized dick.

He noticed my trepidation and smiled. "This is going to hurt. Probably a lot." He rubbed the remnants of the slick liquid all around my entrance, and I gasped when one of his fingers slipped easily up inside me. "But you're going to love it."

I believed him, because I wanted it so much. I'd never wanted anything more.

He crawled right up between my legs, bent one of my knees, and draped it over his arm. The other one he left sprawled on the bed. I looked up at him, scared, and felt myself tense up. He pressed forward, positioning the head of his dick at my entrance and using the weight of his body to push— not going in, but almost. He repeated the action several times, slowly, methodically gaining position within my body. He was loosening me bit by bit, until finally he just went right in.

Kage let out a long, agonized groan as his cock slid in. He squeezed his eyes shut momentarily, as if sheer willpower was the only thing keeping him from losing it.

When the head of his cock popped past the initial resistance of the outer band of muscle, my cry was loud enough to be heard outside the front door of the apartment. But then he was in, and as I adjusted to the sensation of being filled so uncomfortably full, my body began to respond. I wiggled on it just a little, then bit my lip against the strong, pleasurable ache.

"Open your eyes, Jamie," Kage said in a gruff voice. I opened my eyes and stared up at him. God he was beautiful, looming over me with that powerful body. More strands of hair had worked free of their knot and were framing his face. "I want you to see me," he said. "I don't want you pretending I'm someone else."

"There is no one else but you." I wrapped my fingers around his slick biceps and squeezed, thrilling at the feel of those strong muscles moving beneath my hands.

"There better not be," he growled. "Do you feel me? Feel how hard I am inside you? This is what you do to me."

Kage reached down and squeezed my ass cheek so hard it took my mind off of the other pain. Then he moved inside me just enough to make me vocal again. He really seemed to get turned on when I made noises.

"This is my ass," he growled.

I nodded, but that wasn't good enough for him.

"Say it, Jamie." He moved faster and harder, the friction burning me up.

"Your ass," I panted out. "No one else's."

"I'm gonna use your cherry ass to stroke my cock. Show you what it means to be with me."

I reached down and started jerking off, his words lighting a fire in my belly.

He started pounding me hard then, grabbing onto my hips with both hands and banging into me like he truly wanted to do damage. He echoed my higher-pitched cries of pain with his own low grunts of pleasure. I noticed belatedly that I was getting really loud, and that was something I never did. But I couldn't help it. He was forcing it out of me.

He used his powerful arms to slam me down onto his cock at the same time his hips were driving it up into me. It was brutal, and far more painful than I had dared to imagine, but somehow it satisfied a need I didn't even know I had. I stared up into his eyes, balled up my fists and twisted them into the sheets, and just held on as he used my body however he liked.

"Anybody touches you, I'll kill them." His voice was rough with passion, and with rage. I hadn't expected the rage. "Do you understand me? I'll fucking kill them."

"I understand. Yes. Oh, God, Kage. Yes. Yes." The man was hitting me just right. That's all the excuse I had for saying the shit I was saying, because I was agreeing to back him if he committed murder— giving him my unconditional permission to kill anyone who touched me. But God, it felt that fucking good.

Without warning or apology, he pulled out of me, flipped me over, and banded his arm so tightly around my chest I could barely breathe. Then he rammed his cock into me from behind, filling me so completely I thought it would rip me in half. He battered my tender ass until tears squeezed from the corners of my eyes, and still I begged for more. Needed more.

I wondered if this would be the death of me— getting fucked by Michael Kage. It was the most physically demanding thing I'd ever endured. Even the grueling sled drills I dreaded during our workouts paled in comparison. Kage stretched me, folded me, held me down. My muscles screamed for relief, and still I pleaded for him to fuck me harder. He had no qualms about obliging me, shuddering with pleasure as he used my body.

By the time he flipped me back over onto my back and drove his cock back into me, I was completely out of control. I'd never been so lost during sex. Every time before had been so conservative, so planned, so skilled. Using my expertise to get a girl off had been my thing. Not that I hadn't truly enjoyed every minute of sex before, especially with Layla, but this was different.

This was straight-up animal fucking like I'd never experienced before. I had no idea what was going on half the time. At some point, when I'd ridden the edge of pleasure and pain for so long I couldn't tell the difference anymore, Kage began to slow his rhythm, his thrusts becoming much more deliberate and thoughtful. Sweat dripped down his face and onto mine. A drop landed near my mouth, and I darted my tongue out to taste.

Kage grabbed the lube once more, squirted it into his right hand, and wrapped that hand around my erection. Then he lowered his body onto mine, trapping my dick and his hand between our sweaty bodies. He started kissing me passionately, making out with me, stealing my sanity. Loving me.

"Come on, baby," he coaxed. "Come on." Using his hand and our bellies, he massaged my cock in the most amazing way, and I found myself grinding my hips to get it just the way I wanted it, slipping around in the tight, lubed space until I was quivering for release. I was worn out, but still I pushed my tired muscles to strive for it.

Kage was still sheathed to the hilt in my ass, but he was barely rocking, kissing my lips, sucking my tongue, swallowing my moans. Sensing my impending orgasm, he lifted my hips off the bed and started fucking me again, so that he was hitting my most sensitive place on every thrust.

I came like that, with Kage's hand milking every drop of semen out of me, onto my own belly and chest. He watched every second of my orgasm, every expression on my face, and I could feel it inside me when he blew.

In that moment, with our bodies joined, our faces open, and our hearts exposed, I finally saw the clue that I'd been missing. What I saw was that Kage *did* want to hurt me. Desperately. He needed to take all of the pain in his heart and unload it on me.

Because he was damaged. I didn't know exactly what that damage was or just how deep it ran, but it was a big part of who he was. And I had to be willing to accept his pain, and strong enough to take it.

Only then would I ever be able to love him.

Later, as we lay together in Kage's bed, my back spooned against his front, he reached around and toyed with my necklace charm. I smiled dreamily, on the verge of sleep.

He ran his fingertip back and forth across it for a long time before he spoke.

"I want this," he said, so quietly I almost missed it.

"My necklace?" I asked in a groggy voice.

"No." He hesitated long enough that I turned over and looked at his face.

"What do you want?"

"This." He grabbed my necklace again and flipped the Claddagh charm upside down.

My heart got all tingly and warm, and a goofy smile spread across my face. Then, when the reality of what he was asking sank in, I got shy. Bit my lip and looked up at him through my lashes, surprised to discover that I was flirting with him.

It scared me to death, but I wanted it, too.

"Here," I told him. "You do the honors."

He untied the rawhide, flipped the necklace over, and tied it back. Then he admired it for a long time, a hint of a smile on his tempting mouth. Eventually, I leaned over and kissed him.

He cleared his throat. "Did you enjoy the show tonight?"

I chuckled. "Show? *The Rockettes* is a show, Kage. That was a massacre."

"No, it wasn't," he scoffed.

"What? Yes, it was. You totally dominated that guy. And the way you followed my orders… that was ridiculous. I still can't believe it. You were right, though." I touched the cut beside his eye, which didn't seem so bad now that the blood was cleaned up. "I couldn't stand seeing you get hurt. It tore me up."

Kage's expression turned serious. "Jamie, that wasn't really a fight. That was just a show for you. I couldn't really do any damage to the guy in the first round, because you wanted him taken out in the second. That meant I couldn't really get in the zone. I had to keep it together… for you."

"Really?"

"Yeah, really." He put his hand to my cheek and ran his thumb across my lip. "As for getting hit, that wasn't supposed to happen. Not in that fight. But I just couldn't really get into the zone without tearing him to pieces. I was just playing around killing time, and he landed a lucky shot."

"Oh, I forgot about the kick. At the beginning of the fight."

"Now that one was on purpose."

"What?" I stared at him.

He shrugged. "I let him kick me."

My mouth went slack in disbelief. "Why would you do that?"

"Because I like it." He cocked his head to the side and looked me straight in the eyes. "It gets me in the mood."

I didn't have a response for that.

He leaned in and kissed me. I kissed him back, but my mind was preoccupied. I reached up to feel my necklace. Ran my fingers across it in the same way Kage had done earlier, feeling the texture, and wondering if I'd ever really get to know the guy who had just been officially declared my soulmate.

21

WHEN Kage and I pulled up in a cab just after noon, there were so many cars outside my family's house it looked like Thanksgiving. My mother's and father's matching white sedans were inside the garage with the door open, my sister's Mustang sat in the driveway beside what I assumed was her fiancé Chase's pickup truck. There were two strange SUV's parked along the road in front of the house.

The most interesting car of the bunch, however, was a little silver VW Cabriolet with a pair of miniature pink pom-poms hanging from the mirror. I had seen that car more times than I could count. It belonged to Layla.

What the hell was my ex-girlfriend doing at my mother's house?

I didn't get a chance to warn Kage, who had jumped out of the car and gone around to the trunk to get our luggage, because my parents rushed right out to greet us.

Mom looked good. I supposed I had expected the cancer to have altered her appearance, but she looked just the same as the last time I'd seen her. Maybe even better. Her copper hair glistened in the afternoon sunlight, and her freckles were dark enough that I knew she'd still been outside doing her spring and summer gardening.

"I see you've still been working in the yard," I said, trying to keep my eyes from misting at the sight of her. "I forget how much I missed seeing that. Our yard at college barely has grass, and at our place in Vegas, it's all concrete and glass."

"Well, we do have the Grotto," Kage pointed out.

"That's true. You know, it sort of reminds me of the gazebo in our backyard." I looked at Mom and Dad. "You guys are still decorating the gazebo, right?"

"Of course," Mom said. "Come look. It's even nicer this year."

The four of us walked around the house to the backyard, admiring my mom's flower beds on the way. I could tell already she had been hard at work.

"This is beautiful, Mrs. Atwood," Kage said when we came around the corner and passed through the wrought iron archway we'd gotten when I was in high school.

"Thank you," she said, beaming with pride as we admired her handiwork.

White Christmas lights were strung all along the gazebo, and the gardens were fuller and more beautiful than I ever remembered seeing them. Flowers surrounded the gazebo and ran along both sides of the walkway. Small beds jutted out from the foundation of the house. They had added a little wrought iron bench, and a stone fountain with a cherub spitting a stream of water into a round basin.

"It looks gorgeous out here, Mom." I wrapped my arms around her from behind and dropped a kiss on the top of her head. "And you're still as short as ever."

She laughed and slapped me on the arm. "I guess I've tried to concentrate more on the yard this year. Everything has a tendency to get to me, and it helps to have that outlet."

My father chuckled beside us. "You have no idea how much money we've spent on it this year. But I think it's paid off. And what else would we do with the money now that you kids are pretty much out of the house?"

"Um… Buy me a new car," I teased.

"I can get you a car," Kage said, and my parents and I all snapped our heads around so hard I'm surprised we didn't get whiplash. My parents were shocked, but I was mortified. In my mind, what Kage had just said is, *"I'm fucking your son."*

My mom actually giggled like a little girl. "Wow, Jamie must be doing a great job."

Kage didn't even blink. "He is, Mrs. Atwood. You should be very proud. The stipend we pay him isn't nearly what he's worth. I guarantee you when he graduates from college, he'll be pulling down high six figures easily."

"Really?" My dad said, seemingly more impressed with me than he'd ever been.

"Yes, sir," Kage said. "Especially with my reference. I haven't told Jamie this yet, but I got some really good news this morning. Thanks in part to his efforts, I just got picked up for a fight in the UFC. It's my shot at a contract. So if Jamie needs a car, I'll get him a car." He winked at me. "Think of it as a bonus."

I couldn't believe it. I opened my mouth and just started yelling. "Oh my God! Kage, that is so fucking awesome!"

My mom gasped at my language, and my father scowled, but I was so stoked I didn't care. I threw my arms around Kage's neck and gave him the hardest hug I could. He squeezed me back and laughed. I'd never seen him quite so happy. I think in that moment every bit of the darkness was gone from his eyes, and all I saw there was sheer joy.

I backed away from him, and my mind started whirling with thoughts.

"When do you fight? Oh my gosh, can I be in your corner? Can I walk out behind you when you do your entrance? Crap. We have to come up with a walk out song for you. Something to do with fighting, or winning, or hardcore. Yeah, something really hard. Are we gonna wear hoodies when we walk out? I always thought that looked cool. We at least need matching t-shirts. They can say, *The Machine*. Or just *KAGE*. Or *Welcome to the Machine*."

He smiled and looked at me in that special way of his that made my knees weak. "You're babbling again."

"Am I?" All I knew is that I was grinning from ear to ear, and I'd never been so excited in my whole damn life. I wanted to hug him again. Hell, I wanted to kiss him, but for obvious reasons that was impossible.

My parents were just staring at us with bewildered expressions on their faces.

"That's great news, boys," my mom said. "Just great. This is what you've been shooting for, right?"

"Yes," we both said in unison.

"Well, congratulations," Dad said. "We'll have to celebrate with a shot of the hard stuff after dinner."

That made me feel good. It meant my dad thought of me as a man now. I had officially grown up in his eyes.

"That'll be nice," Kage said. "There is one more thing, though. Because of this fight, I have to leave in the morning. I was supposed to leave for camp today, but I didn't want to miss bringing Jamie down here. This is way more important."

"Well, that's awfully sweet of you, Kage," my mom said. She reached out and squeezed his hand. "Thank you. That means a lot."

"Why do you have to leave so soon?" I asked.

"That fight they got me is short notice, because somebody got injured at the last minute. Starting tomorrow, I've got eleven days to lose thirty-five pounds."

"Jesus. Thirty-five?" I asked. "Why so much?"

"I should be fighting Welterweight, but the guy who pulled out is a Lightweight. Gotta take what I can get. Marco's got me signed up for an intensive training camp."

"And that means you have to lose weight?" my mother asked, obviously confused.

"Yes, ma'am," Kage said. "I walk around every day at one-ninety. The weight limit in Welterweight, the class I want to be in, is one-seventy. So I'd have to lose twenty pounds before the fight. That's something fighters do all the time. Most of that is water weight. They sweat it out in a sauna before the weigh-in, then rehydrate over the next twenty-four hours before the fight."

"Why on earth do they do that?" Mom asked.

Kage chuckled. "A long time ago, somebody decided it was a clever way to trick the system. To dehydrate themselves down much lighter for the weigh-in, then use electrolyte drinks and IV fluids to come into the ring the next day far heavier than their opponent. That kind of weight can be an advantage in a fight."

"That sounds terrible," Mom said. "It can't be healthy, can it?"

Kage shook his head. "Not really. But the problem is that everybody started doing it, and now if you don't, you risk being the small guy in the fight. It's a vicious circle."

"And you have to leave tomorrow morning?" I was still hung up on that.

"Don't worry. You stay here and look after your mom, then I'll send for you before the weigh-in. I promise you won't miss anything."

His smile and his words made me feel a lot better. But eleven days? That was a long damn time. I'd gotten used to being with him. Every time he'd disappeared for a couple of days in Vegas, I got agitated. Now we were going to be apart for eleven whole days? I wanted to be there for Mom, but I already knew I was going to lose my mind.

I couldn't say it, though. Not with my parents listening.

THE euphoria of Kage's backyard announcement was short lived for me. In all of the excitement about the fight, and the dread of being without him for so long, I had forgotten about the surprise guest waiting for me in the house. When the four of us entered the back door, we came face to face with Layla and my sister, who were sitting on bar stools in the kitchen.

My laughter died in my throat.

"Jamie," she said, striking a demure pose with her hands on her knee. "It's so great to see you. You look… different."

"If one more person says I look different, I'm going to lose my mind."

"I didn't mean anything by it, papi. Only that you looked like you've really been working out a lot. Your body—" She blushed. "Vegas has been treating you right, huh?"

"I guess. What are you doing here?"

I could see the disappointment on her face at my reaction to her presence, but dammit, I'd broken up with her. Then confirmed it on the phone. So how had she ended up in my parents' kitchen?

"That's no way to speak to someone, Jamie," my mother scolded. "Did you leave your manners in Las Vegas? Layla called to see how I was doing, and I invited her to come and spend the weekend with us while you were in town."

"Oh." That's absolutely all I could manage. I didn't want to be rude or hurt her feelings, but the situation was forty kinds of fucked up.

Kage was standing beside me, but he wasn't looking at me, and he wasn't smiling. He was putting a hole through Layla with his eyes.

My parents were glaring at me, and Layla looked devastated, but my sister Jennifer was twirling a finger in her long auburn hair and smirking evilly at me. She cut her eyes over at Kage and then at me, and that's when I knew. My sister was onto us.

And Jennifer had a big mouth. So there was no telling who else knew.

I shrank about two feet and skulked away into the living room, where Chase the douchebag fiancé was watching TV with my little brother, Paul. Chase was antisocial, always sitting in front of the television at family events instead of spending time with people, so I didn't bother speaking to him.

"Paul, you're not even gonna get up to say hi to your big brother?" I asked, ruffling his red hair.

He jumped up and squealed, throwing his arms around my shoulders. "I didn't know you were here. Where's the wrestler? I want to meet the wrestler."

Paul was only ten years old— the product of a lot of wine and a forgotten contraceptive eleven years after my parents had decided that two kids was plenty. But some accidents are happy accidents, and Paul was definitely a happy one. He had a sunny disposition and a love for all things outdoors, and he was the light in my mother's eye. Her little garden helper she called him, among other things.

"He's a UFC fighter," I told Paul, then turned to find Kage.

He was still seething in the kitchen, listening to my mother explain how her surgery was scheduled for seven on Monday morning, but she had to check in at the ungodly hour of five.

"I mean, what starts at five in the morning?" she was saying.

"Kage," I called. "Could you come over here? There's someone I want you to meet."

Kage dragged himself away from plotting on my ex-girlfriend and came into the living room. "This must be Paul," he said, turning off his anger long enough to be civil to my brother.

"You've heard of me?" Paul asked, and I couldn't help laughing.

"Of course," Kage said. "Your brother told me about you. He said you were a wrestling fan."

Paul nodded emphatically.

"Well, I can show you a few moves if you want. Things to use on bullies if you happen to meet up with any of those."

"We've got a couple at school," Paul said. "They don't pick on me, but one of them is mean to my friend."

"Well, I'll tell you something I had to learn the hard way. It's never good to start a fight, and you should always try to walk away if someone starts one with you. But… if someone does try to pick a fight with you, and you try your best to walk away but they won't stop, it's good to know some self-defense moves. Just so you don't get hurt."

Kage walked Paul over to the large open area at the other side of the living room, and started coaching him. Paul was so thrilled his face was glowing.

I had to admit, I was proud of Kage. Not only was he taking time to dote on my little brother, but he was discouraging fighting except as a means of self-defense. It seemed he did something to surprise me every day.

Most of the time, the surprises were good.

22

THAT night after a supper of delivery pizza, which Kage and I respectfully declined, my father took us into the small room he called his office and pulled a bottle of Johnny Walker Red out of his desk drawer.

"You drink Scotch?" he asked Kage.

"Sure," he said. "Although Jamie and I will be drinking on empty stomachs, so we probably shouldn't have too much."

"Yes." My father gave me a pointed look. "Jamie looks like he could stand to eat a little pizza."

"Dad, I'm fine," I assured him. "I'm healthier than I've ever been. This is what I look like when I eat right. You're just not used to seeing me with so little fat on my body."

"I can see your bones."

"Those are muscles, Dad. And I'm fine."

My mother followed us in and set three glasses on the desk and walked right back out, and then my father proceeded to pour us each what amounted to a triple shot.

"I just wanted to drink a toast to both of your professional futures. I realize they're separate futures, but you both seem to be on your way up, and that's great."

"What do you mean, they're separate futures?" Kage asked.

"Well, I just mean that Jamie will be going back to school soon, and you'll be fighting in the UFC. Then Jamie will graduate and go on to work for new people who need his services, with you providing a good reference, as you said. That is the plan, isn't it? He's done what he set out to do for you, and now that job is pretty much done, am I right?"

"I don't know," Kage said, before knocking back his whisky. I recognized the note of challenge in his voice. "That depends on Jamie. It's pretty much up to him. He's a big boy, so he can make up his own mind." He set his empty glass down on the desk with a thump. "Could I have another?"

I felt my eyes go wide, and I downed my own drink. I figured I was going to need it.

After my dad and Kage both finished off another full drink, I interrupted what seemed an awful lot like a standoff, though for the life of me I couldn't figure it out. "Um, Dad… Is Mom going to drive herself to the hospital? Because at the rate you're going, you'll be passed out when it's time to go."

"No, son. I'm going to bed now to try to get at least a few winks. Y'all had better go to bed soon, too. You'll sleep in your room where you always sleep, and your mother has made up the guest room for your girlfriend. Kage can sleep on the sofa."

"She's my ex-girlfriend." I set my half full second drink on the desk. "We'll go see if Mom needs any help in the kitchen. Goodnight, Dad."

When Kage and I got back to the kitchen, Jennifer and Layla were tidying up the counters and stacking the empty pizza boxes near the garbage can. "We'll take out the trash," I said. "Just leave it."

Mom sat on a barstool watching. "You know, I could get all of this. But I do appreciate you kids making the effort to make things easier on me. I'm fine, though. I've made peace with my decision, and now it's just a matter of finishing it."

"You're not nervous at all?" Jennifer asked.

"A little nervous about the anesthesia," she admitted with a laugh. "I'm afraid I might tell the doctor all of my secrets. They say that stuff gives you a loose tongue, and you'll say all kinds of things."

We all knew she was teasing and that she was probably terrified, but the woman could put on a hell of a front. As calm as she seemed, you'd have thought she was just going in for a checkup.

"Like you have any secrets," Jennifer scoffed. Then she got that look I hated. The bully big sister look, and I knew something bad was coming. She turned toward me with a smile and said, "Jamie's the one who's got secrets."

"Knock it off, Jen." I tried to seem as unruffled as I could, but inside I was shaking. Being outed to my entire family and my ex-girlfriend on the eve of my mother's surgery just seemed too horrific to contemplate.

"Jamie has secrets?" Layla didn't disguise her jealous curiosity well. "I thought I knew *everything* there was to know about him."

And then Kage was pissed. I could sense his short fuse burning beside me without even looking his way. In fact, Layla was damn lucky she was a girl, because it was probably the only thing saving her from getting laid out on my mom's kitchen floor.

"Oh, I'm sure you do. I'll bet you two have some secrets of your own that would make Mom blush."

"Jennifer, you'd better watch yourself," Mom said. "I may be going into surgery tomorrow, but don't think I won't take a strap to you."

I had to take a time out from the drama to address my mother's new saying. "Mom, where did you pick up this strapping people business? It's creeping me out. You never even spanked us."

"I swatted you on the legs a few times," she said.

Jennifer rolled her eyes. "Let's get back to the secrets. For instance, I'd like to know why you're wearing your Claddagh the right way all of a sudden. You've always worn it upside-down. You do know what that means, right?"

"You're still wearing that thing?" my mom asked. "I guess I just got so used to seeing it on you, I stopped noticing it. But you never believed in that superstition, did you?"

Layla stared hard at my necklace, and I brought my hand up self-consciously, toying with it to cover it up. She knew I took it seriously. I'd told her about it. Planned to turn it around one day for her, but obviously that never happened.

I laughed, an empty sound that I hoped would be enough to fool Layla and my mom. "Do I have it on the wrong way? Guess I just picked it up wrong this morning." I reached around to the back of my neck and untied it, flipped it over, then tied it back. I couldn't bring myself to look Kage in the eye.

"Come on, Kage. Let's go out to the gazebo. I'll show you where I used to sit with my friends and listen to music on summer nights. It feels great out there."

We walked out the back door, and it occurred to me too late that my invitation was suspect in itself. There was a perfectly good female sitting in my kitchen— one that I'd been intimate with and who was obviously flirting with me. Yet I'd invited a guy to go on a romantic stroll out to the gazebo. Brilliant.

But there had been no other choice, really. Not only was it what I'd wanted to do, but the alternative might have ended in murder.

"Why did my mom have to invite her here?" I mumbled under my breath to Kage as we crossed the lawn to the gazebo.

"Because she wants you to be with a girl," Kage said. "They all do. This is an intervention, if you haven't noticed."

"What? They don't even know anything about us. Except for Jennifer. I'm pretty sure she knows."

Kage squeezed the back of my neck hard enough to make me wince and guided me up the gazebo steps. "Dammit Jamie, how can you be a senior in college and still be so clueless?"

"What do you mean? They don't know anything. How could they?"

"I don't know. Maybe they're more perceptive than you are."

"You don't have to be an asshole about it."

"Well, you don't have to hide under a fucking rock, either. Or technically I guess it's me you're trying to hide. But guess what? I'm here. I'm right fucking here, standing beside you at your parents' house, trying to support you." He tried to run his hand through his hair and met resistance when his fingers hit the topknot. "Fuck," he growled and ripped the elastic band out of his hair and threw it on the gazebo floor. "I don't know what I have to do for you. I gave you a job, flew you out to Vegas, gave you the best home I could, fed you, trained you, fucked you, fought for you… and still you won't have me."

His voice wavered on the last part, and it broke my heart to hear him sound so rejected. I'd done that to him.

Tears welled up in my eyes, spilled out onto my cheeks, and I wiped them away with the back of my forearm. His words had really struck home. I hadn't been able to see things from his point of view, or maybe I hadn't wanted to, but now he'd held a mirror up to my face, and what I saw there was ugly.

I thought back to every positive step he and I had taken toward declaring ourselves a legitimate couple: kissing in front of the lady hotel clerk on our road trip, confiding in Steve at the Alcazar, sharing a slice of wedding cake in front of Enzo, allowing his psychiatrist to see us together, and coming to visit my family together. It had all been Kage. Every bit of it. I was the one who had resisted, hidden, shied away, gotten embarrassed, and even lied to keep our relationship a secret.

Kage had never once denied me to anyone. He had stepped up and claimed me even when doing so posed a threat to his future—the one goal he'd had since he was a child.

I remembered his words from the afternoon we got back from the road trip, when he'd asked me to go to my apartment and think things through.

I'm the one with something to lose here.

At the time, I had assumed he meant his career. But it wasn't that simple.

I don't give a fuck. I can touch his face if I want. Fuck the cameras. Fuck my uncle, fuck the public...

Self-revulsion roiled the too-still waters of my soul and opened my eyes to the truth. All along, Kage had been trying to come *out* of the closet, and I was the one pushing him back in. He'd taken a chance on me, trusted me, shown me his weakness, and I'd thrown it right back in his face.

"Kage..." I reached out for him, but he backed away.

"I'm not feeling it right now, Jamie." He looked around us, at the twinkling gazebo lights, my parents' house, the nighttime sky. "To be honest, I'm feeling pretty out of place here. This wasn't a good idea. I should have just bought you a plane ticket and let you come alone."

"No, you shouldn't have. I want you here." I put out my hand and stepped toward him, but he backed away again. I felt like I was trying to tame a wild mustang. He was one step ahead and just out of reach, and any sudden move might make him bolt.

He let out a harsh laugh. "You don't want me anywhere except the bedroom."

That one burned like hell going down.

"That's not true."

"You're a fucking liar," he railed. "I told you not to lie to me again."

"Please, Kage. Let's talk about this tomorrow. Let's just go to bed and reset, and then we can work everything out tomorrow."

"Yeah? You want to go to bed, Jamie? Is that what you want? Because I don't have a fucking bed. I get to sleep on the fucking couch. Is that where you want me? On the fucking couch? That cunt gets a bed, and I get the fucking couch?"

"Kage—" I choked out his name on a sob, and that's as far as I got. Because I looked into his eyes, and what I saw there dried the words right up in my throat. It was worse than the conversation over dinner when he told me he was bad, even worse than the fight, when I'd seen him knock that guy unconscious with no remorse.

"You're scaring me," I said, trying to keep my voice calm even though my adrenaline was spiking, and my fight or flight response was kicking in something fierce. "You're not acting like yourself."

"Yeah? Well, I've told you before. You don't know me." This time it was Kage who took a step toward me, and I was the one to retreat. "You don't want to know me. You'd rather live in this little fantasy world of yours where everyone is a good person, and Michael Kage Santori is just an entertaining summer fuck."

He took another step toward me, and when I backed up, my knees hit the built-in bench that ran around the inside of the gazebo. He pressed in so close I had to lean back onto the side of the gazebo rail and catch myself with my hands. His body was so close now, I could smell him, and just like that I was instantly hard— trained to that scent like one of Pavlov's dogs. I felt my nostrils flare and my eyelids flutter, and that uneasy quiver in my belly that told me I was a goner.

"Tell me," he said. "Have you gotten your demons worked out?"

"What do you mean?"

"Your demons. You know. Have you gotten enough cock to satisfy your curiosity? Are you ready to go back to school? Go back to fucking girls?" He reached down between my legs and rubbed my hard dick through the fabric of my shorts. "Mmmm, looks like that part of you is still curious."

I pushed against his hand and let out an involuntary sigh, getting harder by the second. I needed him to touch me more. More contact, more friction. I strained against him.

But instead of giving my cock more attention, he slipped his hand down under, cupping my balls and pushing his finger right up against my hole. The flesh was still aching, still ultra-sensitive from two nights before when Kage had so irrevocably owned my ass. I felt it every time I took a step, every time I sat down, and now the memories of those amazing sensations came flooding back full-force.

I groaned and shifted, trying to give him better access, trying to get more contact. I wanted him to penetrate me. Suddenly I needed more than anything for him to fuck me. If only he would fill me like I needed filling, hit that spot for me and make me come all over us. I drew in a deep, shuddering breath as he pressed up harder with his finger, transforming my entire body into one tangled mass of yearning.

"What do you want from me?" he whispered against my ear, his beard stubble scraping deliciously along my cheek and jaw.

"Fuck my ass," I said, feeling no shame.

"That's what I thought." He removed his hand from between my legs and slipped his fingers under my necklace, snatching it so hard it broke both the cord and the skin on the back of my neck. I cried out in pain as Kage turned and threw the necklace as hard as he could into the woods next to the gazebo. "You think I'm good enough to fuck, but not worthy of being your boyfriend? Well, guess what? I don't want the job anymore. Good luck finding another man for the position. It'll take two to fill the vacancy I left."

He turned and walked away, moving quickly and with resolve down the gazebo steps and onto the lawn. My mind was reeling, my face was hot, I was mortified… and I was angry. Because how dare he treat me that way? To taunt me like that, specifically for the purpose of humiliating me, was inexcusable. And then to destroy my necklace and throw it away.

I ran down the steps of the gazebo and after Kage with only one thought. Revenge.

I wanted to shred him like he'd just shredded my pride. I closed the distance between us in a couple of seconds and tackled him, hoping to take him down and make him suffer. But attacking a brutal fighter trained in multiple disciplines is probably never a good idea, especially if you don't know anything about fighting except the little bit that fighter has taught you.

When I flew at him from behind, I have no doubt he heard me coming like a herd of buffalo and anticipated exactly what I was going to do. To his credit, even in anger, he didn't hit me. He flipped me easily off of his back, deposited me on the ground, and kept walking, stinging my ego even more.

"Are you running from me?" I yelled. I stopped in the middle of the yard, so overcome with anger that it didn't occur to me at first that the people in my house might hear. I glanced at the darkened house. The TV flickered in the living room. Probably Layla and Jennifer watching TV and plotting on me. Kage pulled his cell phone out of his pocket and kept walking toward the house. "Who are you calling? Your uncle?"

"A cab." He was emotionless. Efficient.

Leaving.

"Why don't you come back here and fight like a man, you fucking pussy?" I screamed out of desperation.

He spun around in mid-stride and stalked back to where I was standing. "What is wrong with you? You want me to fight you? I would fucking kill you."

"You don't scare me," I lied. "What have you had, one fight now? It wasn't even that impressive, asshole. You're nothing. They're gonna destroy you in the UFC." I didn't even know what I was saying anymore. Anything to get a rise out of the dark-eyed beast standing in front of me. I knew he could kill me. I knew. And yet I pushed as hard as I could.

When words didn't work, I did the dumbest thing I'd ever done in my entire life. I threw a punch. He let it land. I say *let* because there's no way he didn't see it coming. I telegraphed it from a mile away. I could see where my knuckles had caught his lip, and it was getting pink and swelling up. A bead of blood welled up, and he reached up and touched it.

Then he just looked at me with that cold, terrifying look, then down at the blood on his hand, then up at me again. All I could think to do was run. I ran across the lawn, past the gazebo, and down the small hill in back, out toward the wooded area just beyond our yard. But I didn't make it to the tree line before he caught me.

He grabbed my wrist and spun me easily. Smooth as butter and so fast I didn't know what hit me, he had me face down on the grass with my arm cranked painfully up against the middle of my back. I felt his weight pinning me down, his thighs straddling my thighs, and God help me it was turning me on.

"Kage—" I lifted my hips off the ground as much as I could and pushed my ass back toward him. But I wasn't trying to escape.

"You want it that bad?" he asked, his voice sounding gravelly and just as needy as I felt. He torqued my already screaming arm just enough to make me squeal like a wounded animal, then leaned over me and bit down on the soft spot between my neck and shoulder. He rocked his hips against my ass, dry humping me into the ground for several slow, excruciating seconds, and I could feel how hard he was. Then he sat back on my thighs again. "Jamie, look at me."

He eased up on my arm enough that I could turn my head and look back over my shoulder at him. My cheek was pressed against the damp grass, the scent of earth overpowering in my nostrils.

The sight of Kage straddling me like that, dominating me so completely, made my belly drop like I was on a roller coaster ride. He snapped the band of his shorts down and released his cock, hard and huge and intimidating as hell. He pressed it down into the channel between my ass cheeks, and my muscles spasmed in anticipation.

"Is this what you want?" he asked.

I nodded, my cheek scrubbing against grass and clotted earth. Warm tears collected in the corners of my eyes, and I squeezed them away, feeling the embarrassing tracks they left on my skin.

Kage yanked my shorts down halfway down my thighs with no thought for comfort. I watched him as he spread my cheeks and dripped saliva onto me. The feel of it hitting the sensitive flesh of my hole and sliding all the way down to my balls was excruciating.

He wet his hand and his cock, then he reached under my body, lifted my hips until I was halfway up on my knees, and pushed his thick cock straight in, burying it to the hilt. There was no preparation this time, and there were no apologies. Kage pounded into me with an intensity that put his previous efforts to shame. He kept my body just clear enough of the ground that I could reach beneath me and squeeze and stroke my own painfully hard cock.

Neither one of us lasted long. When Kage let loose, he wrapped an arm around my waist and just quivered there behind me. I felt the strong pulsations one after another and he emptied himself deep inside me while my own cum spilled out onto the grass below.

Just as my body was coming down from the intense adrenaline rush, Kage pulled out of me and stood up. He ran a hand through his loose hair and let out a long, heavy sigh, then pulled his pants up. Dimly, I heard the sound of a car horn in the distance, but my brain was too rattled to register what it meant.

Then, as I lay there recovering, my pants still shoved down around my knees, Kage turned and started walking toward the side of the house. Toward the front yard, where headlights illuminated the road out front, and a car horn blared again.

As I watched him walk away, I realized he was actually leaving. That his cab was here, and he was going to leave. Just like that, without a word to me, and without looking back.

He rounded the front corner of the house and whistled at the cab, lifting his hand to get the driver's attention. That's when it became real and the tears started to well up in my eyes.

Kage— the man I'd only hours ago claimed as my soulmate, the man I'd changed everything for, the man I felt like I would die without seeing for eleven days— was walking out of my life. And all I could do was lie there in my parents' backyard, with my pants around my knees and my heart in my throat, and cry myself dry.

TO BE CONTINUED…

MORE FROM MARIS BLACK:

STANDALONE WORKS:

OWNING COREY

SSU BOYS SERIES:

PINNED (SSU Boys Book #1)

SMITTEN (SSU Boys Book #2)

UNDECLARED (SSU Boys Book #3)

INITIATION (SSU Boys Short)

KAGE TRILOGY:

Kage (KAGE TRILOGY Round 1)

Kage Unleashed (KAGE TRILOGY Round 2)

Kage Unmasked (KAGE TRILOGY Round 3)

MARIS BLACK ON AUDIO:

Audible.com

Sign up for new release notifications at:

MarisBlack.com

ABOUT THE AUTHOR

My name is Maris Black (sort of), and I'm a Southern Girl through and through.

In college, I majored in English and discovered the joys of creative writing and literary interpretation. After honing my skills discovering hidden meanings authors probably never intended, I collected my near-worthless English degree and got a job at a newspaper making minimum wage. But I soon had to admit that small town reporting was not going to pay the bills, so I went back to school and joined the medical field. Logical progression, right? But no matter what I did, my school notebooks and journals would not stop filling up with fiction. I was constantly plotting, constantly jotting prose, and constantly casting the people I met as characters in the secret novels in my head.

Yep. I can blame my creative mother for that one!

When I finally started writing fiction for a living, I surprised myself with my choice of genre. I'd always known I wanted to write romance, but the first story that popped out was about a couple of guys finding love during a threesome with a woman. Then I wrote about more guys, and more guys, and more guys. I was never a reader of gay fiction, and I'd never planned to write it. The only excuse I have for myself is: *Hey, it's just what comes out!*

I adore the M/M genre, though, with all my heart. It feels sort of like coming home. I can't quite explain it. I've always had openly gay and bisexual friends and relatives, the rights and acceptance of whom are very important to me, so it feels great to celebrate that. But there's also something so pure and honest about the love between two men that appeals to me on a romantic level and inspires me to write.

Thank you, men. ☺

I currently live in Nashville, TN with my devoted husband (who just happens to be my biggest fan), my three eccentric children, and a hairless cat named Blu. Life is good.

CONNECT WITH MARIS:

Website: *Marisblack.com*
Facebook Profile: *facebook.com/maris.black.7*
Facebook Fan Page: *facebook.com/marisblackbooks*
Twitter: *twitter.com/marisblackbooks*